SLEEP

SLEEP

Honor Jones

RIVERHEAD BOOKS
NEW YORK
2025

RIVERHEAD BOOKS
An imprint of Penguin Random House LLC
1745 Broadway, New York, NY 10019
penguinrandomhouse.com

Book design by Meighan Cavanaugh

Library of Congress Cataloging-in-Publication Data
Names: Jones, Honor, author.
Title: Sleep: a novel / Honor Jones.
Description: New York: Riverhead Books, 2025.
Identifiers: LCCN 2024018084 (print) | LCCN 2024018085 (ebook) |
ISBN 9780593851982 (hardcover) | ISBN 9780593851999 (ebook)
Subjects: LCGFT: Thrillers (Fiction) | Novels.
Classification: LCC PS3610.O62533 S54 2025 (print) |
LCC PS3610.O62533 (ebook) | DDC 813/.6—dc23/eng/20240812
LC record available at https://lccn.loc.gov/2024018084
LC ebook record available at https://lccn.loc.gov/2024018085

International trade paperback edition ISBN: 9798217045853

Printed in the United States of America
1st Printing

The authorized representative in the EU for product safety and compliance is
Penguin Random House Ireland, Morrison Chambers, 32 Nassau Street,
Dublin D02 YH68, Ireland, https://eu-contact.penguin.ie.

SLEEP

ONE

1

IT WAS DAMP DOWN UNDER THE BLACKBERRY BUSH, BUT MAR-garet liked it there; she was cozy, like a rabbit. It smelled clean—it was funny how dirt could smell so clean. She couldn't see in the dark which berries were ripe, but she nibbled on one anyway, puckered, spat. She rested her cheek against her arm and looked across the yard.

A whoop and a stampede—the boys were running by. They must have spotted Biddy. The bright spot of the flashlight whirled. It made her dizzy trying to follow it. Hammock, grass, basketball net, grass. The flashlight made a photograph each time it hit something—little circles of backyard, punched out of time.

The light lit the door of the toolshed and stayed there, wobbling. She couldn't tell which boy was which in the dark, but one held the flashlight, one went for the door. Tactics, she thought, impressed. They shouted and knocked over some rakes and buckets, but the shed was empty.

Margaret laughed into her elbow. The boys stopped to scheme, and she could see that Danny was holding the flashlight. Danny was her best friend's brother, and so they could almost certainly never fall in love and get married. The boys were making a plan; they had to be more strategic, she could hear Neal, her own brother, saying.

She played with a stick in the dirt, making up signs for the fairy people who would come out later, telling them who she was: *Here lay Margaret, child of man.* The fairies would have tangles in their hair and see-through wings of dusky violet and the pointed toes of Barbies. She didn't believe in fairies, but she liked to pretend.

The light came again, straight into the blackberry bush. For a second it was like being inside a room when someone flicks the switch. The world got solid and sharp-edged and jumped at her—leaves and thorns and shadows of thorns, the dirt so close to her face and suddenly, specifically, dirty. She cringed her eyes shut tight so no one could see them shining like an animal's. When she opened them again the boys were on the other side of the yard.

They'd given up on the ground and were looking into the trees. Biddy would be in a tree, Margaret could have told them that. And it took only a few more minutes before the light found her, pinned her up against the branches. Biddy kicked her sneakers like she didn't care and swung down to the victorious brothers.

But they would never find Margaret. She had known as soon as she burrowed down under the blackberries that no one was going to find her. She was too low to the ground, too good and hidden.

It was fully dark out now. She couldn't see the bats against the sky anymore, the bats that lived in the attic and weren't all bad because they ate the mosquitoes. If she was outside after her own dinner, looking up, she could catch them sometimes sluicing out of the house, so many wings so close together it was like one streaming body, like the house was a factory churning out black smoke. They were up there, eating, but she couldn't see them. She tried pretending them away, but that never worked; you could pretend things into existence but not out of it.

The damp had soaked through her shorts and she shivered. She was bored of flashlight tag. Elbowing her way out from under the brambles,

she shouted, "I win, I win," and linking arms with Biddy, skipped toward
the lit-up house.

THE PARENTS WERE on the porch, around the glass table. "Ice cream's
inside," Biddy's mom, Mrs. Murphy, called to the oncoming children.

"Bring me a bowl too, would you?" Margaret's dad asked her. The fathers were handsome in their off-hours polo shirts, but Margaret's father
was handsomer. And in the doorway her mother in the hot pink sundress—
Elizabeth, commanding the screen. Elizabeth oversaw the children tramp-
ing through, but when Margaret reached the threshold, she put an arm out
and stopped her.

"You're filthy," she said.

Margaret looked at her mother's face to see how she meant it. But it
was safe, she didn't look angry; she looked as if she was thinking of a cute
word, like *ragamuffin*. She glanced down at her T-shirt and jean shorts.
They were smeared with dirt and her knees were brown, but filthy? Elizabeth was always exaggerating. Besides, this was clean dirt, blackberry dirt.
She toed off the heels of her sneakers and lined them up beside the door
the way she was supposed to. She said, "I'm not filthy."

A mistake. Dumb, Margaret. "You are literally," Elizabeth said, "covered in mud."

I'm not, she thought again but did not say.

"Look at yourself."

Elizabeth pinched at her T-shirt as if she had to touch it but didn't
want to. The shirt lifted away from her chest and the air came in. "Take
your clothes off here and give them to me. I don't want you tracking that
mess through the house."

Margaret looked around the porch, at the Murphys, at Danny on the
other side of the door. "Here?"

"Don't be a princess."

Elizabeth took the hem of her T-shirt and pulled. Automatically Margaret's arms went up, like she was still a little kid who was used to being

undressed by her mother. The shirt covered her face, and for a moment it was safe, she was back in the blackberry bush, in the good dark, but then the air was on her. Elizabeth had said she'd buy Margaret a training bra when she started fifth grade that fall. She didn't need it for support or anything yet, but you could see that she would soon; you could see already that she wasn't a child or a boy. "Skin a rabbit," Elizabeth said, reaching for her shorts.

Then Margaret was through the door and up the stairs in her white underwear, moving fast so she couldn't see anyone seeing her. Behind her, Elizabeth was her good mother again, bundling up the dirty laundry, saying to the other kids, still gathered by the door, "Don't forget to put the ice cream back in the freezer. I don't want ichor all over the countertop."

"Don't want what now?" she heard her father asking.

Icker? Margaret repeated the word as she climbed up on the bathroom sink, contorting her knees under the tap. It was a new word. Ick, ick, icker. It meant filthy too, she guessed. Her mother had many words for that, and she was right: Margaret was filthy. The dirt ran down the sink in pleasing long brown lines. But Elizabeth wasn't mad that she was filthy; she was mad that Margaret had said she wasn't filthy. Icker on the countertop, she said to herself, liking the sound of the words.

There was no lock on the bathroom door. There were no locks on any of the doors. Elizabeth had always been afraid, when Margaret and Neal were little, that they would lock themselves inside, that it would happen during an emergency, such as a fire, that locks were therefore a fire hazard. When they'd first moved into the big house, Elizabeth had replaced all the hardware on the doors with matching antique latches—each had a handle of black iron the length of a grown-up's fist and on top of that a tongue you pressed with your thumb. Margaret liked the way the latches rattled into place, but she didn't see why they couldn't have normal doors that locked like other people's did.

Sometimes Margaret would push the dirty laundry basket in front of the bathroom door. The room was quieter when no one else could get inside. She would perch on the counter and look at parts of her face really close in the mirror. Or take her shirt off and turn from side to side. Biddy's nipples were a pale ballerina pink, but hers were much darker, almost brown, an ugly color. It meant her boobs, when she got them, would be bigger—that's what Biddy said. But then one time she heard footsteps and the latch jumped up and down—Elizabeth, trying to get in. She'd had to ram her shoulder hard against the door to push it open. Why should Margaret want to lock her own family out? She got in major trouble for that. That was a big, big fire hazard.

A few weeks earlier they'd all gone to Biddy's house for dinner. The summer nights were like this: backyard, burgers, ice cream, repeat. That night she and Biddy had been playing with Barbies in the basement—they were too old for pretend, so they played with Barbies only in the basement, furtively—when her mother plunged down the steps and pinned Margaret against the wall.

She was yelling something. The yelling wasn't words, it was more physical than that—like the hands clamped around her arms, and the wall knock-knocking at the back of her head, and all over and around it the good-mother smell of sunscreen and Lubriderm lotion that always announced *Elizabeth*.

It was Biddy's brother, Danny, who stopped it. He stood on the stairs, saying, "But wait, it was us. We did it. It was us." He had to shout before anyone noticed. Elizabeth dropped Margaret, looked at Danny, and turned and walked past him up the stairs.

When she was gone, Danny crouched down and told Margaret and Biddy what had happened. The brothers had been making prank calls from the phone in Biddy's parents' bedroom, and some lady had reverse-dialed, tattled to the parents. She had loved Danny long before that night, but she loved him extra now. Not even the dads would stand up to Elizabeth.

Upstairs they could hear the grown-ups laughing, that shouting laughter grown-ups do. "They really thought they'd got away with it," Mr. Murphy was saying. "For a year, in every boardroom on Wall Street." The snorting sound of female disbelief.

"Come on," Danny said. "Let's see if there's dessert."

For the rest of the night she had tried to read Elizabeth's face to see what she was thinking. Was she sorry too? But there was nothing to read—the anger had passed and been replaced; she had on her grown-up-conversation face, then her doing-the-dishes face, then her no-whining, it's-time-to-go face. If the boys got a talking-to, Margaret and Biddy didn't see it.

But why had Elizabeth thought Margaret had done it? The kids were always talking about superpowers—if you could have any superpower, what would it be? Margaret usually said mind reading. But what if she could read her mother's mind, and all her mother was thinking was that Margaret was bad, bad, bad? Better say flying instead.

NOW SHE WRAPPED a towel around her waist and started to leave the bathroom. She needed to get new clothes. She needed to go downstairs and eat ice cream. Biddy would be waiting for her; Biddy was sleeping over. But she stopped at the door and came back. Carefully, with wet toilet paper, she wiped everything down, each thing she'd touched: the sink, the hot tap and the cold, the honey-colored marble that she'd sat on. She had turned the bar of soap brown. Under the clear water she cleaned the soap itself.

2

DAWN HEAVED UP, THE SUN JUST VISIBLE THROUGH THE WIN-
dow. She turned her head. Biddy was on her side with a hand under her
cheek and a stripe of hair across her mouth. One of the rules of their best
friendship was that they always woke at the exact same time. They wanted
everything to happen to them at the same time.

Their parents had been close forever, but Margaret and Biddy liked to
think they would have been best friends even if their parents had spoken
different languages or come from warring tribes. The boys got along because Danny got along with everyone, but it was in Margaret and Biddy
that the bond had been perfected. They had napped together, traded
pacifiers, caught the same fevers, bit each other when angered, thrown
what must have been terrifying simultaneous tantrums of which they
now felt very proud. Once Biddy had said her stomach hurt and Margaret
had run to the bathroom and barfed. It was the meat loaf, but they made
it part of their mythology. They knew where the other family kept the

snacks and silverware and precisely how much patience each parent could be trusted to extend.

Over spring break Margaret had gone on a plane for the first time, to England. Her dad had been promoted, and the children were old enough to appreciate travel. So once a year, Elizabeth said, they would go somewhere enriching, just as she had done with her parents when she was a girl. When Margaret got back, Biddy had refused to listen to a single thing about the trip. If she so much as mentioned tea or castles, Biddy gave her the silent treatment. This was only fair. Margaret had felt the same way when Biddy went to the Six Flags near Trenton with her swim team. Jealous—jealous of the unshared experience.

Every new thing that happened to you changed you; you couldn't take it back. When they were younger, they sometimes got their mothers to dress them in the same outfit, like twins. They wouldn't try that now— it would only draw attention to how different Biddy was from her, how much more concrete, with her curls and her girl-athlete's body. But they had discussed, endlessly, the training bras, how they would wear them on the first day of school.

SHE ROLLED AWAY and then back, coughed, shut her eyes. Then she opened them. And there was Biddy, awake on her separate pillow, looking at her. She waited another second so they could say "pancakes" simultaneously.

Downstairs, the comfort of the kitchen, implements and ingredients all sensibly arranged: spices in the spice drawer, knives in the knife block, mixing bowls nested by diminishing diameter, the cloudy bottles of vinegar and oil. They stared at the Bisquick for a while, hoping Margaret's dad would come down and mix it like he had when they were littler. But they were almost in fifth grade now; they could do it themselves.

They got the stove on, and the butter melted in a skillet. They spooned the batter into circles, poked at the edges with the spatula. The sizzle burned the night away, burned it up in the hot, solid clattering elements of the morning.

"Girls!" Around the corner came Margaret's father, already dressed in another white polo. He palmed the top of her head in his direction and glanced a kiss. "Cooking," he said. "Enough for me?"

He picked a golden one off the stack with a fork, and raw batter oozed up around the tines. "Leave this to the professionals," he said. They were pleased. They considered their fathers' pancakes a tribute to them—the only thing they cooked that wasn't meat. He took over the skillet, turned down the flame, slipped the half-cooked pancakes back onto the heat. "Everybody sleep okay? No bumps in the night?"

"Where's Mom?" she asked.

"Your mother's not feeling well."

So it was one of those days.

Her mouth was full of pancake when her brother, Neal, walked in— Neal with Jane the cat in his arms. He was petting the cat, running his hand down her back and over her tail. It bothered Margaret, though she didn't know why; there was nothing obscene about it. And Jane was purring.

"Morning, Dad," he said.

"Help yourself," their father said. "But could you not pet the cat at the table?"

Neal dumped her to the floor.

Anyone who looked at Neal and Margaret knew they were brother and sister, and yet people talked about Neal being handsome and they did not talk about her being pretty. Maybe her features worked better on a boy, or maybe, at thirteen, he had just grown into them better. Almost all grown-ups admired Neal. He was like a grown-up himself, in the way that he always knew how to be polite. Other kids teased him, which made the grown-ups like him more. It seemed to Margaret that it was Neal's fault he didn't have more friends, but old people seemed to disagree, seemed to think that the kids in their ignorance were missing some rare quality.

Elizabeth loved him more because he was so unlikable. That was just the kind of thing that mothers did.

The girls finished and ran hot water over their plates, sticky with the fake syrup's sweet chemicals. A click and a whoosh and the AC switched on, and Mrs. Murphy honked from the driveway.

AFTER BIDDY LEFT, Margaret went upstairs to Elizabeth with a plate of pancakes like it was Mother's Day. She'd had the idea to pour the syrup into an egg cup so the pancakes wouldn't get soggy, and she was proud of this, of how careful she'd been, and of the goblet of amber nectar that rippled as she walked.

She loved her mother's bedroom, how it was as fancy and formal as the dining room downstairs, with no mess or clutter, no clothes thrown over the back of a chair, no pocket junk on the dresser. There was a satin bedspread in robin's-egg blue that Elizabeth didn't even use as a blanket, just folded down to the foot of the bed each night. On the dresser were treasures: a silver mirror and a silver comb; a shallow bowl clinking with cuff links; an obelisk of perfume. Anything small and delicate and precious to her mother was irresistible to Margaret, and sometimes she was allowed to pick these things up and look at them, and sometimes she was not. But she must never touch the glass box at the center. It locked with a miniature key like for a girl's diary, and inside were the antique dueling pistols her parents had given each other one anniversary. A gold plaque on top read—romantically, worryingly—

> *Hugh and Elizabeth*
> *'til death do us part.*

Her mother was in bed; the room was dark. Margaret put the plate on the dresser and climbed up next to her. "Mom?" She touched her shoulder, then lifted her hand off, touched and lifted. "Mom, are you asleep?"

"Hello, my darling."

"I brought you breakfast."

"Is it late?"

"Pretty late."

Elizabeth rolled over and propped herself half up against the pillows, rubbing her face with her hands. "Hand me my robe."

Margaret bounced down and lifted the robe off the hook on the inside of the closet door. It was so fine and silky, touching it was like touching her mother's skin.

"How was the sleepover?"

"Fun."

"Have you done your chores?"

"I'm going to."

Margaret looked at the novels stacked on her mother's side of the bed. They were all about English girls who worked in bookstores during the war, or about English girls who worked as nurses during the war, or about Italian girls who fell in love with dukes. She hoped Elizabeth wouldn't tell her to go.

Almost a year ago, Elizabeth had stayed in bed for days and days. She had taken too many pills one morning after the kids went to school, Margaret knew, because Elizabeth had told her. She had explained all about it one morning, the two of them sitting in bed as if at story time.

"Sometimes you have to do something extreme so people understand how much pain you're in," Elizabeth had said. *People* meant Dad. It was because of The Affair. Elizabeth used capital letters to talk about it, and so Margaret and Neal did too. Their father did not talk about it at all, though he was the one who'd done it, had it—The Affair.

But Margaret hadn't entirely understood if the pills were somehow an accident—if maybe Elizabeth had been so upset that she'd gotten confused and eaten a big handful of pills instead of something else, some normal food, like popcorn. It was Neal who told her no: that Elizabeth had done it on purpose because Elizabeth had wanted to die. He had turned off the TV to tell her that. He hadn't cried, so she didn't either. "You can't tell anyone," he'd told her. "Not even Biddy."

Elizabeth said their father went away because he was a coward. Neal said he'd come back soon. Their mother stayed in the bedroom. It was much easier to keep the secret than she'd thought it would be. Mrs. Murphy came to check on them. She would stop by in the afternoons, put a casserole or pizza on the counter, disappear upstairs. Three times she picked them up and took them to the swimming pool, where they played sharks and minnows with Biddy and Danny.

"Okay, guys?" she would say when she dropped them back off in the driveway. And to Neal: "Take good care of your sister."

Eventually someone must have called their dad's sister Aunt Daphne, because she drove up from Delaware and took them to stay with her for a week or two. When Aunt Daphne brought them home again, school was about to start, and their father was back, and Elizabeth was up in Margaret's closet, pulling out sundresses. "It's an absolute pigsty in here. None of these can possibly fit you anymore," she was saying, and Margaret had cannonballed on the bed for joy.

She was a kid back then. But she was big enough to understand that when Mrs. Murphy brought the casseroles but not her daughter, it was because she didn't want Biddy in their house. She didn't want her to know that things had gone so wrong. And that made sense, though that first big secret was a crack in the mirror of their friendship, worse than England, worse than pretending she hadn't woken up first.

Margaret hoped, since Elizabeth hadn't died, that she no longer wanted to. But probably sometimes she still did, at least a little bit, and probably it was on days like these, when she didn't want to come out of the bedroom.

"I wasn't in my right mind," Elizabeth had said when she told Margaret about the pills. It hadn't occurred to Margaret before then that you had more than one mind to be in. It was now something that she worried about: protecting, like the pistols in the glass box, the right mind of Elizabeth.

. . .

WHEN SHE HANDED her mother the robe, Elizabeth grabbed her arm. "Margaret," she gasped, "you are absolutely covered in mosquito bites."

All over the white underside of her arm, where the tan never reached, were bright red welts. "It's not that bad . . ." She'd been scratching all morning without noticing.

Her mother held on to the arm, turning it this way and that under the whip of sunlight that made it through the curtains. "You got *devoured*. What will Biddy's mother say? We *have* to get rid of those disgusting bats. The least they could do is keep the mosquitoes off you."

The fussing made the itching worse. Elizabeth put a finger, carefully, right on a bite, and the itch burned up Margaret's arm, so hot everywhere she could feel it behind her eyelids. But she didn't pull away.

Her mother's touch, the whip of light, the close attention. Margaret wanted to cry. Briskly Elizabeth said, "Go into my medicine cabinet and put some hydrocortisone on those right now."

You always feel sadder when you look into a mirror. It's because to the sadness in yourself is added the more generous sadness you feel for another person. Poor thing, Margaret thought about her reflection. The girl in the mirror looked like she was suffering from something much worse than whatever was bothering Margaret.

Weird, Margaret thought, how the ins and outs and shapes and holes clustered at the front of a head made up something this nakedly expressive of thinking and feeling—the face. All that thinking and feeling, Margaret knew, was what Elizabeth was talking about when she said, "Stop making that face." Stop making that face, Margaret thought now at the girl in the mirror. Her eyes were too small and too far apart, and there was something wrong with the mouth; it was all twisted up and trembling. Stop making that face. She splashed cold water on it. She forgot about the hydrocortisone. When she went back into the bedroom, her mother was gone.

3

SHE WOULD NEVER AGAIN KNOW SO LITTLE OR HAVE SO LIT-
tle to do. The mothers had signed up Neal and Danny for a Model UN
camp all summer (Neal: into it; Danny: furious) and Biddy had swim team,
but Margaret wasn't doing anything. She emptied and loaded the dishwasher, took out the trash, emptied and loaded the dishwasher. She went
to the pool with Biddy. She read, endlessly, in the yard, books about special
children doing magic. She daydreamed about Danny, and about JTT from
Home Improvement, and about Calvin O'Keefe from *A Wrinkle in Time*.

She owned a book of poems called *A Child's Garden of Verses*. It had a
red fabric cover and had belonged to her mother growing up. It was a trea-
sure because Elizabeth had won it as a prize at school, the all-girls boarding school she'd gone to when she was even younger than Margaret. Most
of the students came from faraway places, but not Elizabeth. Her parents
lived right there in town. But her father was an important businessman
and her mother threw many parties, and a child at home was a lot of
bother. They wanted their daughter mostly on holidays, Elizabeth said,

when they went to Europe and bought her very beautiful clothes. Both her parents were dead now and it was tragic, like a story. Imagine: having to live at school! Margaret was grateful that no one made her do that. Though in fact Elizabeth always said she had liked the school. It suited her, the kilts and dorms and order, and mass at 4:00 and dinner at 5:00, and the magisterial headmistress with chalk-white fingers who awarded her the book of poems, on the inside cover of which, in a schoolgirl cursive significant as a celebrity autograph, she had written the name *Elizabeth*.

Margaret knew a lot of the poems by heart, and sometimes they played in her head like pop songs. She liked even better a poem that her own teacher had read to her: *Margaret are you grieving over Goldengrove unleaving?* That was a tree. She said that to herself a lot. Margaret, are you grieving? Oh! It was beautiful.

Her historical education came primarily from the American Girl Doll books, which is why she associated the Revolution with redheads climbing trees. About slavery she knew that it was very bad and long ago; about politics she knew only the president's name. She knew about abortion, or at least that people carried posters about abortion. She knew who Kristi Yamaguchi was. The family had one computer, in a corner of the living room, which she had to use to play a game that taught typing and the multiplication tables. Twice with Biddy she had braved the alarm of the dial-up to go on the internet and been equally bored and disturbed by what they'd found there. In health class she had colored in diagrams about puberty but had no idea what it would feel like when her own body changed. They made it sound like it was all little things, hair and pimples, pores and follicles. But she knew it was a bigger deal—more like disappearing, cell by cell, until you were replaced by a whole new body.

She often wondered: What was the point of her? She was ten years old.

One morning Margaret was doing nothing as usual when a car pulled fast into the driveway and Mrs. Ricci from down the road tumbled out. Neal was at camp, their father was at work, and Elizabeth was somewhere in the garden, pulling things out or putting things in. It was only Margaret who saw.

Mrs. Ricci had long hair even though she was a grown-up and had always been sweet to Margaret because she had sons and no daughters, though she probably liked it that way. They lived in a giant brick house behind an iron fence with a driveway that went in a circle around an actual fountain, which Elizabeth thought was very ostentatious, but that was not to be repeated.

"Margaret, get your mother. It's an emergency."

She was ready. She ran around the corner, shouting, "Mom!" And there was Elizabeth, rising from the flower bed. Elizabeth strode down the driveway; she would take care of what was wrong.

Margaret stopped on the porch steps, a polite distance away, and watched the mothers, waiting for their orders. "Lost," she could hear, "sometime last night . . ." Something must have happened to one of the Ricci boys, some gruesome injury—to shy Philip or bullying Jeremy, neither of whom Margaret liked, but neither of whom she wanted hurt or dead either. Mrs. Ricci put her hands up in her hair and started shaking her head from side to side. A mosquito had flown into Margaret's ear once and gotten stuck in the wax, buzzing right by her brain, and she had shaken her head just like that and screamed.

Mrs. Ricci and her mother were friends, but not really. They always said "Let's get together" if they ran into each other. If Elizabeth was watering the flowers by the road, Mrs. Ricci would slow down in her car and say "Your roses are bliss." But the families had been invited to each other's houses only a few times. Elizabeth didn't seem to need a lot of friends.

So it was surprising when Elizabeth hugged Mrs. Ricci, pressed her tight against her chest and held her there. One of Elizabeth's hands was on Mrs. Ricci's back, rubbing up and down, the other cupping the back of her head. Elizabeth was (and this was also surprising) much smaller than Mrs. Ricci. All Margaret could see of her mother were her two hands and a bit of blond hair wisping over Mrs. Ricci's shoulder. She watched in wonder the mother in her mother's arms. The only adult she'd ever seen cry before was Elizabeth.

"We've looked everywhere," Mrs. Ricci said, pulling away. "What if she was stolen?"

Stolen? She who?

Elizabeth, having given comfort, was all action. "Have you called Animal Control? Okay, I'll do that now. And then I'll help you look. Don't worry, she'll turn up."

It was an emergency, but it wasn't Philip or Jeremy who was missing. It was Gambol, their pet pygmy goat.

Gambol lived in a pen in the Riccis' backyard and in theory ate sugar cubes and peppermints out of the palm of your hand, though the few times Margaret had been over to the house, the goat had refused to come anywhere near the fence. They had the goat because Mr. Ricci was allergic to dogs and cats but it was important for children to grow up knowing how to take care of animals. Mrs. Ricci said that as if the goat made the house a farm, like the boys were up at dawn with a bucket in each hand, though everyone knew that this was New Jersey and only pretend.

The goat had a pink collar that read *Gambol*, and her name was also on a gold plaque on the gate of her pen, the gate that Mrs. Ricci was saying now had been mysteriously opened in the night. The goat was so tiny—only as tall as Margaret's knees—not just tiny but freakishly so. People wouldn't expect it. They would run her over in their car before their brains said, What was that? Was that a little goat?

AN OLD MAN MARGARET didn't know was walking up their driveway, though people didn't walk up driveways here; it wasn't that kind of neighborhood. He had gray curls, like her dad's would someday be, but longer and messier than he would let them get. A short-sleeved button-up tucked over a big, hard belly into blue jeans, the blue jeans tucked into work boots.

"Daddy," Mrs. Ricci said.

"Saw the car from the street," the man said. "I walked the road from the back and didn't spot her. Just going to do another loop. Expanding the search party?"

He shook Elizabeth's hand. "Don't think we met before; I'm Stu Elkins, Jeannie's father, from Maryland."

It was strange to think of Mrs. Ricci having a father.

"So nice to meet you," Elizabeth said. "I was just about to call Animal Control."

"Good idea," the man said, nodding.

Elizabeth sniffed, like maybe it wasn't a good idea, or who was he to say so. Margaret understood; Elizabeth wanted to be the one in charge— and she should be, she deserved to be. She was using that tone she used with Margaret's dad, when she was telling him how to fix a situation at work that seemed hard but really wasn't. Elizabeth had never had a job as far as Margaret knew, but if she had, she would have been very good at it. Margaret was proud to have such a competent mother, a mother who didn't fall to pieces when the crisis was someone else's problem.

"Margaret, come here," Elizabeth said. "Why don't you help Mr. Elkins look around on foot while Mrs. Ricci and I drive."

She didn't want to. With a stranger? She wanted to stay with the mothers. But it wasn't a question.

"My daughter," Elizabeth said, gesturing an introduction. "I'll just go in and make this call and get you a glass of water, Jeannie."

Margaret stayed where she was. She looked at Elizabeth, but her mother was already gone. Mrs. Ricci was leaning against the car, taking big breaths with her eyes shut and a hand against her chest.

"This okay with you?" the man asked her.

So Margaret shrugged, okay. She followed him down the driveway and turned left.

"I'll bet you're a kid who knows all the shortcuts and secret spots around here. That right?"

"I guess."

"And what's your name again?"

"Margaret," she said, then: "Margo."

"Now, Margo: If you were the world's tiniest goat, where would you go?"

"Well . . . I wouldn't go far."

"Right. Not on those stumpy legs."

He whistled up and down while she thought.

"I would find somewhere with lots of grass . . ."

"Yup."

"Or clover. Somewhere cool." It was already too hot, the sun stunting their shadows on the road.

"I'll bet that she's barely made it off the property. Let's do another sweep, yes? Of all the cool and shady places."

"Okay. So—you're Mrs. Ricci's dad?"

"I am. I'm visiting for the week."

"From Maryland."

"Good memory. Baltimore."

"Do you like it there?"

He thought it over, as if he was really considering the question. "I do like it, yes," he said. "But my wife died, so."

"Will you move here now?"

"Here?" They had come to the Riccis' driveway. "Ha," he said—not a real laugh, just the word for a laugh. "No."

She felt like she knew what he meant. The brick house was too big, like the goat was too small. They were made not for function or survival, but for something else—to make an impression, to overwhelm or endear. Only someone very rich could have things so frivolously big and small.

They walked down the driveway around to the back, where they stopped and surveyed. There was the stone patio and the barbecue grill. There was the goat's pen and its suspiciously wide-open gate. There was the wall of hedges that encircled the pool, and then beyond it the industrial-size lawn. On either side was a wild strip of nature—five or so feet of forest hiding the neighbors' houses. Hiding the houses was the point of the forest, the only reason the trees had been spared in that landscape of grass and mulched flowers. This was the fanciest thing about the property—fancier even than the pool and the fountain and the pretend farm in the backyard—the fact that there was no visible evidence that other people existed.

"I'll take the right, you take the left?"

Under the trees was a different world, things furling and unfurling, sprouting and decaying, green on top and black underneath. She skirted the poison ivy with its poison-waxed leaves. She was good at identifying which leaves were for sure poison ivy but less good at identifying which leaves were for sure *not* poison ivy, which made everything suspect and walking hard.

She bent down and peered through the branches, clicking her tongue like for a cat. The more she looked for the goat, the more she wanted to find it. She would bundle it into her arms and present it to the mothers. She was proud to have a test, a quest, a purpose. The dads and the boys had gone. The goat would bleat, and she would find it, save it, keep it safe.

But it wasn't there. Maybe it didn't want to be found. She had gone all the way down to the end of the lawn and all the way back up again, and she was thirsty. On the other side of the yard she could see the old man doing the same thing as her. Walking and stooping and looking and walking again. She could take a break. She wouldn't get in trouble for that. She would go put her feet in the pool.

She walked through the gate in the hedge, kicked off her sandals, and sank her feet into the water. Immediately she felt less thirsty. She swished her legs up and down so the cold got in around every toe. Then she looked up. The goat was lying under one of the deck chairs.

In the slats' striped shadows it looked weirder and wilder than she'd remembered. She'd imagined it a sweet lamb, all silky wool and soft rooting nose, like the lamb that sat in Mary's lap in *The Secret Garden*. But it wasn't a lamb, it was a goat, and not just a goat, a pygmy goat. She had thought that being small and fragile would make it cute, but up close it wasn't cute at all. It had dirty gray hair and odds-and-ends-looking legs, joints that made her think of tangled-up bone, and staring yellow eyes too far on either side of its face.

She did not want to bundle the goat in her arms. It didn't look like a creature that could be bundled. It looked like it might bite or die. She felt no desire to protect it. If anything, she felt the opposite: repulsed and some-how threatened. The animal kept looking at her, without fear or curiosity. The pupil in its eye was a thick horizontal line, like someone had drawn a strike through the eye, tried to cross it out to start over.

There was something wrong with the goat, or something wrong with the world to have made it. Its defenselessness was a kind of test, a test that everyone was going to fail or had already failed. The fact that it was so easy to hurt made her feel that someone, maybe Margaret, would have to hurt it. The sun caught the gold on its collar and glinted. Silently, she crept out of the hedges.

4

THE OLD MAN HAD BEEN THE ONE TO RETURN THE GOAT TO the pen. He didn't pick it up. He just hooked a finger under its collar and tugged until it came. He gave Margaret full credit. "Genius," he said, though she'd explained it was an accident. He hit his forehead with his palm and sighed at the grown-ups' stupidity. "Of course it would have been lounging by the pool, like every other kid in this family." He winked, because *kid* was a pun, and getting the pun was almost as good as finding the goat.

Mrs. Ricci cried again when she got home and saw the goat. She ran to it and fell on her knees and nuzzled its weird face. The goat just stood there, tolerating the caresses, the flat line in its eye never wavering. Margaret and Elizabeth stood together at the fence. Elizabeth was still in her gardening clothes, and there was dirt on the seat of her shorts. Her blond hair was wild in the heat, and clipped half back behind one ear. Margaret risked a direct glance at her face.

Her mouth looked funny, like she was moving something gross around inside it, something she didn't want to be rude and spit out but didn't want to taste either. A heavy, satisfied feeling settled over Margaret's head and shoulders. She and her mother had something in common: They felt the same way about the goat. They could never have loved it like Mrs. Ricci loved it.

AS A THANK-YOU for finding the goat—the poor baby could have drowned!—Mrs. Ricci invited them all for a swim after Neal and the Ricci boys got home from their camps. So in the early evening they went back, Margaret heroic in her Speedo. Philip was nice about it: "We heard you found Gambol. Mom must have been freaking out." Jeremy held his palm up and wouldn't put it down until she submitted to the high-five. She would have bet money that one of the boys had left Gambol's gate open. If Margaret did that, she'd be dead meat, but in the Ricci family it seemed like no one got in trouble.

Soon the boys were ignoring her, throwing around a Nerf football, groaning when they dove and missed. Margaret bounced on the diving board, delaying the moment of entry. The water was so clear it might have been a sunk pool of nothing at all. She was just up there, mindlessly boinging. It was nice to be sprung into the air, to jump without trying. At the top of each bounce she could see over the line of hedges, over the prestigious lawn, and down to the road at the bottom of the hill with a tiny stop sign at the end of it as if to say: *That's it, you can't see any farther.* Then down she would go and then up again, ever-so-slightly higher.

She noticed suddenly that the pool was quiet. The boys were looking at her, watching . . . what? Oh god. Had it been sexy, what she was doing? But there was nothing in the Speedo, nothing to catch anyone's attention. She came down from the bounce—it seemed to take forever to come down—and twisted her ankle on the edge of the board in her hurry to get off it. Water everywhere, water up her nose. Stupid pool water, why did it have to be so clear? There was nothing to hide behind but the bubbles of her own exhaled breath. She wanted lake water dark with mud; she wanted to be down in the weeds. She brought her knees to her chest in cannonball position and floated there, refusing to surface.

But suddenly, underneath her, two hands on her ass. She had never thought the word *ass* in relation to her own body before, but now for the first time she did, and just thinking the word seemed to change her body, as if the muscles there tensed into a new shape and would not relax again. Two hands on her ass lifting her up, up through the water and flinging her out of it into the air. The air stripped the water from her skin and her legs flailed open and so did her eyes. She was up in the green landscape of the hedges again, but not high enough to see above them. The black sheen of the boys' heads went by below her, round as river stones. And then down she hit the surface halfway to the shallow end.

She had always loved being thrown in the pool. Her dad would toss her and she'd buoy up laughing, demand to be thrown again. But this was different.

"Don't touch me," she said.

"Just messing around," Jeremy said.

She looked at Neal. "Chill," he said. It wasn't clear if he was talking to her or to Jeremy.

"Hey, catch," Philip called, and held the football up in one hand, cocked it back, mimed the spasm of an arrested pass. But his brother ignored him, and so did hers. "Hey, Jeremy," Philip tried again. "Let's play."

Jeremy lowered himself so that only his nose and eyes were above the surface.

"I don't want to be thrown," she said.

He ducked his head under and swam. Something about his too-broad white back coming toward her freaked her out. It was like a shark but grosser. The ripples made the edges of the colors wiggle, the blue of the tiles penetrating the skin and the skin penetrating the tiles. He just wanted to play. He wanted to toss her in the air like a football. What was the big deal? But she thought she couldn't bear for him to touch her again. She kicked backward, but there was nowhere to go; she was trapped between the pebbles of the pool wall and the smooth, rubbery wetness of his body.

"What the fuck did you do?" Jeremy shrieked. Now Jeremy was the one sputtering out of the water like something had shocked and hurt him there. Across his chest and shoulder were red lines, dark with blood, each scratch surrounded by spreading, stinging, valentine-pink, as if trimmed with a border of ribbon. She lifted a dripping hand out of the water and turned it around, inspected her fingernails. A lot of his skin must be under there.

Right then the mothers walked up. Margaret swished her hand underwater. Mrs. Ricci had a pitcher and cups on a tray, Elizabeth a pile of white towels in her arms. Behind them came the old man. The mothers looked young in an ancient way, Margaret thought, like serving girls painted on a wall. She looked hard at the mothers so she didn't have to look at Neal or Jeremy. She thought the word *mural*. No, *fresco*. It had something to do with their bare shoulders, and the miniature green leaves of the hedge behind them, and the white stone under their sandals. They looked like serving girls painted on a fresco in a temple in Rome, which was a place Elizabeth had visited as a girl and always wanted to go back to, because that's where you could really see history, in the ruins.

Elizabeth placed the towels down on a chair and then she saw Jeremy. She looked from the cuts to Margaret and back again.

"You're bleeding," Mrs. Ricci said.

"Margaret! Did you do that?" Elizabeth assumed it was Margaret, and this time she was right. She looked at Neal, and he shrugged: Yeah, it was her.

"Why were you playing so rough?"

"He threw me," she said.

"So?" asked Elizabeth, genuinely baffled. "Apologize to Jeremy. You hurt him!"

Whatever credit she had gained with Mrs. Ricci for finding the goat was gone. She had saved the goat but scratched—perhaps scarred—her son. He heaved himself out of the pool like a wounded soldier coming out of some trench in her dad's war movies. The mothers bustled around him. They pressed a white towel against his chest, as if they needed further proof that the blood was real. When it came away red, they looked even more surprised.

The old man had sat down on a lounge chair, and he was looking at his daughter, who was looking at her son. Margaret couldn't tell what he was thinking. He wore the same short-sleeved button-up but had exchanged his boots and blue jeans for swim trunks. His white legs were skinnier than she would have expected. Under his chair, the shadows lay in jungled stripes.

Elizabeth stepped to the edge of the pool. The sun was behind her. "Apologize," she said. Her hands twitched, but she couldn't reach Margaret; she was too deep in the water. "Come here right now and say sorry."

Margaret took a step forward but then stopped. No. She wouldn't come. She wasn't sorry. She had made those marks in the surface of the world. She had not been thrown again.

She backed away instead, step by step, to the far side of the pool.

Mrs. Ricci had her hands on her face again; apparently that was just a thing she did, it didn't take much. Margaret hated her then, and the old man too, who had been so nice but now couldn't possibly like her anymore. Even Elizabeth had made a fuss about the goat, and now Margaret hated her most, for being so concerned that it was safe, for joining in the motherly fluster.

"Come back here this instant. Come back here or you'll be—"

Margaret had reached the other end of the pool. She put her palms behind her on the edge, lifted and scooched her new ass backward.

"Margaret, don't you dare."

But she was running for it, running home, not bothering with a towel, through the hedges and down across the lawn, grass clippings sticking to her feet and legs, knee-socked in the cut-down green.

5

THE NEXT DAY THEY WENT TO THE MALL. THEY NEEDED NEW shoes for the school year, new jeans and tops too, and Elizabeth didn't want to leave it to the last minute. Their dad was supposed to come— he'd told Neal they would go to Brooks Brothers together—but had too much work at the last minute, so it was only the three of them, the children and their mother.

Margaret was bothered by the mall. There were so many things she wanted, but she couldn't have everything—it had to be something Elizabeth approved of, and even within that category it was so hard to decide: Why this thing over that thing? And still when they walked into the expensive air, she wanted it, that, maybe that thing over there.

The mall was a square, and the stores were arranged in order of ascending (or, if you walked in the other direction, descending) expense. You could start at Old Navy, where the shirts were piled in bins, and then walk up to the Gap, where the same shirts were on hangers, and then to

J.Crew and Banana Republic, with their soft sweaters forever refolding. In Abercrombie & Fitch, body spray hung in the dark rooms like rain. Would Victoria's Secret have training bras? She was too embarrassed to ask; the posters out front were angel porn, and Neal was openly staring.

Finally, at the pinnacle, was Nordstrom. Oh, Nordstrom! At Christmas they bought gloves from glass cases for their oldest relatives. As if it were another century, it even sold hats—hats for horse races, with wide brims and ribbons, and jaunty black ones that could be meant only for lady detectives. Margaret had never seen anyone shopping for hats, but it was crucial that the hats be there. From the Estée Lauder counter they would buy Elizabeth's face cream in its precious white jar. And then they would go up the elevator to the floor where Elizabeth bought her dresses.

Elizabeth did not believe in the color black. She did not believe in anything cheap or skimpy. If it didn't cost enough, she wouldn't buy it. She liked a tailored sundress. She liked buttons and belts and visible stitching and silk linings. When she really loved a dress she would buy it in multiple sizes—a six for herself, a zero for Margaret, and a two for Margaret to grow into. This was why Margaret had many dresses that would have been appropriate for a husband's boss's cookout or an evening at the theater but none of the low-rise khakis (cheap) or spaghetti-strap tops (skimpy) that she deeply desired.

After an hour in the mall Margaret no longer desired anything except to be free of desire, to desire nothing ever again. By the time they made it to the shoe section she was the new owner of a knee-length A-line belted sundress in blue and white toile that would have to be taken in because she was too short-waisted and a duckling yellow sheath dress with a matching cap-sleeved jacket that Elizabeth called a bolero. Neal had three sweaters that he wouldn't be able to wear for three more months. Her throat hurt. She felt like she was breathing in the threads of his sweaters, some airborne slurry of acrylic fibers and ground-down sequins. Her throat was like the inside of a sleeve. She wanted to sit down; she really wanted to sit down.

. . .

"MY DAUGHTER despises shopping."

"I don't, I'm just tired."

"Oh, you'll see, she hates it."

"Mom, please don't tell people that. I really don't."

The salesman, on his knees to check her size, had big wrists and quills of gel-hard hair and a firm hold on Margaret's ankle. "We'll just have to change her mind, then, won't we?"

Margaret's feet were right on the line. She could wear the largest kid sizes or the smallest adult size. How to proceed? She definitely wasn't going to wear light-up Disney sneakers, but she wasn't going to wear purple velvet stilettos either. She finally chose a pair of navy Adidas that showed up on both sides of the age divide, which seemed therefore ageless, and which were very similar, actually, to a pair Danny had worn the year before. "I love them," she said, and kissed Elizabeth's cheek. "Thanks, Mom."

"A kiss! I *never* get any kisses," Elizabeth told the salesman.

"Ma'am, I find that *very* hard to believe."

"Now," Elizabeth said, "go choose two more pairs."

"What?"

"If you want these sneakers, you also have to choose two more pairs. Nice ones. Leather ones."

"But—why?"

"You need at least three pairs of decent shoes for the year, and I don't want to argue about it."

She tried anyway. She had many shoes and listed them for Elizabeth, who didn't care. "If you want to get the sneakers, you need to select two others. Simple enough."

She was acting playful, but she wasn't joking. She'd made up this game, and Margaret had to play it. The salesman was in on it too, like they'd planned it out together in advance. Neal was sitting a row away with *The*

Lord of the Rings and the same white tennis shoes their father wore in a smaller size, undergoing no psychodrama.

Margaret looked at the blue sneakers, nestled back in their box. She could refuse them. She could take her mother's bet, face her down. She could get nothing and win. But she wanted the sneakers. Elizabeth knew how much she wanted them.

Also she didn't want to make a scene. You had to be really, really mad to pick a fight with Elizabeth. You had to be maximally, disproportionately angry, and she knew she didn't have that kind of fury in her.

"Better get shopping," Elizabeth said.

Margaret looked at the shoes, rows and rows of them, square-toed pumps and two-dimensional flip-flops and running shoes as inflated as tires. There were kitten heels and funky heels and sexy heels, and boots like smooth brown amputated legs. It didn't seem possible that all of these were meant for actual feet, for actual walking. That Margaret would choose any, would wear them on her body to walk through the dirt— absurd. She stood in her socks surrounded.

But Elizabeth was watching her, the salesman smiling along. "I can always choose for you," Elizabeth said, waggling a loafer, black and awful with a big gold buckle.

It occurred to her then that it wasn't a game—it was a punishment. Of course it was. Dumb, Margaret. Elizabeth had made her write an apology letter that morning: *Dear Jeremy and Mrs. Ricci, I am very sorry that I did not control my temper in the pool yesterday.* Elizabeth had added a PS, inviting the Ricci boys to come over whenever they liked. They had dropped it in the mailbox on their way to the mall. That was the punishment for scratching Jeremy. But this was the punishment for defying Elizabeth.

"Can't you just hurry up?" Neal said. "I'm hungry."

The salesman fit her three shoe boxes into two big paper bags. "That wasn't so bad, now was it?" Elizabeth said. Margaret promised herself that she would never wear the shoes. She knew she would wear the shoes.

· · ·

LUNCH WAS ALWAYS at Café la Mer. It was the nicest restaurant at the mall, which meant that it almost felt like you weren't at the mall. The restaurant accomplished this by being windowless and very dark. A bare minimum of light trickled out from the gold lamps on each table and the sconces on the wall and dripped onto the silverware and the tense surfaces of the water glasses. Their bags barely fit under the table. When Elizabeth went to the bathroom, Margaret said to Neal, "She's being so intense today."

"What was with that shoe thing?" he asked.

"Yeah, how come she didn't make you get so many?"

"Probably because I'm not a girl," he said.

When she's being a little mean to me, I think she's having fun, she thought but did not say. She wouldn't betray Elizabeth, not even to Neal. She kicked her feet against the bags so they crinkled and the boxes inside made a hollow beaten sound.

Elizabeth came back and paid the bill. This was Margaret's last chance to bring up the training bra, but she didn't want to mention it in front of Neal. Besides, she was worried that her mother would make her buy ten bras, twenty bras, ones like the angels wore in the ads, with lace and matching underwear, the kind that went up your butt.

Instead of going back the way they'd come, they took the short way to the car. They walked around the corner and into an empty area. The stores must have been under construction—their windows were opaque, the insides covered with white paper. Their footsteps echoed. A column stood in the center of the hall, surrounded by big shiny ferns. It looked like it was meant to display a map, with a red dot reading *You are here*, but there was no map. The plain white stone made it significant, like it was the mall's own monument. Instead of the plants she felt there should have been some kind of sacrifice there, an offering, a pyre of burning shoes. She could dump her bags out onto the floor, everything she'd wanted and everything she hadn't. Was this the lesson of the mall? That to get what you asked for, you had to take more than you asked for? Maybe wanting was always like this: Perverted. Stuffed down your throat.

"Margaret, hurry up. Big steps."

On the other side of the column, the mall began all over again, like an error or a joke, and suddenly they were at Claire's, where a dozen girls were waiting for their piercings in a line outside the door.

6

HAD IT ALWAYS BEEN THERE? IF IT HAD ALWAYS BEEN THERE, why had she never noticed it before? But if it hadn't always been there, when had it gotten there, and how? It was an empty square in the wall, right down by the floor, maybe eight inches tall. It was like a door for elves or fairies—some kind of passageway. Margaret was washing her hair in the shower one afternoon when she noticed it. She rinsed off her face, looked again. It was still there.

The shower was on one side of the bathroom and the hole was on the other. It was the guest bathroom, technically—the one the kids used. Above it were shelves stacked with towels, the tissue box, the Q-tip jar, the cotton ball jar, the candle in a glass cup painted with white lilies. But beneath the ordinary arrangement: that empty square. She needed to go look at it, but she didn't want to get close to it. Something could come out. A rat, maybe. Maybe lots of rats. Or something worse. Margaret didn't want to think about it.

She turned off the shower, wrapped a towel tight around her chest.

She took a step toward the hole. What would she see if she looked through it? She'd see the room on the other side of the wall, of course, the guest room with the blue quilt, and the rocking chair that Elizabeth didn't like enough to put anywhere else, and the chest at the foot of the bed where Margaret kept the dolls she was too old to play with.

Or maybe it would be like in *The Lion, the Witch and the Wardrobe*, when the snowflakes float by the fur coats. Maybe she'd see inside the blackberry bush. Maybe she'd see nothing, just a black void forever, and the wind would whistle through it and suddenly all the bats of the attic would wake up and come winging.

But there was something in the hole. A step closer, and she could see it glinting. She thought of a jewel, of a genie's lamp. She thought of an eye. But it was round and as still as glass. She got on her knees and put her hand in the hole and pulled it out. It was a video camera.

MARGARET PUSHED the wastepaper basket in front of the hole. She hid the camera for days. She hid it in the guest room chest, at the very bottom, under the Barbies' prom dresses. Every few hours she would close the door and fish it out and stare at it.

It read PANASONIC, and it was boxy, glossy black, with a row of buttons down the top that she didn't dare touch. She lifted it up to her eye, pulled it away. It was like finding a hole within the hole. She thought of the men she sometimes saw at intersections, with those cameras on stilts that counted how many cars went by. Maybe it was something like that, with a practical purpose that Margaret just didn't understand. Maybe Elizabeth was planning to remodel the bathroom and the architect had asked for a video?

She touched the sides of the hole, and they were rough, more uneven than they'd looked at first. That part of the wall was thin, the wall between the guest room and the bathroom shelves. It made a hollow sound if you knocked on it. It looked solid enough, but a little saw could cut right through it, a saw like the one on a nail in the basement where her father kept his tools.

She tried to believe in these different possibilities, but it was hard, and when she caught Neal searching her bedroom, she knew. Basically, she knew.

—

"Why are you wearing a blazer?" Margaret asked Neal one morning a few days later over breakfast. Their dad had left for work an hour earlier. Elizabeth was paging through a fat book of upholstery swatches that she'd borrowed from the fabric store. She was thinking about redoing some armchairs. Neal looked like such a dweeb. "You look like such a dweeb," she said.

"I'm wearing a blazer because we're picking teams today for the final debate," he said, "and the more professional I look, the likelier it is that I get on a successful team."

"Just because you're wearing a blazer doesn't mean people will think you're smart."

"Margaret, don't be obnoxious," Elizabeth said. "Maybe you and Danny will be on the same team," she told Neal.

"I hope not. Danny's a nice guy and all, but he's kind of a behavior case."

"A *behavior case?*" Margaret was outraged. "What's that supposed to mean?"

"Look, I know you're obsessed with Danny," Neal said to her, "but you know he has ADHD, right?"

"So?"

"So he's not exactly a winning asset, that's all."

Margaret fumbled for a comeback and came up empty. "Shut up," she said.

"Margaret," Elizabeth said, "if you're going to be a bitch to your brother you can leave the table. He's not being nasty to Danny; he's just being honest."

Margaret wanted to damage Neal; she wanted to scratch him, worse. "He is nasty," she said under her breath.

"Young lady, what did you say?"

"I said, *He is nasty.*" She set the sentence down crisply on the table, and they looked at it there, solid as a cut of meat.

Margaret could feel Elizabeth's anger cohering, her mind flicking through the possible punishments like they were pages in the book of swatches, flick, flick, flick. She was searching for something suitable, something that would make an impression. From Neal, nothing. He took a bite of his toast. She hadn't scratched him at all. So she said it.

"Did you lose your camera, Neal?"

He was out of his chair, around the table. "Where is it?"

She wouldn't shrink from him; she forced herself not to. "I hid it."

"Where is it?" He was yelling. He couldn't make her say. Could he?

Elizabeth's head was turning between her two children. "Margaret, did you take your brother's camera?" The same conversation they'd had a thousand times, ten thousand times, as brother and sister and mother. Who took whose toy. Take turns. Who hit, and why. Say sorry. The words were reflex, symbols connoting a commitment to fairness if not its actual attainment. But they didn't apply—Elizabeth couldn't make them apply—to this new conflict, whatever it was. She stopped, confused. "Neal . . . what camera?"

Margaret would show Elizabeth the video camera and what was on it, whatever was on it—herself, Margaret knew, herself in the shower was on it, her body there for anyone to see. She would show Elizabeth, and Elizabeth would understand, and then something would happen. That wasn't Margaret's responsibility. Her brain was moving fast now. She had to be careful; she had to be strategic.

If she moved to get the camera, Neal would get there first. He would tackle her. He was stronger. He would take the camera and crack it on the ground and she would have no proof. She felt sick but also full of a coiled-up energy, like some kind of ninja, a spy, the hero in the story. Neal whipped out of the room. She was smart, she let him go, she waited until he was in her bedroom and she could hear him searching through her drawers. And then she went up to the guest room and quietly brought down the camera.

When she handed it over to her mother, that boxy black hole of a device, she felt she would be safe. Her mother would say, That's weird, Neal, that's not appropriate. Would he get in big trouble? He'd probably have to go to boarding school. She hoped it wouldn't be too terrible.

Her mother would hire a carpenter to fill in the square in the bathroom and a painter to paint it white again. Deeply shocking: that Neal had damaged Elizabeth's house. Bad enough when they failed to hang up their jackets—it was like their mother could sense it from across the house, felt exactly when the jacket hit the floor, the disturbance in the air made by that rippling fabric. Neal had sawed through the wall, and their mother had sensed nothing. Margaret felt sorry for him then, for what was coming his way.

Elizabeth held the camera as far from her body as possible. "What is this?"

"It's a camera. I found it in the bathroom."

"Did Neal forget it there?"

"No. It was hidden. There's a hole in the wall."

"A hole? In the wall?"

"Yeah, Mom, the camera was in the hole."

"Neal," her mother called. "Come back down here."

"No!" Neal would do something; he would confuse Elizabeth before she could begin to understand.

But he was already in the doorway.

"Is this yours?"

"No, it's Jeremy's."

Jeremy Ricci's? Was this payback for the scratches? But they were just scratches.

"I need to return it to him," Neal said. "It's his father's, actually. Can I have it back now?"

He was so calm. How did he act so calm?

"Why did you put it in the bathroom?"

"No reason, it was just a joke."

"A joke," Elizabeth repeated.

"Mom," she said. She needed to be gentle. Elizabeth was in the mud, Elizabeth was sinking, Margaret threw her facts like a rope: "I think there might be something on the camera; I think he—they—filmed something, in the bathroom."

Elizabeth looked at Margaret, a look she didn't understand because there was no anger in it. "Okay," she finally said, and examined the black surface of the camera, shifting it around. "How does it work?"

Neal reached over and took it neatly out of her hands. "You just turn it on," he said, sounding hassled, a middle-aged IT guy having to explain the obvious. He did it; he pulled the screen out and to the side and pushed play. Margaret didn't want to but had to come closer to see.

A girl, her leg lifting higher and higher, filled the square.

It wasn't Margaret. It was a cartoon. It was Sailor Moon in her pleated skirt, her pigtails streaming, kicking a man in the face.

Elizabeth breathed out.

"See?" Neal said. There was nothing to see. He shut the screen. He walked out with the camera and whatever was on the camera. Maybe there was nothing on it. Maybe it was two hours of Sailor Moon and only Sailor Moon. Maybe it *had* been a joke, ha ha. After all, the camera had been off the afternoon when she found it. Maybe she should apologize to *him* now, for being so crazy, for acting so rude.

And yet the camera had been waiting for her. Most days she showered in the morning. If anyone had wanted to catch her, they'd have known when to look. Most days she showered quickly, sleepily. She tried to think how long it could have been there without her noticing. Maybe morning after morning she'd been caught on that screen: Margaret naked in the shower, Margaret sitting on the toilet, pulling her shirt over her head, bending over her socks, frame after frame of her body recorded over the cartoon right up to the moment when Neal pushed play.

Elizabeth hadn't rewound the tape, so now they would never know what was on it.

Whatever happened next, no one was going to protect her. Too late, Margaret understood what Elizabeth's expression had meant. She had been asking for help, pleading with Margaret, just this once, for a really big favor. She'd been saying, Please don't make me look.

7

IT WAS VERY LATE IN THE AFTERNOON AND SOMETHING SMALL
was in the grass. "What is that?" Biddy bent down.

"Don't touch it."

It was a curled tip of black fur, soft, pettable, as plush as the velveteen
lovey she used to rub against her face to fall asleep at night, but fresher. It
looked both strange and very familiar. Bits of dark were splattered on the
grass around it.

"Oh my god," Margaret said. "It's Jane's tail."

"What do you mean, Jane's tail?"

"Look."

"No."

"It is, though, isn't it? Just the very end?" It was the exact same black.
She looked around. "What if there's a wolf?"

"We should go inside."

"No . . . Jane could be hurt." Margaret imagined the hurt cat limping,
foreshortened, needing her help. Or a more horrible thought: the wolf had

eaten her up and only this little bit of her was left, remnant of cat, silky pelt in the grass.

"What do we do then?"

Serial killers tortured cats. That was how they started, when they were kids. Everyone knew that. You could prove someone was a psychopath if as a boy he'd cut up cats.

Mom? Margaret thought. Elizabeth had known what to do about the goat; she would know what to do about the cat. Mom was who you asked for help. But instead she said, "Let's get Danny."

Danny came out and nudged the black fur bravely with a stick. It turned over, revealing a bare belly and pink hands, its snouty pink countenance. He couldn't stop laughing. "It's a rodent," Danny said. "I think it's a mole."

It did seem to be a mole. It was definitely a mole. But Margaret kept feeling at the same time that it was part of Jane. She couldn't be sure until she saw the cat again that she was alive, safe, whole. Biddy and Danny wanted to bury the mole, give it a funeral, but she wouldn't let them. They had to find the cat first.

They searched the house—under the beds and sofas, in the basement where the litter box was—and then the yard, under all the bushes and the porch.

At last there she was in the grass near the toolshed, every inch of her unharmed tail waving proudly in the air. "Janey," Margaret called, and went to pick her up, to bury her face against the cat's soft back. But the cat was busy with something in her paws, punishing or playing with something that looked exactly like a bit of her own self, biting and batting it down in the dirt.

Oh god—don't look—the mole.

Biddy covered her eyes and screamed. Danny grabbed Margaret's hand and pulled her back, away from the horror on the lawn. They ran to the porch, and by the time they got there, their shrieks had turned to laughter. "Jane!" Danny was saying. "What a beast!"

"Thirsty?" Margaret's dad said, not bothering to ask what they were running from because kids were always running from something. He was standing at the patio table with Mr. Murphy and a blender full of strawberry daiquiris.

Their dads had grown up together. It was easier to imagine the dads before they were dads—the jobs they'd had, the jokes they'd made. It was the mothers who'd come out of nowhere, who'd had to be found, wooed, incorporated. But it was the mothers Margaret and Biddy cared about.

Now Margaret's dad handed her a glass of strawberry daiquiri. Biddy and Danny said no thanks, they wanted sodas. The drink tasted cold, then sweet, then bitter.

"All right, Hugh," Mr. Murphy said, "now let's deflower this virgin."

"Ew, Dad," said Biddy, and the dads laughed, because this was a favorite gag: making their daughters uncomfortable. Margaret's dad picked up a golden bottle, and the liquor glugged into the blender just when Mrs. Murphy walked out.

"Hugh! What are you doing? I already added the rum."

"Oh shit." Her dad put down the bottle. "I thought you made it virgin for the kids?"

"No! Not this batch. Margaret, you're not *drinking that*, are you?"

She lowered her cup. Danny swiped it and chugged.

"I can't taste any rum," he said.

"Margaret, please tell me you didn't drink any."

"*I* didn't get to drink any," Biddy said.

"Your mother is going to kill me."

"Oh, Becks, she's perfectly fine," Margaret's dad said. "In fact: Where's Neal? He's actually old enough to try this."

"Hugh," Mr. Murphy said, "you remember that time with the Long Islands—"

"Oh boy. Were we even in high school?"

"Am I drunk?" Danny asked.

"Could everyone please try to be serious?" Mrs. Murphy looked around. "Hugh, Frank, finish this off with me. Margaret, I think we'd better not mention this to your mother."

"Don't worry, Mrs. Murphy, I won't."

The grown-ups divided up the evidence, and Mrs. Murphy took the empty pitcher back inside.

"This is so unfair," Biddy said. She sniffed the cup. "What do you feel like?" she asked Danny.

"Like nothing, really. Like a little fun."

"Walk in a line and touch your nose."

Danny had drunk out of her cup—that was what Margaret was thinking. He'd put his mouth right there where hers had been. She wished she could take it back now, run her tongue along the rim.

"What if one of those mole things climbs on us while we're sleeping?" Biddy asked. All summer they'd been planning to camp out on the porch, the four kids, and this was the night.

"Obviously Jane will kill it," Danny said. "Can you believe we were worried about Jane? That cat is *savage*."

"What about wolves?"

"Don't be dumb, there aren't any wolves in New Jersey."

"Margaret said there were wolves."

"I just said *what if* . . . Besides, whenever you're afraid of one thing, it's always a totally different thing."

Danny nodded, like that was a smart thing to say, and Margaret's mouth tasted all over again of daiquiri.

"Is that supposed to make me feel better?" Biddy said. "Come on, let's just sleep inside like normal."

"Don't be a baby," Margaret said. "You promised."

AFTER DINNER Elizabeth oversaw the thorough application of bug spray. If they needed to come inside, it was perfectly fine. But Margaret wasn't afraid; she would never go inside, and Biddy would never leave her. Though in case anything crawled up, Margaret agreed to put her sleeping bag on the outside, the dangerous side, near the porch railing.

The boys were in the living room playing Nintendo. They were allowed to stay up as late as they wanted because they were twelve and thirteen, which wasn't fair; ten wasn't that much younger. She and Biddy had complained about it, loudly, all through dinner. But truthfully she was happy to be away from Neal. Since the camera, she had spoken to her brother only when she had to. It was surprising how easy it was to stop speaking to him; she just left any room he was in.

But she wasn't thinking about that now. She was trying not to think about it. She was happy to be alone with Biddy, happy to be out late with a flashlight in the strange night air that got inside her sleeping bag and made her shiver.

Biddy kept hearing sounds, asking, "What was that?" in the voice she imagined teenage girls used in horror movies. Margaret knocked her knuckles against the railing when Biddy wasn't looking. "I think I heard footsteps," she said, making a wide-eyed face. "Is someone out there?" The headlights of a car roved down the street and over her face. Biddy froze and then threw her pillow at Margaret. "It was you, I know it."

They played Would You Rather. "Would you rather have tiny wings on your back or tiny horns on your head?"

"Would you rather have tiny horns on your head or a tiny tail?"

"Would you rather die or never be born?"

"Would you rather have to wash your mouth out with dish soap before and after every meal or have every meal only ever be broccoli? But not the tops of the broccoli, only the stalks. And *no ranch*."

Biddy was a master. Biddy made you cringe. Every option she came up with was equally horrifying, but you had to pick something, you had to choose. They took turns making terrible choices until they got sleepy, then quiet.

Margaret thought about the goat in its pen and all the wilderness between them. Foxes, probably, and trundling possums, and raccoons poking their heads out of trees. The bats, everywhere wheeling. Along the tree line, lightning bugs were igniting, setting green fires in their bellies. That was how they communicated, Margaret knew from school. She wondered what it would be like to talk that way, if words were something you could see. You couldn't pretend you hadn't heard. But then again, you could see and still not care. Or you could be looking the wrong way or blinking. Flash flash *what?* She fell asleep.

A NOISE. She thought first of the animals, but it was a human sound. It was necessary that she not move until she knew what it was. She had kicked her way out of the sleeping bag at some point, and the night air was slick. Someone was awake; someone was moving around. Danny? Maybe Danny wanted to sleep near her. Maybe he would lie close and when she woke in the morning he would look at her in a new way, like she was a princess in a bower. The plastic hiss of a sleeping bag, a creak, the shifting air, a hovering presence. She lay stiller than sleeping, stiller than breathing.

A finger was touching her. She should have jumped up, rolled away, curled into a ball, shouted. But in her confusion or fear she didn't. And then it was too late; almost immediately, it was too late.

It was just a finger, but she couldn't have stopped it or dodged it or flung it aside; some power had tapered to a point to pin her down, to keep her frozen there. The finger touched her breast, or what was almost a breast, touched the nipple, and then kept touching, down her ribs and belly and lower, to the flat space between her legs.

Her body locked into an even more rigid paralysis. It must have been noticeable, the lack of movement its own kind of movement, the tension so extreme it couldn't possibly have looked natural. Because the finger lifted. There was the sense of a withdrawal, a footstep.

Part of her was safe in the darkness, part of her wasn't. It was like the beam of the flashlight, the line of the finger down her body, like everything it touched was lit, stripped, cut away. Biddy was safe and sleeping. Her mother, her father, probably, were sleeping. She would have to look for herself, and so she did; she made herself slit an eye. She saw a shirt, elbows, the blank back of a diminishing head. It wasn't Danny. It was Neal.

It was Neal who would come into her bedroom six, seven, maybe eight times that bad summer. He would only ever put his hands on her, only ever when she was sleeping, only until she stirred and flinched and felt the blanket around her knees like shallow water. There was a sparking, shrinking feeling in the spots where he had touched her, like the spots in your vision after a bright light strobes past or a ringing in your ears after a violent sound. It kept happening like that after he was done.

She didn't count the times she slept straight through to morning and wondered only after—because the door was cracked, though she was sure she'd shut it tight; because the blanket seemed folded down, not kicked away—if he had come and gone without her knowing. And those were the worst days. It was not good to wake that way.

She knew that it would happen again if she did not move to stop it, and yet she did not move to stop it, did not scream during, did not tell after. She did that for Elizabeth. She kept the lights on. She kept awake as best she could into the long hours of the adult evening and then later, past that, into the dark bereft. She pushed things against the door—backpacks filled with books, her bedside table—until Elizabeth yelled at her about fire hazards, very dangerous fire hazards, and so she had to stop.

In the fall, then, three times in a row she headed him off, heard his footsteps coming and stomped coughing around the blazing room. Each time he turned back from the door, and after the third he gave up, losing interest or bowing to her vigilance. She won, though what happened remained a secret and sleep a peril.

That first night, she lay awake long after the sleeping bag hissed again. She waited until all was quiet, and then she set her face toward the yard, toward the deeper blackness there. Here lies Margaret, here Margaret used to lie.

TWO

8

THE GIRLS WERE SLEEPING—THEY HAD FOUGHT SO HARD OVER
whose turn it was to take the top bunk that in the end they were both in
the bottom, sleeping head to foot. Margaret went in to check on them.
Helen was turtled under the blankets. Jo was the opposite—legs bare, her
arms thrown one way and her hair the other.

She had spent half an hour tidying the apartment; it was so small it
never took much longer. She could disinfect the whole place with half a
packet of Clorox wipes if she wanted to and sometimes did. There were
two small white bedrooms with airshaft views and a sunny living room
with five feet of kitchen against one wall and a couch against the other.
Between them was a pinkish rug with a pattern so faded it was only a
rumor, darker patches that could as well have been stains or shadows as
design.

The apartment had been renovated for roommates in their twenties,
not mothers and children. So there was no hall closet for a vacuum
cleaner, no bathtub, and a stove so doll-size it was basically decorative.

The rooms did not reward close inspection. Gaps under the windowsills and behind the radiators bulged creamily with the insulation she'd sprayed from a can to keep out the drafts and the mice. But she liked living with the girls in those white boxes, how snug it felt. Shipshape, she sometimes let herself think.

What was it about watching her children sleep that made Margaret feel so safe? It was like she was both the mother keeping watch and a third girl in the bed, like she was standing guard over herself too. Helen shifted under the covers. She had brought Margaret running with the cry of "Mommy!" but it was only a dream. She was murmuring now. Margaret couldn't make out the words, just the cadence of a complaint. When the girls were sleeping at their father's, did they know to call out "Daddy" in the night? No, Margaret knew they didn't, knew it was always Margaret they first shouted for, whether she was there to answer or not. She battened down the pain, watched until the child settled back to quiet.

She had to get some work done. She dimmed the hallway light to the agreed-upon dimness, took her laptop back to the couch, and began reading. Dear editor, please consider. Dear editor, the time has come to. Dear Margaret, I never wanted to have to tell this story. Dear sirs.

Someone shrieked. Outside the open window Thursday night went past, the sound like blue buffetings of fresh air. She wished she could be out there too, going somewhere, with the night air lifting up her skirt. She felt antsy in a way that was almost hormonal, a teenage itch. She couldn't make out what people were saying, but it didn't matter, she got the gist. Someone was slagging someone else, someone was telling an outraged story, someone was discussing the logistics of the night. Distance abstracted the language from the units of its content, turned it into tone and meter and nothing else. She was surprised how much she could understand without understanding a word.

Once, she'd heard a man speaking, his voice abnormally deep and loud—stentorian, she thought. It was an Elizabeth kind of word, and she could hear her mother's voice in her head for a moment, clearer than the man outside. He wasn't talking to anyone else, you could tell. She thought, at first, a madman. Each phrase seemed to draw up the next, a dissonance that built and built and hung there, suspended, until he spoke again, answering. That was when she realized, no—an actor. He was reciting. She'd been folding laundry; she stopped and listened. "Tomorrow and tomorrow and tomorrow—" she wished. "To die, to sleep; to sleep, perchance—" Nope, she couldn't make it out. Yet she was moved by the voice without knowing what it said.

She submitted to her inbox, opened another email, read the pitch: "I decided I finally had to share what happened to me because what ensued was a textbook case of the everyday violence women experience in places like offices and literary events. It speaks to the traumatizing effects of toxic male power . . ." She skimmed the submission. Lord, it was long; it just kept going. She skipped to the end, to the call to action: We can no longer, the cost of silence, the head in the sand, the blind eye. "We must not continue to be complicit in the violence lest we let the perpetrators win."

It had been a few months since the Harvey Weinstein news had broken. She was the only senior editor on staff who was also a woman, so as long as the news cycle lasted, it was her job to tell all the variations on the story, to find new ones in ever more nuanced and disturbing iterations. She edited essays about predators at school, at work, on sidewalks and subways, at concerts and grocery stores, reassessments of desire, reassessments of consent. She believed, of course, in the importance of telling these stories. But she didn't experience the full shock and outrage that others seemed to feel. She wasn't surprised—that was the trouble. If anything, she was relieved.

Of course the men were wrong. But they were wrong in a tidy way. These were not the kinds of transgressions that proved that underneath the guise of human love and caregiving was a roiling pit of filthy horror. That other people were so shocked—it comforted her. The hidden truth was coming out, and one thing it revealed was that the world was not as sick as Margaret had feared, that in fact it was full of still-innocent people. The bad news had broken, and it was not quite as bad as she had always thought it would be.

She didn't want Jo and Helen to know about Harvey Weinstein. Not yet. But if she was going to have to pick an introductory predator, a sort of textbook example, he was a good choice. In a perverted way, she liked to look at pictures of him. He was so big and lumpy, with that bulbous nose and medievally pitted skin. What had he had, the pox? It was reassuring how much he looked like an actual monster, an A-list demon. His awfulness was so predictable, so easy to imagine, it didn't frighten her. How could she prepare her children for the awfulness that couldn't be imagined? How could she prepare them without ruining their lives? Ezra, their father, wouldn't help. He had no experience of such things; she was the worst thing that had ever happened to him.

She knew she couldn't tell anyone about this sense of relief. Recently, in her cubicle, she had turned to the young editorial assistant next to her and said that it was just not possible for her to read the word *survivor* without hearing that song by Destiny's Child. The woman had covered her mouth and said, "Oh my god. Margaret."

Or maybe she was just tired. The stories that she edited seemed too neatly packaged. And that was her fault, of course. She was the one who made sure they had all the right components, that they were different enough to keep readers interested but not so different that they weren't recognizably the same thing. It made her think of the cardboard and clear-plastic containers the girls' toys came in—Happy Hour Predatory Ken Doll, with fashions and accessories. If the story departed too far from the standard, it wouldn't be relevant. It might not even be believable.

Above all the stories had to have a villain, and it had to be obvious that everyone would be better off if they were revealed and punished. But in real life it wasn't always like that. Sometimes the right thing to do was not to make a fuss—if you could be certain that they wouldn't do it again, if you could be certain that you'd been the only one damaged.

She looked back at the submission. Was this a new angle on the story? Did it make her see things differently? Was she interested in this person's trauma? No—she wasn't. And there was that awful phrase: *lest we let.* By speaking up we, by telling our stories we, never again will we. How did one become part of it, speak on behalf of it—that confident plural voice?

"I'm really sorry to say we're going to pass on this essay, but thank you so much for giving us the chance to consider it," she typed out. She copied the rejection and sent it back to all the day's Dear Margarets. The apartment in the light of the one last lamp was no longer white but blue with shadow. Outside the crowds went by, the words *Where to? Where to?* like the song of some small darting bird. But now she didn't want to join them—she liked that they were out there and she was in here and no one else could get inside.

In the morning, the street noise would be different. In the morning, it was always children shouting, and they always sounded just like Helen and Jo. The girls would be sitting at the table, eating breakfast or coloring, and at the same time they would be crying out for Margaret on the sidewalk. You would think you knew your child's voice, that you could never mistake some stranger for that sound. But that wasn't how it was. Every crying child sounded just like her own. She would have to stare hard at the girls, she would have to touch them or ask them something so they would lift their heads and look at her, to keep herself from running to the window. When they were with their father, it was so much worse. All day she heard them and could not go to them.

On Saturday she would see Duncan, the man she'd been dating. On Sunday she would take the children to the Natural History Museum with Ezra. But first one more day of work and camp. She had signed up the girls for the cheapest option in the neighborhood, which still cost many thousands of dollars, and as a result they were spending the summer in T-shirts that came down to their knees in a stuffy classroom at the nearby Catholic high school, throwing water balloons at the playground for an hour each afternoon. Was it better or worse than her own childhood summers, lying on the lawn? Better. It was better than that.

But what did they think, what did they feel, about their lives? She always wanted to know, was terribly afraid of finding out. Earlier that day

Jo had had a meltdown because she wanted bubble gum. She was face down on the sidewalk, shouting about bubble gum. But what if it wasn't about the gum? "Is something else making you sad, JoJo?" she'd asked. "Are you"—say it—"missing Daddy?"

"You never buy me candy," Jo had wailed.

If Jo or Helen was confused or bereft about the divorce, Margaret didn't know how to tell, let alone what to do about it. Children accepted almost anything. They knew perfectly well that things would happen to them and they were powerless to do anything about it. And so they needed to exert themselves in moments like this, when they could, in a small yet crucial fashion, get their own way. Her understanding of this, her ability to accommodate this, was what made her a different mother from Elizabeth. She got down on her knees. "Fine," she said. "Let's buy the gum."

It was the wrong thing to do. Obviously it was the wrong thing to do. Children needed firm rules and boundaries to feel safe. They shouldn't eat candy every day. Jo was too young for gum; she could choke. Tomorrow she would be a better parent. Next summer, the girls would do something cooler, something more enriching. She would have to ask Elizabeth for some money. She could do it; for the girls she could do that. Her mother didn't like to talk about how much she'd inherited from her own parents, but she had made it clear that when it came to her grandchildren, she could easily afford to be generous.

Margaret would bring it up next weekend, at the birthday party.

Jo wanted just one thing for her fifth birthday: a pool party at Elizabeth's house. Margaret had tried her best to tempt her into other options, dangling a park hang with pizza and cupcakes and friends, then upping the offer to expensive spaces they could book with trampolines, ball pits, climbing walls. A Broadway show! Tea at the Plaza! Jo wasn't having it.

Elizabeth had installed the pool the previous year, and the girls didn't understand why they weren't in it every moment of the summer like Neal's son, Charlie, who lived just down the road. It was the one reason Margaret was glad they couldn't afford a car in the city. It gave her an excuse to say no. But she couldn't say no to the birthday party. So all of them, Ezra included, would go to Elizabeth's for a weekend. The date brooded there atop her calendar. It was just two days, she told herself as she leaned back in bed, as the laptop lay on her belly and burned.

A sound, a disruption in the darkness, a hand on the edge of the mattress. Someone had come into the room. She knew it without being able to do anything about it. A basic part of her brain was sending flares of panic down the coiling nerveways. But the rest of her mind remained slack with oblivion, far off in the soft void of sleep. Neuron over neuron, limp and slow and stupid, the mind hauled itself back into consciousness. Synapses twitched, and twitched, and twitched, and suddenly her brain sluiced back in her body and all the signals went through and she woke and went rigid with the old familiar terror.

But in yet another moment it was over. She began to see, and to hear, and understanding followed. A small tousled head was looking down at her, sniffling. Fear, then guilt, then the redemption of action. Margaret lifted the blanket and tucked the child against her body.

Almost immediately, Jo was asleep again. Her feet were cold, and Margaret was glad; this gave her a job to do. She pressed her legs against Jo's feet, and by the time they were warm, her panic had abated. She always woke into fear, but it wasn't so bad; in no time the world began to bustle about, calmly and sturdily putting the room back in order. The dresser, the door, the closet ajar, the black lampshade, the sleeping child, the open window, and through it she could hear people again, on their way home now, drunk and laughing and calling out something that sounded almost like her name.

9

SHE HAD SPENT A SIGNIFICANT PORTION OF THE AFTERNOON on the phone with a writer and fact-checker trying to determine how to compare the influence of a podcast, as measured by monthly (self-reported) downloads, to that of a nightly network news show, as measured by daily (estimated) viewership. Could the writer say for sure that the podcast was more popular? Was that fact or opinion? The writer was at first accommodating, then annoyed, then outraged, and finally defeated, as unsure of herself in the end as everyone else had been in the beginning. "Just tell me what it should say," the writer said.

This happened sometimes. Eventually the sentences, exposed to so much light and heat, were leached of all meaning. It was like looking at yourself in the mirror too long. What you understood as your features—nose, mouth, eyes—decayed in the face of the face, and you were left with planes of bone and deposits of cartilage that had no recognizable significance. What was this story even about? The fact-checker asked how the writer knew for sure whether it was "shocking" that an actor so long known for bro-hijinks and dick jokes could have produced such a hit mindfulness podcast. "I think we're good on that one, Jaime," she said, swiveling in the mesh confines of the cubicle chair. "I feel comfortable with all this now."

She hung up, added the requisite caveats, published the story. She always felt like there should be some kind of sound effect for that, a ding or a whoosh. But it was silent, seamless. "I can't wait to get this out into the world" was a line she often used on writers when she wanted them to look at her edits more quickly. But what did it mean? Mostly that once it was out in the world, she could move on to something new.

Maybe it would be different if she was a writer instead of an editor. She had wanted to write, once. But she was good at this, at letting someone else's thoughts run through her, at speaking in someone else's voice. If you wanted a person's story to be persuasive, believable, here was how you did it: you made the bad parts sound a little worse, but the worst part, the very worst part, you made that sound a little better.

Recently, at some book party, she'd been introduced to a man with a masthead look, one of those tall men too old to be described as gangly, presumably bald, though it was hard to tell from so far below. He'd looked confused and repeated her name like it sounded familiar. "I only recognize you as an email address," he said.

"Well . . ." She did a *ta-da!* with her hands—as if some demonstration of embodiment had been called for—and immediately regretted it. She'd disappointed him. You could tell that she'd meant more to him as an email address, had more power, seemed like the kind of person who had the right to go around telling people no to their faces. Now she was just a woman with a skirt and a ponytail. Would he ever take them seriously again—her emails, with their cold voice of authority?

But who was *he*, anyway? She didn't know him as a person or an email address, so there. When he reached to deposit an empty glass on a passing tray, she ducked under his arm and escaped.

She left the office early to get the kids from camp. The heat, so welcome at first, was moments later a crisis. The sun ricocheted off the jammed-up traffic. She made a block of shade with her hand and felt her way down the subway stairs.

She liked this time of day, she liked going to the school where the shitty camp was held, she liked the security guard in her benign blue uniform. More than anything, more than taxes or voting, walking into schools made her feel like a citizen. She liked being bossed around, and waiting her turn in the gentle chaos of the pickup line, and feeling like she didn't have to be the only one in charge.

The guard recognized her and said, "Helen and Jo?" and there was always something funny about it, like it was her regular deli order, her kids the sandwiches she ordered every day. "Helen and Jo—again? You don't want to mix it up, try something different? Some Sloane? A little Oliver?" No, no, they were the ones she wanted. And then out they would come down the hallway, dropping their water bottles at Margaret's feet, balled-up drawings in their hands, sticky with whatever snacks they'd been given, the proof of what she could not share, the residue of their separate, mysterious weekdays.

"Are we going to Grandma's now?" Jo asked, as she had every day for a week already.

"Not today," she said, and, sensing the mustering whine, kept talking. "Today is Friday. Today is almost over. Tomorrow you'll be home with Daddy. Sunday we're going to the museum. Then a few more days of work and camp, and just a week from today we'll go to the train and be at Grandma's by dinnertime." They weren't pleased with this timeline, but they accepted it.

"Can we play at the playground?" Helen asked, and she said yes, for a while.

The playground was attached to the school by an encircling chain-link fence, but it was not of the school—it was the city. This was a subtle but important distinction, and it had to do with the fact that out there the parents were responsible for making sure that nothing went wrong. And yet so much did go wrong. At the playground was a child whose father had accidentally thrown a ball into his face and then snapped at him to stop crying. At the playground was a child who often seemed hungry and would boldly ask for a granola bar if she saw your own child eating one. At the playground was a child who—she'd been told by someone who knew someone who knew his parents—had been touched, once, by a homeless man in the bathroom of that very playground.

So did Margaret watch the girls all the time? Did she keep her eyes peeled on them and spot them on all the ladders? Even knowing what the world was, she did not. She got distracted, looking at her phone. Duncan had sent her a video from the beach near his house in the Rockaways, and she watched it three times in a row, the white-fuzzed waves and the far-off horizon so small on the screen. The image of the sea just made her think of his body, how he put his fingers inside her mouth sometimes to get them wet.

A mother whose name she forgot, whose son was in Helen's class, approached, looking timid in a barebacked sundress. "Er, I think your younger daughter is eating something off the ground," she said.

So she was. Jo was under the bouncy bridge, foraging for scattered Goldfish.

"Jo, ew," she shouted. "Don't eat that!"

Jo looked right at her and put her hand to her mouth. Margaret had been texting with a man while her child ate literal trash. What would Ezra think?

"I have snacks right here," she said, holding up her bag.

"Do you have Goldfish?"

"Well . . . no."

Jo ate another one.

She squatted under the bridge. "If you stop, I'll play tag with you."

Jo, striped with blue shadow, considered this. "You better run," Margaret said. "You better hide." Jo shrieked and ran. Margaret stomped the Goldfish into orange dust.

She tried not to worry about what the other mother thought. Of course she was being watched. There was the Ezra in her mind, the superego ex-husband. There was Elizabeth, shocked by the divorce, shocked by the apartment, shocked by the decision to live in the city in the first place. And there were the other parents, the married parents. She wanted them to think she was careful, playful, never bored, a little hot, maybe the babysitter. She chased Jo up a ladder and pretended to try to grab her leg through the bars. Was she faking it? Did it matter, if performing being a better mother made her a better mother? She was so sweaty the lining of her work skirt felt like cling wrap against her thighs.

When Margaret was out of breath from running, she found the sun-dress mother on a bench and sat down in hopes of rehabilitating herself. She tried to take a drink from Helen's water bottle, but it was empty. "Whew, these kids," she said. "How are you?"

"It's been a tough summer, to be honest," the mother said. "Actually I've been meaning to ask you something. Tell me if this is too personal."

She had heard Margaret was divorced. She wanted advice. Women often did. Margaret didn't mind. She liked to hear about people's lives, was curious about how they lived and whether they were happy. It made her sad, though, or maybe angry—the way they tested out the word *divorce*. Like they were kids on the monkey bars, skinny arms shaking, and change was a faraway rung.

It wasn't like she was some kind of divorce promoter. It wasn't like she had some kind of investment in other women's choices. But when she talked about her divorce—especially with their mutual old friends, those deeply concerned couples—she was careful to reveal no hint of uncer-tainty or regret, no crack of doubt. In the beginning, even Biddy had asked: "Are you sure you know what you're doing?" She had sounded just like when they were in high school and college, whenever she thought Margaret was falling for some guy, putting her future in his untrustwor-thy hands. Except there had been no guy then—only her own choice, her own life. Are you sure you know what you're doing? As if her own life were a dangerous older man.

Biddy had been afraid that Margaret would be punished, that Ezra might do something crazy, like try to take the children away. She'd just seen the movie *Carol*. "Don't worry, it's not the 1950s anymore," Margaret had told her, though of course she was afraid of being punished too.

Recently Ezra had made her a proposal. He'd sent her a link to an article on a law school's website about restorative justice that he thought could serve as a sort of model for them. The Person Who Has Harmed creates space for the Person Who Has Been Harmed to talk about the impact of the wound and seek answers about how and why it happened. The Person Who Has Harmed makes amends. The Person Who Has Been Harmed offers forgiveness.

She had traumatized him, he explained. This was the least she could do.

She hadn't taken it well. "I'm not a criminal!" she'd texted back. "I'm not the apartheid government of South Africa!"

He said he wanted to understand how and why. She could have gotten the fact-checker to help with that, to call the sources, review the data. But Margaret didn't think he wanted answers. Asking the questions extracted some suffering, and that was what he really wanted, to spread around the pain. He had every right. She just didn't like it when he asked: What kind of person could do a thing like this? She could live with him calling her a monster so long as he didn't phrase it as a question, so long as he didn't try to make her agree.

The other mother was still looking at her, waiting. "I'm so sorry, that must be really hard. I'd love to talk it through. But I should get dinner started." Fuck, what was the woman's name? "Let me give you my number. Text me, we'll get coffee. We can talk all about it."

She just didn't feel up to it then, the how and the why and the hypothetical lawyer's rates. Helen was standing in the turret above the slide, leaning over the rail, her camp T-shirt billowing. She looked proud and solitary. Margaret was about to call out to her, to tell her to get her backpack and her sister, it was time to go home. But she stopped.

Helen was illuminated, blasted with the six-o'clock sun, the familiar, unfathomable face undergoing something private and essential. What is it? she wanted to ask her. What is it that you feel? Instead she turned her face in the same direction, felt the same sun hammer it to gold. She forgot about the woman behind her, forgot about the other parents on the playground. The moment was a gift—not for her, not to keep, but a gift nonetheless. The game of tag was still going on, and below Helen the younger children churned, chasing then fleeing then chasing then fleeing.

She could wait. She could wait until they told her they were ready.

10

SHE HAD BEEN RELIEVED, THE FIRST TIME SHE SAW IT, THAT Duncan's house was a shitshow; if it had been clean, she would have been in danger of wanting to marry him. She was pretty sure she wouldn't want to live alone forever, but she had no interest in picking a man's clothes off the floor. She could never live with another man who didn't clear off his kitchen counters to clean them, who just pushed the accumulated piles back and wiped in front of them. She could never live with a man who let a sink scum over with the spat-out foam of so many days of toothpaste or left underwear on the floor that she would have to inspect to know if they were clean or dirty. Even now, on her knees on the carpet, a part of her was aware of how badly it needed vacuuming.

But then again: his cock. She was surprised by how much she thought about it. Not just about sleeping with him but, specifically, about his cock; specifically, inside her mouth. She had never minded giving blow jobs. She was generally a person who liked to be proficient and who liked to please. She had given plenty when she was still a virgin and the occasional one during her marriage, especially after the babies were born, when the breast-feeding hormones had left her too dry and depleted to want anything inside her. But this was different.

Maybe it was the combination of submitting to him while also being in control. She would have hated to have him pull at her head and gag her, and she knew he never would. Or maybe it was science, some pheromonal magnetism based on his particular smell. Or maybe she just liked it, the delicacy of the skin, his hard pulse, the length of it all against her tongue. It was called giving a blow job, but she wasn't trying to give him something; she wanted something from him. In fact, she would probably like it if he made her beg, if she had to say please.

She couldn't tell other women this because they wouldn't believe it. And she couldn't tell men because they would. There was nothing unusual about wanting to be dominated in bed. But liking to be told to do something wasn't the same as liking, simply, to do it, to fill her mouth with him, her mouth that was normally so full of all the things she didn't say.

EARLY ON, she had been afraid that something might be wrong with her, that she might be damaged. She was grateful that it hadn't turned out that way, that ever since she'd had her first real boyfriend, she'd liked sex, it had made her happy, mostly. Wanting something, and getting it, and wanting more—that was sex. The fulfillment of desire never depleted the desire; it only intensified it. She gathered that this was normal, though it sounded crazy. Duncan's cock inside her made her want his cock inside her.

Once, in her very early twenties, she'd been invited to join a book club full of glamorous older editors. She'd worn corduroys and felt like a child, and they'd read *On Chesil Beach* by Ian McEwan, about British virgins who love each other but can't consummate their wedding night because the boy is proud and clueless and the girl is traumatized. Her father raped or molested her in some way—the book doesn't say exactly. Margaret wondered how McEwan had done it, described with such precision the girl's horror at the prospect of being touched again. The new husband ejaculates, prematurely. The girl frantically tries to wipe the cum away but it's too sticky; it congeals, another layer of skin; she can't get it off herself; she has never been able to get it off herself.

"Nobody could recover from something like that," a woman in the book group said.

Oh, Margaret had hated that. That wasn't what the story meant at all. "There was hope for her." It literally said that; a line in the book said that. She remembered, cross-legged on the floor in the position of maximum deference, flipping through pages. "But he writes, 'There was hope for her,'" she interjected. The woman—she had a sweater with a hole in it and a job at *The Paris Review*—looked down at her and said, again, "No way. Nobody gets over that."

Fiction wasn't about what happened, she thought. What happened only happened to show you what could have happened differently. That was why there was hope. Ian McEwan put those people on that beach and they couldn't cope. But change one thing, anything—oh, if the boy had only called her name—and it would all have turned out differently.

She would have been interested in talking about this, if only she could express the idea properly. Even now, so many years later: the problem of expression. "How was the book club?" Ezra had asked when she'd gotten home to their apartment, that first gloomy railroad. "I dunno, they were kinda snobby," she'd said. She had never gone back; in fact (it was silly . . .), she'd never gone to any book club ever again. Duncan would talk to her about *On Chesil Beach*, about the hope in the plot, if she could remember what she'd been thinking about when she was finished.

Duncan lived in the Rockaways in a house full of books like a literary sea captain. He surfed, even in winter, and taught in the architecture school at CUNY. He'd lent her his copy of *The Waves*, and she realized only at the very end that she'd forgotten about Woolf having drowned. Of course she had. And yet Margaret somehow didn't believe that her life had ended that way, with stones in her pockets. Or she believed it on the internet but not in the books. She would talk to Duncan about that too; he would be interested in that feeling.

She'd been to the Rockaways before, of course, to go to the beach. She liked it; it was full of all kinds of people, as if someone had tipped a subway car sideways and tumbled New York out onto the sand. But she'd never seen Duncan's part of town until she started dating him. It was wild and desolate there on the bayside—old people living in the same houses they'd grown up in, silver junk in the front yards and shacks in the back. Rats in the salt grass. Abundant street parking. She did something new with her tongue.

That afternoon they'd paddled across the bay in his canoe. He owned a canoe with a crack in it that he stored under the bushes in a neighbor's backyard. Rain had threatened all day, and as soon as they pushed the boat into the water the wind picked up, great humid gusts of it.

"What do you think?" Duncan had asked, knee deep, assessing the sky, holding the canoe and her in it.

"I think we paddle fast," she said, and so that's what they did.

They had wanted to go out to a little island before the storm hit. But when she looked back in the direction of the city she could see it already—the bad weather plopped down in the sky like a fat black island itself. The wind snatched at her, and she laughed. She liked a storm. It was just the right amount of emergency.

She put her hand into the water and the fingers disappeared; she couldn't see three inches down into it. That gave her a buoyant, upside-down feeling, like the sky was deep and dangerous while the bay was pure surface. It was blue, then gray, then blue, then gray, then suddenly green as a field. If she'd gone overboard, she wouldn't have sunk—she'd have lain there beside the boat while the wavelets rustled around her.

Duncan had been talking about his kids, Willis and Louie. They were a few years older than Helen and Jo, and surfed with their father, and built bonfires on the beach. A fantasy clambered into the canoe, and it dipped and shimmied from side to side. She and Duncan would blend the kids into one raucous and bohemian family, and instead of the Catholic classroom, her girls would spend their summers here, with the bonfires and the bay. Her marriage would fade into a sweet but misguided phase she'd gone through, and Ezra would be an old friend and not an angry man whose home she'd destroyed. She would have, once again, the coherence of a single life, instead of this division in which she was either mother or woman but never both at once. She would have a future again, instead of just a past.

But then Duncan's ex-wife, whose feelings he still talked about with a proprietary intensity, reached a hand out of the bay. Ezra followed, enumerating his many concerns. Then, last of all, the boys, the brothers, the terrible risk. She plunged her paddle down through the murk, down among the unseeable crabs and turtles and whatever dank reeds had managed to cling to the shifting silt. The paddle resisted; she rowed against the real beneath.

The rain had started, and they'd had to turn around.

Her hair was still wet, which was helpful now—it stayed in a rope down her back and she didn't have to tie it up. She wondered what the kids were doing; they would be out at the playground (she hoped—not watching television). Would they have eaten any vegetables? She would need to get groceries.

But then Duncan put a hand on the back of her neck, a point of contact so gentle there was no weight to it. "Oh," he said softly, and once again the current of her desire was rising and sweeping the thoughts away until all that was left was her own building rhythm. His hand trembled, and he made another sound, a sound of wondering pleasure. It was good that she was on her knees. She swallowed.

11

I HAD SAID NO SO MANY TIMES, TO SO MANY THINGS—THE massages, the oral sex. That scene made no sense. But the movie would never have been made if I hadn't agreed to go topless."

She turned off the radio. "Disgusting," Ezra said, and his fingertips rose off the steering wheel of their friend's borrowed minivan, as if even the upholstery had somehow been corrupted by the crimes of Harvey Weinstein.

She was glad the girls were napping in the back; she didn't want them listening to this. What Weinstein had done to the actresses had nothing to do with her, it was not sex—it was a different category altogether—and yet the word *oral* still made her twitchy. She could feel Ezra glancing sideways, sensing it on her—what she had done and liked. Before she'd left, Duncan had asked her, "Will you be okay?" meaning during the day ahead with Ezra, during the weekend with her family. His worrying about her was a kind of lingering possession. He'd forced her legs apart with his knee and she really shouldn't be thinking about that right now.

Ezra was turning in to the museum and then down, underneath it. A guard stopped them at the entrance of the parking lot, gesturing through the closed window. He opened the back, and hot air blasted in while he poked around under the collapsed stroller. Then he crouched down out of view. What was he doing? She craned her head to see. He was shining a flashlight under the car.

"Are they really looking for bombs?" she asked quietly, but Ezra didn't answer. Of course they were looking for bombs. The girls were stirring crankily in the back seat, suffering through the onset of consciousness. "Are we there yet?" one of them asked, and for once she got to say, "Yes!" Though it took about twenty-five more minutes to find a spot and resurrect the stroller and steer them all into the elevator and up to the lobby.

She hoped they would never modernize this museum. She loved the swashbuckling antiquatedness of it all, as if Teddy Roosevelt himself might stomp in at any moment with a dead cat over his shoulder. It was a bit horrible to think of all the animals as corpses with the meat scooped out, but it was horrible in an honest way. Everything was mimesis, but this was as close as you could get—not just resembling but reassembling. There they all were with their own precious claws and teeth.

Margaret and Ezra had been coming since Helen was an infant, before she could even focus her eyes. It had felt like something parents did, though now Margaret would hardly consider carrying twelve hot pounds in a sling parenting. Since the divorce, they'd come, if anything, more often. They agreed that continuity was important. The museum distracted the girls from any parental tension, and the fear of losing sight of the girls in the crowds distracted the parents from each other. At least, that was the theory. And so they carted out the old hide of the nuclear family, stuffed the slack bits with cotton, reinforced it with pins, asked the children, "Where to first?"

"Space," said Helen.

"The whale," said Jo.

Would Ezra make a divorce joke? Did he remember watching that Noah Baumbach movie together? The whale and the meteorites were in completely opposite directions, but it didn't matter. "Okay," she said, and they just kept going the way they were already going.

"I READ somewhere that the biggest threat to the museum now is moth infestations," she told Ezra. "Remember we got moths that time, and we had to seal all the sweaters in bags? It's the same moth; they eat the taxidermy."

Ezra gave her a look like, Don't remind me of our happy past, though she hadn't remembered the moths as a particularly happy episode.

What really interested Margaret was the idea that even the dead animals weren't safe, that even in the simulacrum the decay was real. But that wasn't the kind of comment Ezra would appreciate either. Ezra mostly liked the museum because he could demonstrate that he knew which antelope was a waterbuck and which was a springbok without looking at the plaques. She thought this and felt bad about it.

Ezra hated the idea of her having ideas about him, of her making any assumptions about what he thought, or felt, or what interested him. They had agreed for a dozen years that they knew each other better than anyone else in the world, and they had loved to say to each other things like: You'll hate this; that is so you; I could tell from your face; I knew you were going to say that. Then they broke up and agreed that they didn't know each other at all. Now they were supposed to treat the other's private, interior life as if it was too dignified and mysterious to presume to encroach upon, and to pay each other the respect of having no idea what the other thought, or felt, or might do next.

Her phone buzzed, and she took it out of her back pocket. Duncan. She would tell him about the moths in the simulacrum; it was exactly the kind of thing that would interest him. Reflexively she opened her email for five seconds, got overwhelmed by the scroll of bold unreads, and stuffed the phone away again. What had she been about to say? Oh shit, where was Helen?

How could she let this happen? A blur of backpacks and T-shirt slogans and other people's children. What was Helen wearing? The dress with the strawberries? No, Jo was wearing that. Face after face presented itself: that one was old, that one bearded, that one a waxen Inuit figure in bobsledding furs. She discarded each face, looked for another. Body after body and all of them too big to be Helen's until— There she was.

She had her hands clasped behind her back, professorially, and her head was tilted up so her ponytail swung loose. She was looking at a grizzly bear. It was posed on its hind legs, but it wasn't rearing to strike so much as gazing around dopily. Margaret wheeled the stroller, smothered the panic, took her daughter's hand.

This was Margaret's favorite part of the museum. Being provincial, she liked the North American mammals best, the bears and beavers and wolves, all that fake snow dusted on real fur. She liked the mountains in the background and how the painted stalks of grass became real stalks of grass rooted to the floor. She liked to flick her eyes back and forth between the real grass and the fake, back and forth over that line where the illusion began.

Then Jo said she was bored and Helen said she was tired. At eight, Helen was far too big for the stroller, but she demanded a turn in it anyway. "My legs hurt so much they feel wounded," she said. Good word, *wounded*. It was time for the Hall of Ocean Life.

EVERYONE LOVED the Hall of Ocean Life. The diving, the splashing, the dolphins: so playful. All that movement suspended on wires under blue lights, and the impossibly fleshy sea lions with their proud rolls of neck fat. The girls could dart around without her worrying that she would lose sight of them. The blue light really did make you feel like you were underwater, or at least under something. She and Ezra leaned against a glass sea and watched their daughters. The phrase *companionable silence* entered her mind. They were watching their children in companionable silence.

Margaret had told Ezra that she wanted a divorce in dead winter. It had been barely 5:00 but already somehow night, the air so cold and dry it felt contentless. Words, breath, heat, the day—the second they left a living surface they were gone, voided. Outside the cab, everyone was doing the same thing they were doing, what they were always doing: going home with their shopping, their groceries, their kids who'd been expensively stimulated by their afternoon extracurriculars. Margaret had thought about the sheer physical effort expended to do the tiniest fucking thing. The circuits to the fibers, the muscles tugging at the bones.

They got home, and she sat the girls in front of the TV in the living room. (Their shared apartment had been big enough to have a proper living room and kitchen.) She started unpacking the groceries. He asked her if something was wrong. It wasn't typical of him to ask, or it wasn't typical of her to convey that she needed to be asked. But that day he did, and/or she did, and after only an agonized hour or two—poof. The whole framework of their life was gone.

It didn't shatter or fall to pieces. The marriage was simply there, solid, a real-life fact, and then it was gone, and in its place the four of them were just out there on some two-by-fours, dangling their legs in the void.

She sometimes thought that if Ezra hadn't asked if something was wrong, maybe it would never have happened. Maybe she'd be in that kitchen still, stacking a can on the highest shelf. Why had she done it? He might never stop asking. If he asked again now, she could say it was like she had been behind a sheet of glass, suspended on wires, making, forever, some suspended representative gesture. But then something had gotten inside, something had set her swinging.

He wanted an answer, though, not a simile. It was the least she could do—explain why. And he said she couldn't or wouldn't. And she said, I tried, and I am.

They hadn't seen much of each other lately, beyond the regular hand-offs. With Jo's birthday weekend coming, Ezra thought it would be good to spend some time together before spending more time together. This outing was a practice run. To make sure it didn't end in whisper-fights or worse. Margaret and the girls planned to take the train to New Jersey on

Friday, and Ezra would follow on Saturday. It was probably going to be terrible. But at least the girls would be happy. At least Elizabeth's house was big enough for them to sleep as far apart as possible. At least Elizabeth and Ezra had always been close. They could talk, if not to her, then to each other.

A GUIDE WAS EXPLAINING to a group that the whale on the ceiling had been renovated in 2003. They'd added a belly button. The tourists had their heads cranked navel-ward. All she could see was their throats.

She tried to gauge how Ezra was feeling. She had done this throughout their marriage, like a diabetic monitoring blood sugar, and it was hard to stop. She tracked his moods, parceled out sweet wifely snacks—granola bars, juice boxes, tenderness. Everything, it seemed, was going okay. Gratitude welled up in her. She loved him. In this way, she would always love him.

Immediately the feeling was counterweighted: she was too easy to please, she didn't need to be so desperately relieved that a grown man was able to keep it together for his kids on a summer Sunday in the American Museum of Natural History.

When they still did things like this as a family, Margaret had to suppress a need to stop the other people in the room and make sure they didn't get the wrong idea: Us? No, we're divorced. She hated that people would think she was Ezra's wife or, worse, that she was pretending to be, that she was ashamed of her decision. She wanted her own plaque: *Divorced mom; North America; early twenty-first century. This terrestrial omnivore reared two offspring and was found well preserved in frozen ground.*

Helen and Jo were darting around, grabbing each other's arms, whispering in each other's ears. What was it they were pointing out? Probably butts. Still, Margaret wished she could hear, could see what they saw, could be, for a moment, one of the sisters. She wasn't anybody's sister. She wasn't anybody's wife.

A worse thought intruded, one of those bad thoughts you had at least once in any crowded public space, as if it were handed out with the ticket: What if someone did blow them up? What if one of those drivers in the lot below had hidden his bomb so well beneath the trunk detritus that even the guard's assiduous flashlight had failed to expose it? The floor would explode beneath them. They would rise up into the air and then descend into disaster, the glass of the dioramas shattering and water pouring out, though of course water was not what they were filled with.

She tensed against the wall, tracked the girls more vigilantly. Whatever she did, whatever Ezra said, they would always be a family in the fundamental sense that both of them would rather die in her hypothetical conflagration of fire and water and taxidermy than walk out without one of their children. Ezra said she had thrown away their marriage like it was nothing, like it meant nothing, or worse, like it never happened in the first place. Why? Because. Because she had wanted to. It was a child's answer, but it was true. And yet it would always be Ezra she trusted to carry their children from the burning museum. She felt like this should make him feel better, though she knew it probably wouldn't.

She wanted to say something to him now, she wanted, at least, to try. About why it was necessary, to know, to feel, how nonetheless—

But he was already speaking. He was saying, "Can't you at least try to make conversation?"

12

"A PLATE?"

"No."

"An apple."

"No."

"The flowerpot."

"Mom, be serious."

"A . . . book?" she said, through a crackling yawn.

"But *which* book?" Helen asked.

"That's impossible, I can't guess that."

"Okay, okay, but try to guess if it's, like, one of our books or one of yours."

She'd only guessed a book because there were so many at hand, and she was tired, so tired, just incapacitated by fatigue after the day at the museum, the day with Ezra. She was so tired . . . her legs felt like sacks of cat food. She wished she was back at Duncan's, lying face down in his bed.

"Mommy, guess."

All she knew was it was an object, it had some kind of mass, that it was weighing her down, but not by much, that it was light and flat, that it had a decent amount of surface area. Inside, who knew, but if she had to guess: colors and pictures, caterpillars and tigers. "Yours," she said.

"You did it! Mommy wins," Jo said, throwing herself on top of her.

They were playing a game called What's on My Butt? You played it by lying half asleep on your stomach on the couch and letting your kids put random household objects on your butt. It was their second-favorite game right then, after Blindness, which they played by closing their eyes and trying to move around the apartment. Interesting, Margaret thought, that they were drawn to these tests of proprioception. Where is my body in the world? Can I trust my senses to keep it safe? What's on my butt?

The girls had a basket of stuffies, a basket of dolls, and a box of magnetic tiles they could stack into towers, but there wasn't much room in the apartment for toys. What they played with more than anything else were chairs: the four kitchen table chairs and the two countertop stools, which they rearranged in endless iterations around the living room/dining room/kitchen. They made: rocket ships, trains, limos, factories, pet stores, forts. They put the chairs in a line, then in a circle, then covered them with blankets. The mess drove Margaret nuts, but she loved to watch them do it, how they made the room itself a game.

Elizabeth had strong feelings about their lack of toys. She was always buying them dolls and dress-up clothes, sticker books and craft kits filled with glitter that immediately went all over the carpet. Margaret was always making her take them back to New Jersey. She had finally, finally, found a constraint that Elizabeth had to accept (though in fact she did not accept it, pushed, constantly, against it, sending her real estate listings for nicer, more expensive places in the suburbs every week). They lived here, in this small white space, and Elizabeth simply could not make it any bigger.

A few weeks earlier she'd asked her mother to babysit. She had to go to a colleague's goodbye drinks, and Ezra couldn't trade nights. When she got home, the girls were sleeping and Elizabeth was lying on the couch with an arm over her eyes, an audiobook playing. It was one of her romance novels, read by a lady with the cozy English accent of Angela Lansbury as the teapot in *Beauty and the Beast.*

Elizabeth sat half up as the voice said, "The duke drew her to him and clasped her small hand." Margaret hugged her hello.

"A hug! I never get a hug."

"I'm hugging you right now."

The voice said, "She entreated him. 'Stop,' she said . . ."

"Where is that phone? I'll turn this off," Elizabeth said.

Something in the apartment felt different, displaced. What was it? The chairs were all where they belonged. The backpacks were on their hooks, the dishes in the sink.

". . . but he could not stop. 'I have seen you sit a horse,' the duke said . . ."

"What are you listening to?"

"Oh, some smut." She found the phone between two couch pillows.

Margaret noticed two trash bags on the ground. "What's that?"

"I sorted through their outgrown clothes. Margaret, their closet was an utter disaster."

"But, Mom, we've talked about this. Please don't reorganize our things."

"They're not your things, they're the girls' things. And really, a thank-you would be nice. I spent all afternoon doing it."

"But this is one of Helen's favorites." She pulled from the top of a bag a green T-shirt that read *I won a ribbon at the Race for Social Justice.*

"It's too small."

"It's not, though."

"It's skimpy. I ordered some new things anyway; she doesn't need these."

Margaret turned away. She went into the girls' room and opened the dresser drawers as quietly as she could. Everything was beautifully tidy, piled into careful rows. Many people would have paid good money for this service, but the fact that Elizabeth had done it without asking made her want to jam her arm in and fuck the neat piles up.

Elizabeth was standing in the doorway. "Mom"—she tried to keep her voice low—"please listen . . . What's that?"

A new dollhouse stood in the corner of the room. It was the kind of dollhouse built like a box, with a hinge down the middle and two halves you could pull apart to reveal the interior. It was like that now, three stories of pink rooms splayed wide open. Bending down to look, Margaret realized that it wasn't a normal house. Instead of living rooms and bedrooms and bathrooms for the dolls to live in, it had stores. Racks and registers were painted on the walls, and different styles of doll clothes were stuck there with ingenious Velcro patches. Dolls in various states of undress were lying through the rooms.

"It's a doll mall. The girls love it. They played the whole time I was cleaning."

"Mom, I'm grateful to you for helping out with the kids, but"—she went back into the hallway and closed the bedroom door behind her—"you have to listen to me. No reorganizing clothes. No big toys. Please."

"You can't have it both ways, Margaret. You can't ask me to come and then dictate to me what I do when I get here."

"Can't I, though? It's my home. They're my children."

"Stop shouting at me," Elizabeth said.

I'm not shouting, she thought but did not shout.

The childhood fantasy never went away. She would have given anything for a witness, an umpire, Angela Lansbury, Danny, anyone, to say it wasn't she who was acting unreasonable.

"If I can't trust you to listen to me, I won't feel comfortable asking you to come."

"What are you saying?"

Margaret squeezed past her through the hallway. She wanted to shift the conversation away from the girls, back into the kitchen, but Elizabeth wouldn't budge.

"I'm not saying anything, except what I already asked."

"Are you saying you won't let me see my grandchildren?"

"Of course not." How had this escalated so quickly? There was too much feeling in the hallway. She felt trapped, jammed with her mother in the barrel of a white gun. "I'm not threatening you, Mom, calm down."

"I can't calm down. I need them. I need them like medicine. If you take them away I don't know what I would do."

For a horrified moment Margaret thought her mother might fall to her knees, and how would she bear it? She had never been able to bear Elizabeth's feelings. All she could say was "Shhh, Mom, you'll wake the girls."

Elizabeth went and grabbed the necks of the trash bags. "I'll just go, I'm going," she said. Margaret said sorry, sending her apologies trailing down the stairwell, the green shirt in her fist.

That weekend would be the first time she'd seen Elizabeth since that argument. It was one of Elizabeth's best qualities that she didn't hold grudges. She seemed to forget fights as soon as she'd won them.

"JoJo, you're smooshing me," Margaret said now, trying to shift the child off her back. "I need you guys to play something without me. Why don't you play with that mall?"

"We hate the mall," Jo said.

"Really? Why?"

"Jo ruined it," Helen said.

"Ruined it how?"

They went to see. Jo had scribbled all over the rooms, great nubbly scrawls of crayon and black marker slashes. Margaret got down on her knees and laughed. She knew she should act stern, but she was delighted. "It's like graffiti. Come here, you little punk, you little anticapitalist."

"Anti what?" Jo asked.

"I like what you did here," she said, touching an orange stripe that started in a room of ballgowns and trailed down the hall. It was so bright its edges seemed to vibrate. Jo had clearly spent a long time on the stripe, going over and over it. A stub of orange crayon lay nearby, having put so much of itself into what it made.

"We're not in trouble?" Helen asked.

"No, it's your toy, you can draw on it, I don't care. Oh, but please don't draw on our actual walls, okay? Then I would be mad."

"Okay," Jo said, unconvincingly.

The girls wandered off, but Margaret kept looking at the desecrated mall. She imagined that orange stripe running through the mall of her childhood, from Old Navy to Nordstrom to that odd blank space, the constructionless zone. She ran her finger down the line. She hated that Elizabeth had called her children medicine. But she knew exactly what she meant.

13

THURSDAYS WERE USUALLY EZRA'S NIGHT, BUT TODAY WAS HIS girlfriend's birthday, so he'd asked Margaret to swap. She was glad to do him a favor, gladder still of the bonus night. She wanted as much time with the girls as possible before they all went to New Jersey for the weekend. She wanted to stamp in their minds that they were *her* children, that they lived in Brooklyn, that they didn't belong to Elizabeth's house with the marble counters and the swimming pool. At 5:00 she buzzed his building, and before she'd even climbed the first grim stair she could hear her children. "Mommy!" They hung above her on the banisters, one leg each dangling into the cavernous stairwell.

"Careful," she said, raising her hands up in a pointless gesture of caution. "Careful."

"How was the afternoon?" she asked Ezra, panting from the stairs.

"Jo had that playdate but wouldn't play," he said. "She just wanted to look at my phone."

"That's weird," she said. "Jo, you didn't want to play with your friend?"

Jo didn't answer. She and Helen had each wrapped themselves around Margaret's legs, and she was lifting them like heavy shoes.

"Jo," Ezra said, "it's rude not to play. We can't keep scheduling playdates if you won't play with your friends when they get here."

Margaret bristled. Ezra was always so concerned about offending people who weren't a part of their family. He was thoughtful, that was why. More thoughtful than she was. And yet in this one way he reminded her, a little, of Elizabeth. "She's only four," she said. "She'll be more interested next year."

"She's five in two days."

"You can't make her want to play," Margaret said, trying to pry her daughters off her legs. She didn't want them overhearing. "Guys, go get your stuff," she said, pointing her toe and trying to lift one sneaker out of the crisscross-applesauce trap it was caught in. The girls just laughed. "Try to walk, Mommy," they said.

"Girls, get off." She lost her balance, reached out to grab—no, not Ezra, pivot to the bookshelf—and it was terrible, her foot came back down half on Jo's leg.

"Ow," Jo said. "You hurt me."

You made me, Margaret thought but did not say. She knelt and kissed the leg. "I'm sorry. Ouch. I didn't mean to."

Jo was crying, but not much. Margaret gathered her up and set her down on her feet. "Seriously, go get your stuff."

Ezra never got them ready to go before she arrived. She wasn't sure if it was because he didn't think to or didn't want to or if it was more intentional—if he liked prolonging this time with her. It was never pleasant; she was never so sweaty and shrill as when she was trying to get her children's shoes on. "Socks and shoes! Socks and shoes! Helen, how many times do I have to say it, put on your socks." Maybe it was somehow helpful to him, seeing her struggle so ineffectually like this.

"What's wrong?" he asked her.

"Nothing," she said, meaning: this.

Ezra was a managing editor at *The Really*, which he described as a small, tech-focused digital magazine, though in fact it was published by a branch of the PR department of the world's most powerful social media company. In his seven-year tenure, the magazine had cycled through many names: *Ikon, Aria, Interrobang.* He seemed to spend most of his time in meetings brainstorming new names, or in meetings about best practices for future meetings for brainstorming new names, or in meetings to discuss the demographics of those future meetings and how to ensure that everyone participated equally in the important work of brainstorming new names. Occasionally he worked on an infographic about disinformation.

He had a graduate degree from Columbia Journalism School and was paid as much as an entry-level coder, which was to say, far more than she was. She could ask him for child support but didn't want to, and he hadn't offered for the obvious reason that the divorce was her idea. He wore black hoodies and cared about all the right things and was widely admired professionally for being almost entirely egoless.

But Margaret had found it frustrating to be dominated by a husband who acted so insistently uninterested in power. When he faded into the background, he expected her to fade too, bundling up her wifely skirts and following him down the dim passageways of self-effacement.

When she'd gone into labor with Helen, and her water broke, and it was immediately clear to her that she needed an epidural right that absolute second, he'd made her walk around the apartment for twenty more minutes, because all the pregnancy books said that labor would come on slowly, and it was best to pass the time at home, rocking back and forth on an exercise ball and getting lower-back massages. She had known exactly what Ezra was worried about, and it was not (at least not primarily) the imminent arrival of their baby or the already-remarkable pain that heralded it. His concern was that Ezra and his wife would bother the healthcare providers of NewYork-Presbyterian before it was absolutely necessary to do so.

She had finally, between contractions, picked up her own overnight

bag and walked out the door, the picture of entitlement. By the time they
made it to the hospital, she was listing against the walls.

RIDICULOUS TO BE RESENTFUL of that still. This was what came of
lingering. What on earth were the girls doing? Helen was lying on the
floor coloring. One sock was on one foot. Jo was in the bathroom. "Ezra,
can you help with Helen, please?" she asked him, in the fed-up-wife voice
she knew he hated.

"You don't have to use that voice," he said, as she'd known he would.
"I'm already helping," he said, though he wasn't.

"JoJo, what are you doing? We need to go eat dinner."

"I want some scream."

"What?"

"Some scream." She was rooting around in the medicine cabinet. She
knocked over a bottle of mouthwash. Band-Aids and hair ties rained down.

"What?"

"Some scream."

Margaret was trying but failing to pick things up faster than Jo knocked
them down. A jar of antiaging moisturizer clanked into the sink, the overnight evidence of Ezra's girlfriend. Margaret was worried it had cracked,
but it hadn't. She picked it up and thought about opening it. She wanted
to know what it smelled like. But that would be weird and invasive. She
opened it anyway. It smelled good—warm and citrusy, like cream and
oranges. She badly wanted to touch it, but that would be weird and invasive and perhaps even, in the girlfriend's eyes, unsanitary. She touched it
anyway—stuck just the tip of a finger into the whipped pearlescence.

She was happy that Ezra had a girlfriend. Delighted, actually. Though
the thought of her—a teacher named Anaya who wrote out grocery lists
for elaborate dinners with different-colored gel pens that he persisted in
magneting to his refrigerator—did seed a terrible panic that in ten years
he would be happily remarried while Margaret would be alone with a vibrator with cat hair sticking to it. "What birthday is it?" she'd asked Ezra,

about Anaya's celebration that night. The answer: her thirtieth. Margaret rubbed the cream into the skin between her eyes, into the wrinkle that was forming there.

Jo knocked over Ezra's electric razor, and his beard trimmings went everywhere. "Okay, enough, enough," she said. "Jo, stop touching everything." Guiltily, she put her finger back into the cream and smoothed the surface flat, as if covering up a bootprint in the snow. She screwed the top back on and tried to remember which shelf it had fallen from. "I'm begging you, go get your socks."

"Some scream," Jo said. She was holding up a tube of toothpaste.

"She means sunscreen," Helen called from the other room.

Ah. "You don't need sunscreen, JoJo," Margaret said, taking the toothpaste from her hand. "It's dinnertime, the sun is already going down."

"I like it," Jo said.

This was demonstrably false. Every morning before camp Margaret had to forcibly hold Jo down to get lotion on her face while she kicked and screamed. Alternatively, Margaret could sometimes swipe some on, nonconsensually, if she was distracted enough by the TV or breakfast. But usually that ended with Jo screaming anyway and rubbing it into her own outraged eyes.

"Tomorrow morning we can put on so much sunscreen, I promise," Margaret promised. "Shoes and socks!" she said again, in a bright desperate voice. She picked Jo up and notched her onto a hip, moved sideways through the door so she wouldn't bump her head.

Helen stood in her single sock, taping her picture up against the window. The sky outside was golden with late-day sun, but the light stopped abruptly at the glass. Inside was already beginning the blue evening, shadows padding the corners of the room. On the couch was Ezra, watching her, looking more cheerful than she'd seen him in weeks.

"Mommy, come see," Helen said. "I drew a picture of Grandma's house."

THREE

14

ELIZABETH STOPPED RIGHT WHERE SHE WAS, AND SO MARGA-ret had to stop too. They were in a hurry, but this was more important: her mother had to have the last word. But Margaret too had to have the last word. She dug her heels into the floor, down into the stone of the station concourse. Commuters in their routine rush streamed around them, the flow splashed through with antic rivulets of anxiety, the darting men about to miss their trains. But neither Margaret nor her mother moved.

"Stop shouting at me," Elizabeth said, "and come back here." Margaret never shouted. Did she? Why was her mother always accusing her of shouting, just because she wouldn't give in? She would never give in. She stood as tall as she could; she looked proud and disdainful. She was ten paces off; she thought of honor, and pistols cocked and aimed, and blood in the snow. Whatever happened now, she would not walk back to Elizabeth.

Margaret had wanted to wait for the train in the Amtrak concourse; Elizabeth had insisted they go down to the New Jersey Transit waiting area, that they would head off the lines that way and be sure to find better seats. Why Elizabeth had even insisted on coming into the city that day was a mystery. She had said something about shopping but also, confusingly, something about a doctor. She carried no bags. "We'll ride the train home together," she'd said. "Start the birthday weekend early. Won't that be nice?" And Margaret had said, "Mm-hmm." She wasn't even saying that her mother was wrong about New Jersey Transit, only that they were sure to get seats regardless, that it didn't matter, that honestly, it made no difference whatsoever.

Elizabeth was looking around the concourse as if for allies, as if hoping to catch someone's eye so she could plead for their sympathy, so she could gather their defenses to her side. All yellow hair and golden buttons shining from her pale blue dress of eyelash tweed, she mustered her charm about her. But no one paused; no one looked.

Ha! This was Margaret's city. The city frightened Elizabeth, but it did not frighten Margaret, and sometimes that made her feel magnanimous pity toward her mother and sometimes it made her feel glorious and vengeful. "Don't be so *anxious*," she liked to say to her mother, when they were here together, on an outing, waiting for the subway or a car, trying to get through the crowd to a restaurant or museum; "everything is totally *fine*"—knowing it filled Elizabeth with a sizzling red mist of absolute rage.

MARGARET KNEW she should be more sympathetic to her mother's fears. Planes, trains, intersections, ski mountain chairlifts—they all made Elizabeth nervous, and it wasn't hard to guess why: Because of all that traveling with the parents who hadn't loved her better. Because of being dragged to Europe in new dresses when all she wanted was mass at 4:00 and dinner at 5:00. But couldn't she just get over it?

What Elizabeth liked was houses: big houses with elaborate basement storage systems and curtains with tassels and trim. She never hired a decorator—she picked everything out herself. And Margaret, even at her most resentful, was proud of that. She felt that her mother was, in a sense, an artist. Like when you saw the line of a painting, or read a sentence, and you knew that only one person could have made that mark, only one person would have done it quite that way. You opened the door to Elizabeth's house and *bam*, there was an antique cabinet painted with scenes of medieval Florence, topped with the white-on-green-grass of family wedding photos, and dangling from one of its handles a Christmas ornament—a wooden soldier doll that flung his legs in the air when you pulled the string between them, as if dancing along to a song called "Elizabeth."

You had to respect it. It just wasn't Margaret's style. The older she got, the more she suspected it was sumptuous in a way that tipped, almost, into bad taste. For instance: What was with all the Chinese villages? Margaret swore, every time she visited, yet another armchair had been reupholstered with pagodas and people in Oriental hats. This was maybe racist, right? But she couldn't tell her mother that. It was a beautiful print, she would say. She was only coordinating colors.

Margaret didn't think of going there as going home anymore. Her parents had renovated the house so many times. It was a very gracious house now with sunlight in the foyer and the right number of bathrooms and its own swimming pool dug out of the yard, but there was something blurred about it—you knew it had been something else before and something else before that, and that was disorienting, you couldn't quite trust it. The back staircase: gone; a new half bath; a bigger kitchen with (count them) three separate ovens; something her family unironically called the great room.

It had been a few years now since the last redo. Margaret wondered what Elizabeth would do next. A new chair. A new addition. But always, in theory, the same home. She must have liked the idea of change in small, controlled doses. Or maybe she was just bored and had too much money.

Elizabeth's parents had spent a fortune on a series of pieds-à-terre and then on an assisted living apartment in South Beach. Margaret remembered, vaguely, her one and only visit: how her grandparents had sat stiffly in armchairs and complimented Neal on being handsome and polite, as old people always did. When they went away for good and died, they left Elizabeth a lot of money. It paid for the big house, and for the endless improvements to the house, and still there was more left over.

The people who'd owned the house before them had been artists. Elizabeth, who'd majored in art history at Barnard, had probably liked the idea of that. But she hadn't liked the art they left behind. Margaret had been six the first time she'd entered the house, following the boxes of their possessions through the door and into the dining room. There she saw, at the head of their own familiar table, a life-size sculpture of a totally naked man. She'd stared for only a moment before Elizabeth had ordered the movers to take the statue away, but she remembered him as beautiful, his body tense with muscle, his monumental face staring out the window.

The room held nothing now but the dining set and the Christmas china, a picture of horses, a picture of an angel. Still, whenever they sat there on holidays, no matter what else had changed, Margaret couldn't help but see, in place of whoever was carving the roast, that indifferent stone cock.

STRUGGLING AGAINST ELIZABETH ALWAYS made her feel like a teenager—weak, and mad about it. What must Helen and Jo be thinking as she gripped them by the hands? This wasn't a safe place for stopping. She could feel them being tugged this way and that by the current of the crowd, eddying uncertainly about her legs. They could go one way or another, but the going was imperative. They wanted to get on the train. They were excited about a summer weekend at the big house in New Jersey. They didn't know that in the past it had been a different sort of house. They *liked* their grandparents. They liked their cousin and their uncle Neal.

"I'm sorry Mommy and Grandma are disagreeing," she told them quietly. Helen shrugged. Jo didn't seem to be paying attention; she was watching the slow-motion chomp of the escalator teeth. Margaret could never quite tell if grown-up disagreements (she didn't like to call them arguments) upset them. They must, because she remembered her own agony as a child in moments like these. She would have been staring at the station floor, wishing she could fall right through it into the squirming rat pits below.

But when she asked her children if they were bothered—by a tense inter-action between Margaret and her mother, or Margaret and Ezra—they would never say. She tried not to force it. Maybe they were as stubborn as she was. "Mom," she said to Elizabeth, "you're being ridiculous." (She knew she would *hate* that.) "Let's just go," she said.

People somehow kept walking between them, as if they couldn't feel the leaden air, the high-pressure front their battling wills were creating. She knew exactly what her mother wanted to say now. She could practi-cally see the word in Elizabeth's mouth, passing like a sour lozenge from one cheek to the other, but she was trying hard not to let it out, and Mar-garet appreciated it, that was something at least—the word *bitch*.

If her mother would only come now, Margaret felt, she would be quiet. They would go down the stairs toward New Jersey Transit. They would stoop through the low-ceilinged hallway, where the light was such a grimy yellow it might have traveled, as if from a distant star, straight from the 1990s. And they would wait in the tunnels for the submission of the train, the roaring body coming to heel, hissing, ticking, compliant, tame. They would enter and take their seats.

"Come *back* here," Elizabeth said again, but Margaret would not, would never. The world was on her side now, both instinct and reason tilted toward her. She was standing by the stairs they had to go down—that, in fact, Elizabeth had insisted they go down! Margaret could stand there until they missed their train, if her mother wanted to. Point number two: the children were holding her hands. It was wrong to make them take sides, wrong to conscript them into this endless battle against Elizabeth. It was wrong and yet they were *her* children, they were holding *her* hands. Speaking, purely, of the arrangement of their four bodies on the floor of the concourse, it was three against one. And Elizabeth knew it too. She was weakening, Margaret could see it. Sensing her power, she took one step backward.

If only Elizabeth would come now. If only they could stay on the train forever and never get to the house in the suburbs, then maybe they could get along. The girls could build a nest of jackets to sleep in and chat up the conductor until he let them wear his hat and steer. Elizabeth could—what? Reorganize everyone's luggage.

She wouldn't have time to talk about the divorce or the girls' need for more space and stability. Margaret in turn wouldn't be filled with the desperate temptation to throw her own childhood back in her face, the things she'd borne in silence to spare her mother's feelings. And the stations would pass by unmentioned, undwelled-upon, like the wrong note in a conversation, something a generous person shrugged off, forgot. They would move on through the mudflats, past the sullen factories burning off whatever it was they had to burn off. And Margaret would let Elizabeth talk about how she had been right—they had headed off the lines—because she would know that she had won: there was nothing to argue about.

15

LEANING AGAINST THE THRESHOLD OF HER OLD BEDROOM, SHE watched the girls sleep. The curtains were different. The blanket was different. But the bed was the same number of footsteps from the door, the window the same black squares of pure suburban night. Outside, unseen, the wind muddled the branches of the cherry tree. They'd arrived in time for Hugh's roast chicken, and the girls had had the rare luxury of a bath in Elizabeth's great cauldron of a tub. In a few minutes Biddy was coming to get her, to take her out for a drink.

Biddy had moved back to the neighborhood when her daughter, Alice, was born and lived in a sweet yellow house with her husband, Steve. They were no longer bothered by the fact that their lives had diverged. This was because they were grown-ups; they didn't need to dress like twins to be friends. Though she had to admit it would have been harder if one of them hadn't had children. Motherhood allowed difference because it made them so categorically the same.

Her relief now at getting away from Elizabeth's house fizzed up so hard it made her feel a little drunk. She should get a little drunk.

She went downstairs, by the chess set made of lead and the soldier doll dangling from the cabinet. She passed the glass box that kept the antique dueling pistols, which stood now on a side table surrounded by baby pictures, and touched the words *'til death do us part.* The older she got, the less romantic it seemed, that dare between two people who should never have been armed in the first place. She found them in front of the TV, their backs to her, watching a Viking heft a broadsword.

"Hey, do you mind if I go out for a bit? Biddy's coming to get me. The kids are fast asleep."

Elizabeth turned around and laid her arm on the back of the couch. "Turn the volume down," she told Margaret's father. "Not down, Hugh, I said *off.*"

Then: "We were hoping to spend some time with you, Margaret."

Warlords flickered as they looked at each other across the expanse of the great room. It was the train station concourse all over again. This would never be happening, they all knew, if Margaret was still somebody's wife.

Her dad broke the tension, broke it with the blessed ease of someone who didn't notice, or was pretending not to notice, that there was tension in the first place: "Tell Biddy to come in and say hi."

"Absolutely," she said as he unmuted the show and she went outside to wait.

THE DARK SMELLED damp and sweet as watered flowers. The toolshed, the roses, the coiled green hose, the bushes dense with memory—it was all too precise to be real, as if each backyard landmark had been reconstructed to her exact specifications, just for Margaret, just to trick or delight her. Elizabeth didn't do her own gardening anymore—she had a lady she paid to plant and weed—but the flowers were the same as always. The new pool was tucked out of sight. She tried to see where the lawn ended, what happened there at the property line, but all she could see was gloom and darker gloom. She ducked. Something overhead—a swoop, an unbirdlike unflutter. She covered her hair with one hand and looked up. Nothing.

For years, the attic had been infested with bats, the upside-down masses of them living right above her bedroom. You couldn't pretend they weren't there, because there was evidence: a pile of guano accumulating day by day near the eaves outside her bedroom window. If she was patient and timed it just right, she could see them spill out of the house like black runoff, straight out of the gutter and into the gloaming. Seeing them was better than not seeing them, and seeing them as a colony was better than imagining one alone, crawling headfirst down the wall, fiddling with its dark little hands along her windowsill, its face . . . No, not even in nightmares did it have a face.

The attic had been cleared long ago, but the bats were still there; they must live somewhere. She looked up at her old window in the room where her daughters were sleeping. She had cracked it open before she left. Should she go back and shut it? No, she was being paranoid. The fresh air was good for them. And anyway here came Biddy in her silver minivan.

Biddy had gotten her license seven months before Margaret and had been driving her around ever since. They navigated the gearshift to put their arms around each other.

"My dad wants you to come in and say hi, but please don't make me go back in there."

"But I love your dad."

"But you love me more."

"True. How are you holding up?"

"Work is crazy. Elizabeth is Elizabeth. Ezra is coming tomorrow. About how you'd expect."

"Steve and I are in a fight about one of your stories."

"Which one?"

"The one about the startup guy. Did you work on that one? The guy who apologized and then deleted his apology? I hate how that guy looks. A man should have some bones in his face, don't you think? Which way am I going?"

"Cocktails? The hotel?"

"Perfect."

"What was the fight about?"

"Oh, I don't even know. We keep switching whose side we're on, but we fight the same amount regardless. Also, he's weirded out by all the puzzles."

"Puzzles?"

"It's my new coping mechanism."

"Coping with what? Anxiety?"

"Oh, more like rage."

"How many puzzles are we talking? Is this an every-night thing?"

"It's every night."

"Okay, but what's *on* the puzzles? Don't tell me cats. Covered bridges?"

"Anything. Literally anything. It doesn't matter what's on them."

Margaret nodded like she was making some kind of professional assessment, like she was the handyman of middle-aged marriages: Yes, ma'am, I see your problem right there. She enjoyed, for a moment, the pleasant idea that her life was not necessarily so much more screwed up than everyone else's. She thought Steve should throw the puzzles out the window and fuck his wife. That, or she thought Biddy should throw the puzzles out the window and fuck someone else.

"I do the puzzles on this big poster board so I can slide them under the bed when I'm working on them," Biddy was telling her, "because if I leave them out Alice will get them."

"Right. Smart."

"But the other morning she was playing in my room, and she went under the bed and found one and tore it up. It was a bad week at work. I had to throw a retirement party because, listen, my boss says I'm the cultural center of the team. I was like, Fuck you, I'm a portfolio manager, I don't plan parties just because I'm a woman. Anyway, but I planned it. So each night I'd been doing this puzzle; it's like two thousand pieces. I walk in and Alice is just throwing them everywhere, stomping on them; they were in her hair, in her mouth."

"Jesus, Biddy."

"Yeah. And you know what she said? 'Sorry, Mommy, it was an accident.'"

Margaret was imagining Alice like a demented flower girl, throwing petals into the air.

"For a second," Biddy said, "I mean truly, for the tiniest second, and I never would, but for a sliver of a second, I wanted to slap her."

Margaret put her hand on her oldest friend's shoulder, and they contemplated the intersection. "Of course you wanted to," she said.

Then: "Do you want to get a puzzle right now? We can get ten." In her filthiest voice: "We can get a room and do them all over, on the bed, on the floor. We can do them all night long."

There were no other cars, no streetlights here. The road felt abandoned, though Margaret knew that just out of sight the houses were lousy with families, the trees packed to the branches with congregating deer just waiting to blunder into traffic. The fact of her sleeping children rushed over her. She had left them behind at Elizabeth's house. How could she? They should turn around right then. But Helen and Jo were safe. Weren't they? Just the fact that she worried, just the fact that she was afraid, was keeping them safe. Right?

"You know what Jo said to me the other day?"

"What?"

"She sort of stroked my face and said, 'Mommy, I dreamed your life.'"

"What kind of mystic shit is that?"

"I know, right? Don't you wonder, like, what they must think of us? When they're older, I mean. Will they understand?"

"No," Biddy said, parallel parking in front of the hotel in one try. "They won't."

In high school, Biddy knew a guy called Joey—Joseph Spacatto Jr. Joseph Spacatto Sr. owned a company that manufactured construction supplies and accessories—nuts and bolts and rebar, that kind of thing. Their parents were friends, and Joey was in college, but he couldn't have been very popular because when he threw parties at the warehouse, Margaret and Biddy were always some of the only girls there.

Still, the parties were amazing, if only for the *Night at the Museum* thrill of being unsupervised in the warehouse after hours. Margaret and Biddy would sneak off to explore the aisles, through the merchandise packed all the way up to the fluorescent lights. They padded around in their ballet flats, reading the labels: snap tie; super tie; super tie wedge; articulated in-corner (six- and three-foot lengths available); articulated out-corner; push-pull prop; guard rail; safety clamp.

It felt strange to be tipsy under such bright light. The nights had the thrown-together, mixed-up quality of dreams, like they'd snuck into some canyon of grown-up masculinity and they were these little fish way down in the trickling riverbed. Now and then, they'd make a tear in the cling wrap and work a finger through, touch the metal. Whenever they came across a ladder, they climbed it.

But mostly they talked. "When I live in Paris someday," Biddy would say, "you'll come stay with me."

"You'll smoke and sleep with artists and put flowers in old wine bottles."

"I'll be a high-powered executive and you'll write famous poems."

Biddy would indeed study abroad in Paris in college, though Margaret never visited her there. Margaret would indeed write poems, though no one outside her college workshop ever read them.

They would talk until the beep of a forklift alerted them that some drunk kid had turned it on and they needed to get off the floor if they didn't want to be crushed or speared. They'd dart up the clanging metal steps to a lounge filled with black leather armchairs that smelled like manly cars, where they'd sit in boys' laps and take sips from their cans of spoiled-tasting beer. Sometimes Margaret kissed someone, but usually not. When a cute boy wanted her, she felt more pity than desire, and when an unattractive boy wanted her, she was filled with a confusing, righteous fury. She was still waiting for someone, anyone, to be as beautiful as Danny.

One night Biddy got wasted and Margaret couldn't find her. She'd been distracted by a game of quarters, and when she looked around again Biddy wasn't in the lounge. She wasn't answering her phone either. Margaret went back down to the warehouse floor and called her name quietly. Then louder. "Biddy!" She flipped her head upside down and snapped her hair into a ponytail. "Biddy, it's not funny." She walked, then jogged the perimeter, but it was deserted—nothing but tools and light. By the time she stomped back into the lounge she was worried.

"I can't find Biddy," she told Joey.

He shrugged. "She's around here somewhere. What are you nervous about? Just chill."

She could feel eyes rolling, a smirk going around the room. She didn't care. None of them belonged there on the echoing factory floor surrounded by grown men's props—all that metal and the blades sharp enough to cut through it. "Don't tell me to chill," she said.

She knew from Joey's expression that something had entered her face, a do-not-fuck-with-me tension, an almost maternal threat.

"Did you check the workout room?"

"Where?"

"Upstairs, at the end of the hall."

She was almost there when she heard someone coughing in a bathroom. She backtracked and went in and there was Biddy in one of the stalls, bending over the toilet, barfing. "Hey hey hey hey," she said, gathering Biddy's hair in her hands.

"Ugh."

"You okay?"

"Ugh."

She stayed there a few minutes, in a wobbling squat, and then Margaret helped her up. She pulled her ponytail loose and gave Biddy the hair tie. "One of your earrings is missing," she said. Biddy put her hands to her ears and made a disgusted face. They both looked into the toilet bowl and there it was, the hoop twinkling silver through the bile.

Margaret rolled up her sleeve and fished it out.

"Oh my god." Biddy was laughing so hard she had to lean against the toilet paper dispenser. Margaret flushed and grinned, pushing past her to the sink, pumping and pumping the industrial-grade soap.

"I can't believe you did that," Biddy said. "I seriously cannot believe you did that."

She rinsed the earring, handed it back to her. "Where have you been? I was starting to freak out."

"Oh my god." She poked the pin back through her ear and then cupped her hands under the faucet and made a bowl of clear water to drink from, rinsed out her mouth, kept talking. "Joey and that guy Kyle said they'd show me the workout room—did you know there's a workout room?—and I was just hanging out and fooling around on the machines, but then Joey left and the other guy tried to kiss me, and I said no, because I was starting to get the spins. I told him I thought I might throw up. And this guy Kyle—"

She was laughing again, too hard to talk, had to press her forehead against the mirror to catch her breath. "This guy Kyle says, 'Lie down and take your pants off. If you take your pants off, you'll feel better.'"

"No. Biddy. That is seriously fucked up."

They left the party without saying goodbye. Margaret wished she had done more than reach into a toilet bowl of puke. She wanted to murder that guy Kyle, drive an articulated out-corner through his stupid skull. "Let me rip your jugular out, Kyle! It'll make you feel better."

They went back to Biddy's car and spent the rest of the night in the Dunkin' Donuts parking lot, trying to sleep. Margaret would have told her parents she was staying over at Biddy's. Biddy would have told her parents she was staying over at Margaret's. At 6:00, they got donuts and sweet coffee. At 8:00, they decided it was late enough not to look suspicious. They went home to the mothers, who were waiting inside to ask, "So did you girls have fun?" and to make sure they took off their shoes before going in the door.

16

SHE WOKE UP IN THE DARK IN THE GUEST ROOM. SHE HAD heard something, but what? It was a hard limit of consciousness that you never knew what woke you. You could deduce it from the next sound you heard. If you heard a baby crying, then it was a baby's cry that woke you. If you heard a clanking radiator, then it was the heat kicking in. If you heard footsteps, then someone was in the room. It wasn't certain, but it was reasonable to assume that a cry followed a cry, a footstep followed a footstep. But if the noise didn't happen again, you would never know, and that was the case now, though she lay and listened in the dark, and something that was not quite memory reverberated inside her. Whatever it was had happened to her body, not her mind. She was awake and she didn't know why.

She could have been ten again, or sixteen, except for the small, warm weight beside her that proved, no, she was thirty-five. Biddy had dropped her off around 11:00, and Helen had gotten into her bed sometime after that. Over her daughter's head, she looked at the wall. Elizabeth had arranged a photo gallery there. All in a line were pictures of sleeping children: ancient ones of Neal and Margaret as toddlers, and then the three grandkids from oldest to youngest.

She remembered taking the picture of Jo. Elizabeth had asked her for it, to complete the collection. She'd turned on the light, dimmed it, tried different angles, furtively, while Jo slept. She'd caught the eyelashes on rosy cheeks and the dimpled hand on a pillow, but not the essential thing— that stubborn, private self, the inaccessible solitude of the child's dreaming life.

A stomp in the hallway, the handle of the door rattled, and there she was, Jo hurtling toward the bed. "Shhh, JoJo, your sister is asleep, come on my other side," she tried to say before it was too late, but it was too late. Jo clambered straight over her sister, lay on top of them both, and said: "Pancakes."

"Happy birthday, you," Margaret said.

They turned on the lights as they descended. She found the Bisquick and the butter and the bowl; she took the skillet down from its hook above the island. Her father had told her during dinner about the renovation they were planning. A new stove would go where the cabinets were and the sink would go where the stove was. This was because the built-in fridge and freezer were getting old and needed to be replaced before they broke down, but Sub-Zero no longer made them in the same dimensions, so the cabinets surrounding them would need to be replaced, and if they were already doing that, they might as well tear the whole thing out. "That makes sense," Margaret had lied.

She made an excessive stack of pancakes and put two on each girl's plate. She and Helen sang—softly but not softly enough for the hour— *happy birthday to you.*

There was nothing sinister now about the big, quiet house as the morning sun idled into the room. The light concentrated: first a diluted white, then cream then suddenly golden. It rose up the doomed cabinets and set the stovetop gleaming. The warmth drew something out of everything it touched, drew it up to the surface—a nectar. That was what shone, not the sunlight—the essence of each object made manifest, the sunlight only circumstance. When the light reached the girls, it gathered in their hair, in their overnight knots, and in the pools of syrup on their plates, giving everything from the child to the dust suspended in air its own nimbus, a haloing she could hardly bear because it was already fading, the beauty the morning gave her in the house of her childhood, until finally the light hit the butter dish at the far end of the table and the sun was contained, an ignition in white china.

"More syrup," Jo said.

"What do we say?"

"Please."

"But look, you've got so much there already. Finish that first."

"I want more now." She reached for the syrup.

"I said no," said Margaret, moving to intercept her, but too late. The jug was fumbled and tipped. Syrup oozed across the table. She tried to catch it in her hands.

"They would listen to you if you set better boundaries." It was Elizabeth, of course, in a white tennis skirt, her hair still damp from the shower. She was rubbing lotion up and down an arm, smelling of health and competency and the impossibility of sorrow. Margaret was wearing one of Ezra's old shirts and bike shorts with batter on them. Paper towels were sticking to her hands.

Elizabeth picked up one of the sodden towels between finger and thumb. "What an utter disaster," she said. "Go get a bowl of warm water; you can't just wipe it up."

"I'm soaking it up and then I'm going to do it with water."

"No, no, it won't work that way, if it settles into the cracks it'll be impossible to get out." Somehow Elizabeth had got hold of the paper towels and removed the girls from the table and was trying to hand Margaret a stack of plates. "Hurry up and help me," she was saying.

"Mom, I've got it, I'm already doing it," Margaret said.

"She has to learn that actions have consequences," Elizabeth said, her face bowed to the wood now, scrubbing. "She's just exerting her independence." Meaning: Don't let her.

"But I want her to exert her independence," Margaret said, exerting her independence. "And anyway, it's her birthday." She tried to take the roll of towels from under Elizabeth's arm, but her mother shifted it, like a football, out of reach.

Elizabeth was right: the syrup was indeed settling into the cracks of the table, as if remembering that it belonged there, longed to return there, sap in the tree. Elizabeth was trying to dig it out with a fingernail, scrapings of hardened amber going everywhere. Fine, Margaret would give up, surrender the mess to her mother if she wanted it so badly. *Ichor on the countertop.* It was gross, she thought, how ichor was both the ambrosial blood of the gods and also a wound's watery discharge. Margaret licked her fingers.

"When's Daddy getting here?" Helen asked.

"Let's text him and find out."

Just then her own father came down the stairs, already in his polo shirt. "Where's the birthday girl?" he thundered. And to Margaret: "You want me to get him from the station?"

It was a kindness, the closest he came to mentioning the divorce. "Thanks, Dad, but I can do it." She got out her phone, wrote, "eta?"

"When's Charlie getting here?" Jo asked, starting to jiggle with birthday excitement.

"Your cousin will be here by lunchtime," Elizabeth said. Now that the sun was all the way up, the kitchen seemed somehow darker. Elizabeth turned on the overhead light to inspect the table. "I've got some special things for the swim party. Who wants to see?" The girls squealed on cue. A text came back from Ezra. He was on his way.

17

THE CAKE WAS VANILLA WITH STRAWBERRIES IN CREAM AND on top pink roses around the pink words *Happy Birthday Josephine.* The aproned lady behind the register showed it to Margaret, tipping the box toward her before taping it up so she could admire the roses and check the spelling.

She dropped off the cake in her parents' car then stopped at the grocery store for milk and hot dog buns and candles. Whenever she did errands in her hometown she felt sure that she was about to run into someone from high school, that they would have to approach each other in the aisle, sizing up the weight gain and the offspring and the outfits, herding their shopping carts together like skittish livestock. She felt nervous about the prospect and then a bit disappointed that it never happened. Part of her quite wanted to be sized up. For years, through college and after, she'd fantasized about bumping into Danny, but it never happened. He did something technical in Silicon Valley now, and had a partner but no children, and only came home for Thanksgiving.

The heat had come down suddenly over the parking lot. It had been a crisp morning when she entered the grocery store, but now that day was over. The sun had pushed the blue sky lower and lower until it had finally taken shelter under the cars and she could see flickers of it cowering in the shadows there, and in the blue stripes of the corralled shopping carts, and in the blue silhouettes of the shopping people moving slowly toward the trunk doors that lifted automatically but languorously at the touch of a button.

Dumb, Margaret! She should have gone to the grocery store first and the bakery second; the cake would be melting inside the car. The roses were probably oozing, the petal edges bleeding over the white icing, the letters blurred, the birthday ruined.

But no, it was fine, it was probably fine. It wasn't even hot in the car yet. She resisted the urge to open the cake box and look.

SHE HAD ANOTHER FIFTEEN MINUTES until Ezra's train arrived. She turned left. Between the shopping center and the station was a residential area, filled with fine old Victorian houses. Around a green corner she passed Kendra Cleary's house, the finest, oldest, Victorianest of them all. She wondered if Kendra's parents were still there. Kendra had been cool, brazen; she wore tube tops all year round. It would be interesting to meet her again at thirty-five, see if she'd become more or less herself.

Kendra had thrown a party one night their junior year when her parents were out of town. The cops had famously busted it, just as half the kids were skinny-dipping in the pool. Margaret had fooled around with guys, but she'd never seen one completely naked before that night. It should have been sexy, the pool packed with all those incipient bodies, everyone giggling and stealing glances. But it wasn't like that.

As soon as they'd decided to do it, everyone got very serious. The moonlight fell like a silver veil over the teenagers stepping out of their shorts, and she felt, despite the DMX pumping from the house, that she was being inducted into something spiritual and formal, some austere ritual. She couldn't remember a single intimate body part, just a silver glimmer as they all dove under. And she remembered the water, the all-encompassing everywhere touch of it. Then she surfaced and Biddy said, "Run."

And she had. No memory of getting out of the pool, just the screeching static of the police loudspeaker and the swiftness that followed. Biddy and the others had paused long enough to try to put their clothes back on and by then it was too late; they were surrounded by a phalanx of cops with nothing better to do than smirk.

But not Margaret. Margaret got away. She plunged naked into the bushes at the back of the property then ran in the direction of home, through backyards that got progressively bigger until they were more like fields. The moon was so bright it felt audible, a white ringing bell in the sky. Now and then a car went by, its headlights sweeping the trees. She'd hit the ground and lie there, face in the grass, just hoping it grew high enough to cover the pale rise of her ass. When it was quiet she would get up and run again.

Being on the cross-country team that year really paid off, she thought; she could have kept going and going. She reminded herself to loosen her hands and shake out her shoulders and to run lightly on the balls of her feet. She passed only a few lit-up windows, someone awake way too late, the color wheel of a TV screen inside. She hugged the landscaping, two miles, three, America's least-wanted minor fugitive.

At last she got to her own road. She jogged across a lawn, leapt a stone path, and entered the shelter of some trees. Not just trees—a forest. A few steps in and she couldn't see an end to it, could barely see anything at all, not even her own feet in the leaves. She knew she must still be moving parallel to the street she drove down every day of her life, and yet what was this place?

She breathed through the cramp in her side and kept walking. Her hands brushed against trunks, some rough, some furred with vines. It was hard—shuffling over roots and fallen branches and the unseeable-down-into undergrowth cracking and compacting beneath her feet—not to trip. Many sharp things seemed to be touching her at once. And then she stumbled out into the Riccis' backyard.

Was it? She hadn't been there in years, at least not since Neal had left for college. There was the colossal house and the hedge around the pool but no sign of the fence or the shed or the goat. It made sense now that she thought about it—pygmy goats probably didn't live that long—but it was still surprising, the way they'd wiped its existence clean off the land. In place of the pen was a new sunken patio with a firepit at the center. She padded over and peered inside and saw that it was brimful of ashes.

And just then everything went bright, the lawn neon, every blade of grass an exclamation of shadow. She looked down and saw her skin glowing as if lit from within by its own green light. She froze. Her body, which had been all movement, was once again flesh—breasts, belly, legs, the one dark space between them. She took short shallow breaths.

Nothing moved. No noise from the house, no alarm. It was just a motion-activated floodlight, to scare off burglars or raccoons. She turned and ran out of the glare.

No more than ten minutes later she was in bed. She'd rubbed the worst of the mud off her feet in the grass then let herself into the house, tiptoed up to her bedroom, and climbed, filthy, under the sheets. She would wash them in the morning. Elizabeth, thank god, was away visiting Neal at college, but she was still too scared to turn on the shower and risk waking her father. And she was tired, tired, unbelievably tired, awed and exhausted by what she'd gotten away with. Her whole body tingled in the way skin does right after it's slapped, before the pain sets in.

Only when she went to take a shower in the morning, after she heard her dad's car pull out of the driveway, did she realize how bad it was. Twigs and brambles had clawed red lines all over her body. Her legs were the bloodiest, but the cuts went everywhere, across her torso and up her neck. She stood under the hot water until a puddle of mud surrounded the drain. Once she was clean, she looked even worse.

Biddy—when she called at 8:00 to make sure Margaret was still alive—

couldn't stop laughing. The cops had called Kendra's parents, but the other kids got off with a warning. No ticket or anything. A few of them had gone to Wendy's for late-night fries and Frosties. Biddy had grabbed Margaret's shoes and shorts, but she couldn't find her top; she'd have to ask Kendra at school.

A day later the poison ivy started itching, and it was everywhere. Her skin turned pink then red then bubbled up into oozing patches that grew and grew until the healthy skin was reduced to little white pathways between the poison. She could have hidden the scratches under baggy pajamas, but there was no way to hide the poison ivy. "What happened?" Elizabeth shrieked when she came home. She held Margaret by the wrists, pushing her sleeves up and up and up.

Elizabeth took her straight to the doctor, where she got a prescription for an extra-strength steroid cream. She served her cool drinks and let her watch movies on the couch in the dark. For once she didn't yell, or not nearly as much as Margaret expected her to. She seemed satisfied. It was the perfect punishment, like a hangover or a pregnancy. Margaret's body had taught Margaret a lesson.

Now out of the crowd of exiting passengers came Ezra. She had always liked how he looked when he needed a haircut. He had on a black hoodie and the same backpack he'd carried since college. He saw the car right away. When they'd been married she would have gotten out of the front seat and walked around, kissed him hello, passed him the keys so he could drive. But now it felt strange to ask if he wanted to—a return to abandoned archetypes. She waited until he got in and then, unsure what else to say, asked him anyway.

"I don't care," he said.

A silence.

"I picked the cake up."

"Good."

"It's pretty, Jo's going to love it." She didn't mention the heat, the potentially ruined roses.

"Jo excited?"

"Excessively."

She tried to think of something else to say. She passed Kendra's house again, driving the same way she'd run. The quiet thickened between them, in the cup holders, in the air vents, pushing up from the brake pedal. Against her will she breathed it in. Every second the possibility of speech seemed more remote. With a great effort she said, "I was just thinking about that time I got poison ivy, and how nice Mom was about it."

"Was she nice?"

"Bizarrely nice."

"Well, people can sometimes surprise you." They turned into the driveway now. They were doing a pretty good job. They had spoken. They would make it through the party. A new car was parked out front—Neal's.

She often ended up telling people (men) the skinny-dipping story. It was funny. Also she was naked in it. She'd tell them about hiding in the bushes while amused cops corralled the scattering teenagers. She'd tell them about the irony of the poison ivy, if irony was what it was—the successful escape and the punishment that came for her regardless.

But she always failed to tell the truth about that night—that by getting away she *had* protected something, if only the dignity of those first few moments of moonlight and immersion. She hadn't let the cops get hold of that. She hadn't had to stand there in her body while they told her she was wrong. No, instead she made the story a joke, so everyone could agree that it was all very Margaret, the way that, by saving herself, she'd made everything so much harder.

18

THE CHILDREN WERE MAKING MORE NOISE THAN SHE WOULD
have imagined possible. They were being tossed through the air, landing
on the couch, and lining up to be tossed again. Jo then Helen then Neal's
son, Charlie, and at the fulcrum of it, Neal: bending and lifting up children, the motion like shoveling dirt or snow. He wore white socks, and
complicated sneakers, and khaki shorts belted tight around a polo shirt.
He was as slight as he'd always been. His hair was the same color as her
own. He never changes, she thought, and at the same time, he might be
another person entirely, she couldn't say; it was difficult to look straight at
him, her brother.

The couch was freshly reupholstered, and beneath the kids the pattern roiled. Charlie was rolling off the cushions while Jo landed right behind him, the embroidered people in the embroidered villages staring up
with embroidered concern at the incoming bodies. Helen was next, reaching up her arms to Neal, when Margaret called across the room, "Daddy's
here!"

They hugged, everyone hugged. It was mandatory in the family, the hugging. Neal moved in with his arms open. Margaret held on to the cake.

After, he turned to Ezra, shook his hand.

"How was your trip in? How's the city?"

"Oh, hot. But not too bad. Not too bad."

"Uncle Neal, keep playing!"

"Why don't we give Uncle Neal a break," Margaret said.

"Nooooo," her daughters wailed.

"We can go swimming," Margaret suggested.

A cacophony of "Can we?"

Margaret said she would find the girls' swimsuits as soon as she got the cake in the fridge. It was always a shock that her kids thought Neal was fun. But he was, when he wanted to be—he made silly faces and joined in all their games. It made her wonder if his childhood reserve had been just that—shyness, awkwardness, not pride or disdain—and she would feel an awful rush of withheld sympathy. But then he would say something proud and disdainful, and the sympathy was gone.

In the kitchen, Neal's wife was doing something on her phone. They hugged a brief hello. Neal was talking about murder. Someone had been shot, or perhaps many people shot, in some place where you didn't expect that to happen. "Right outside," he was saying, "in the afternoon." He was very invested in the city considering he had never lived or worked there. "You didn't see that story? Sweetheart, send them that story." The mayor—he wanted to talk about the mayor. The general theme: cities, what were they coming to, and people who just couldn't seem to help themselves.

While she rearranged a shelf of leftovers and the Anglophilic condiments Elizabeth bought but never seemed to consume (horseradish, salad cream, mint jelly, every jar of it long since expired) to make room for the cake box, she listened as Ezra tried hard not to sound like he in any way disagreed.

Then her father came up from the basement. Elizabeth had found him a particular kind of woven basket with little compartments for carrying wine bottles, and he had this dangling from a hand. He gave Ezra a hearty handshake. Everyone was always glad to see Ezra.

On the matter of urban violence, their father agreed with Neal—or rather, Neal agreed with their father. And yet their father didn't like it when people seemed too sure of themselves; he felt compelled to complicate and caveat whatever had been said, even if that meant proposing the opposite of what he actually believed. He would argue the point so stridently that Neal would have to declare himself persuaded, at which point their father would say, "But come on, that's ridiculous."

She almost enjoyed it, their dad swinging his wicker basket like a contrarian Red Riding Hood while he pleasantly demolished any sincerely held point of view. But she felt sorry for Neal. The only person he ever deferred to was their father; criticism or correction from anyone else was unacceptable, intolerable. And yet, poor Neal, his submission meant nothing to the man. Their father barely noticed. He thought he was just having a conversation. He tried not to let on, but it was obvious to Margaret— and perhaps to Neal, and to Neal's wife as well—that he enjoyed talking to Ezra more.

They seemed to have pivoted to religion. Or novels? Her father was saying, "So the gods become mortal and it turns out they're all kinds of drunks and losers, but a few of them decide to go into business together, as private eyes, and they're solving these crimes—"

"Great books, great books," Neal said.

"But total trash."

"Guilty pleasures."

"And yet, they really are kind of genius."

"Sui generis."

"Actually—you should know this, Neal." (At the sound of his name, his wife looked up from her phone, but then lowered her head again, so quick it could have been a nod.) "Didn't you read them too? He ripped the whole premise off a series about a wizard who's a detective in Chicago."

"Well, I'll definitely have to check them out," Ezra said.

Margaret managed to get the fridge door shut. "We're going swimming," she told her sister-in-law. "Do you want to come?"

"Oh, no thanks," she said. Then: "I can't. I have to order groceries." She tipped the phone in Margaret's direction so she could see the shopping cart, the future food on the screen.

"I can take Charlie if you tell me where his swimsuit is."

Neal answered for her: "He's wearing his trunks already."

It was always like this between Margaret and her sister-in-law: blank politeness. She did not, Margaret felt, seem altogether well. She found small things overwhelming and took frequent naps. A better person would have tried harder to get to know her. But Margaret didn't, couldn't. She was too much a part of Neal. Like she had a wire up her chest, or cameras for eyes. Like because she was his wife, he could see out of her face.

Margaret went to find the swimsuits, a snarl of polyester at the bottom of their bag. At Duncan's house she'd left a bikini so tiny you could almost see her C-section scar, but the suit she'd brought here was high-necked and athletic, basically the same Speedo she'd had as a child. She pulled it on in the bathroom and then chased Jo down to change. Helen went in last.

Helen had asked for a two-piece that year for the first time. Margaret was trying not to make a big deal out of it. But when Helen wore it, Margaret could see that her body was already, ever so slightly, starting to change. Something was beginning in her legs and higher, a definition. She thought the word *pert* and her stomach cringed, shrank away from the empty space that was opening up inside her.

THE POOL was the most disorienting of the changes the house had undergone. A thicket of forsythia used to grow in the spot where it was now. In the spring she had liked to part the boughs and cram herself inside with all those yellow flowers. Now the cousins cannonballed into the same space, straight into the giving-way blue. Helen dove under, fleet and fast and sharp as a fish. Jo and Charlie in their floaties popped right back up to the surface.

Margaret reached for her phone: "Everybody look at me, say, *Happy birthday, Jo!*"

It was important to do this kind of thing, document the moment. When the girls had been babies, she'd taken thousands of photos and slipped the best ones into the sleeves of leather albums. She didn't anymore. She knew she would regret it—that the girls would be hurt someday when they noticed that the seven stages of Helen's tummy time had been meticulously recorded, her first foods, her first toppling steps from mother to father in the days of their marriage—and then nothing. And yet still she didn't do it.

Because the photos didn't work. In photos they always looked like someone else's children—squinting, awkward, sometimes even ugly. Or worse, if they looked beautiful, then the photos were like bad commercials for the past—someone else's performance of someone else's life. What was real in them was only loss.

But no, that wasn't always true. Sometimes you saw something in a photo—like the bend in a crawling baby's dimpled knee—and the vision was real again, and she would think not of the apartment that Helen was crawling through, or the stress of cooking Thanksgiving dinner, but only of how it had felt to lift that pre-toddler weight in her arms, the dense, round core of them before their legs went dangly. Looking at the bend in Helen's knee in the corner of a photograph, Margaret lifted her again and again off the ground.

"Charlie, move over a little. Jo, get in front." Helen grabbed the straps of Jo's floaties and towed her into position. "Perfect, now on three, two, one." She would print this photo, frame it, hang it on the wall. She would remember this: the way the kids' wet shoulders glistened as if they'd been dipped as much in light as in water. They waved and smiled for the camera just as the garden gate on the other side of the pool swung open and Elizabeth came through it.

"Guys, wait, just a sec. Mom, stop—" Too late. Everyone turned to look. Elizabeth was dragging something behind her, something black and swollen. Margaret thought at first it was a trash bag. But it was too big and yet not heavy enough for that. Maybe a trash bag filled with balloons? But it was enormous, it kept coming and coming until it got stuck. Elizabeth tugged and tugged and then with a rubbery squeak it popped through and bounced on the deck, its red mouth grinning.

It was a pool float in the shape of a dragon. The kids went ballistic. Margaret gave up, put the phone away, slid back into the water.

The next twenty minutes she spent helping kids onto the dragon, which had handles down its back and was almost as long as the pool was wide. The kids fought over who got to sit in front while in back the rubbery points of its barbed tail kept bumping into the walls.

"I wish we lived here," Jo said.

"This isn't our home. And we love New York. We have work and school and friends in Brooklyn. Charlie, don't do that, we're taking turns."

"Why not just the summers, then? It's better here."

"We can always visit. Charlie, stop, you could drown someone like that." She always tried to treat him like her own kids, but he was being a real only child about this dragon situation. He had hold of Helen's leg and was trying to pull her off. She kicked him in the face.

"Helen, careful, remember you're bigger."

"It's no fair you grew up here and we have to grow up in apartments," Jo said.

"Yeah, in apartments with, like, no toys," Helen added.

"Yes, fine, okay, it can be your turn now," she said to the furious boy, and lifted him up to the front.

Then: "The pool wasn't here when I was growing up," knowing that wasn't anyone's point.

AFTER LUNCH the kids played in the house while the adults congregated in the kitchen talking about the regulatory system.

"Consumer protection is such a misnomer," her dad said.

"Consumers won't feel so protected when they can't get a loan," Neal said. "Though of course I'm not saying some protections weren't warranted."

"Well, perhaps, but this is America; the paternalism—"

"Maybe these people need some paternalism."

"I certainly agree with that," Neal said. "Financially speaking, and perhaps generally speaking, they're illiterate."

"That's a bit harsh, though. I'm not sure *we* could make sense of one of these subprime loan agreements. They're criminally obtuse."

Oh, this was a tough one. Neal was so proud of being shrewd, of his certainty that no one would ever get the better of him. Would he agree with his father on this, would he go that far?

Ezra, graciously, came to the rescue. "I guess we're just lucky we don't have to."

For Hugh, politics was a game, which was repugnant, of course, but she found it hard to get that offended by him. That was just the way their father was—charming even while offending.

Neal, on the other hand. Behind the policy and data points she glimpsed something fanatical, the bright red rays of a violent vision. If it had been another century no doubt he would have argued for the stocks, for cutting off the hands of thieves, for drawing and quartering in public squares. Hard labor for unwed mothers, unwanted babies drowned like cats.

"Zero tolerance," he liked to say. "Zero. Tolerance." As if that were the highest virtue, to forswear tolerance. As if he was making a sacrifice and not confessing a deficit. She blamed Elizabeth for that.

"Margaret," Elizabeth said now, "finish that coffee because I want to show you the most beautiful cyclamen I planted."

Elizabeth wanted to show her something! She felt a glow of pride and pleasure. Enough of Neal, enough of politics. Her mother wanted to show her something pretty. It was because she was happy, Margaret could see. Having all the children in the house had filled her up, she was brimming over, and little splish-splashes of happiness were hitting even Margaret.

They went outside and looked at the cyclamen. They had hot pink petals that grew straight upward, making the plant seem cheerfully alert, a whole bed of them, throwing up their petals in surprise. Margaret loved them, she thought. "I love them," she said.

"If only you had a garden. Now I need to turn the sprinkler on. Can you deflate the pool dragon?"

Sure, Margaret liked to have a chore. Her feet were bare, the clean grass hot between her toes, a reminder that it had been like this some-times too—she had been cared for.

19

EZRA CARRIED THE CAKE OUT TO THE PATIO, THREE OF ITS
five candles still blazing. In the end it was a perfect cake—white as plain
sugar, as sugar incarnate. He set the platter in front of Jo, and her eyes
gathered up the pink roses. For this moment at least her face was worth a
thousand visits to Elizabeth's house. "That's my name," she said. Elizabeth started them singing. The children crept closer and closer to the
cake so that by the three syllables of *Jo-se-phine* they were practically face-
planting in the icing. Jo blew out the candles and shouted, "I get the first
piece! I want a flower!"

"Hold on just a sec," Margaret said. "Let me get a picture."

But on the other side of the table Elizabeth also had her phone up, saying, "Everybody smile."

"Mom, stop, I'm already—" But Elizabeth was holding the cake knife
above her head so the late-day sun dazzled off the blade. "Cake, cake,
cake," the kids chanted. Under the blue shadow of the umbrella the cake

was a lunar white, so white it seemed to glow. Elizabeth brought the knife down, lower and lower, sank it in. The children cheered. Everyone had a slice but Neal's wife, who never ate sweets.

Her father was telling Ezra about someone at the office who knew someone else at the office who knew a thing or two about charter schools. Ezra, who believed charter schools were a leech on the public education system, was nodding politely.

Neal kept trying and failing to interject into the charters conversation. Charlie went to private school. But now Neal glanced over at his son. "Charles, disgusting, stop doing that right now." The boy had put down his fork and was licking the icing off his plate. "Charles. What did I say?"

"I want more," Charlie said, peeking over the rim of his plate.

"You've had enough, don't be a pig."

"But, Dad—"

"Put the plate away. I said enough."

Neal stared down his son. His eyes never moved toward their parents, but Margaret felt certain that that was where his attention was focused, that was what he was truly reacting to: the intolerable pressure of their inevitable judgment.

"I mean, there's plenty," Margaret said, gesturing at the cake. She knew she should have shut up. If it had been one of her friends, she never would have intervened. But with Neal she couldn't help herself. Besides, more than half of the cake was still there, and the open face of it was so pleasing, the pink stain of the strawberries. She wanted more too.

"No," Neal said. "Charles, don't make me repeat myself." Fun Uncle Neal was gone, and she could see once again Neal at fourteen, his need for order and deference, the part in his hair that had never moved a millimeter right or left in nearly forty years, the severity that in a boy seemed sad and in a man seemed something else.

"Can I have another too?" Helen asked.

Margaret picked up the knife. "I don't see why we can't all have seconds. It's a party."

"Your kids can have all they want, that's your prerogative. But mine has had enough cake. And if I hear one more whine out of you—" He looked at Charlie. But Charlie, being six, had only just begun to whine. He started kicking his chair with his feet and nudging his plate around the table with small outraged motions.

"I'm still hungry," he said.

"If you're hungry, you can have an apple."

"I don't want an apple. I want cake." Neal's wife pulled the plate out of reach and, shushing him, tried to take his hand. "No no no," he said, and swatted her arm away.

Neal was out of his chair, around the table. "Don't you dare hit your mother."

"I never—" the boy said, but it was too late, Neal had one hand clamped around his arm and a forearm around his stomach and had lifted him up and away from the table. "You want to get angry? I can get angrier than you can get." The boy was writhing, slamming his heels backward, bucking his head to try to hit his father in the face. Margaret was used to tantrums, but Charlie was less like a child now than an animal trying to escape from a trap, twisting his small body horribly against its restraints. Neal stood there, taking the blows against his legs, craning his face out of reach, righteousness or viciousness blazing out of it. The harder Charlie fought, the tighter Neal held him.

They sat at the table and watched, Margaret, Ezra, Elizabeth, Hugh, none of them doing a thing, the child's feet kicking just out of reach, the only sound his furious crying getting more and more ragged until he gagged on his own screams and had to stop to dry heave, and then wailed one last time in despair, and went limp and hung there, weeping.

The phrase *charter schools* crept back across the table. Her father was speaking determinedly. Ezra seemed to be listening, though his eyes were flicking at her. Neal's wife was as unreachable as a statue or a doll. Elizabeth was stacking plates. Helen and Jo were watching Margaret, the shock in their faces like a brand-new flaw.

If he had hit the boy, she could have said, You can't do that. What he had done was in some way more terrible, the domination that they were all pretending was discipline. But Margaret hadn't moved, she hadn't done a thing.

"Apologize to your mother," Neal said.

"I I I I I'm suh suh suh sorry," Charlie said through the spasms.

Now that Charlie wasn't trying to get away, Neal let him get away. He deposited the child back into his chair, where he put his head straight down on the table.

"Pour me another glass?" Neal said to their father, who passed the wine.

"He's only six," Margaret said.

"Margaret, keep out of it," Elizabeth said.

"But that was so . . . unnecessary."

"Margaret, I told you to move on. Don't make a bigger scene than Charles did."

I'm not making a scene, she thought but did not say. She looked at Ezra for support, and she could have killed him, she could have divorced him all over again—he was looking at his phone.

But he must have felt her eyes on him because he put down the phone. "Movie time?" he said. "Should I turn it on? What are we watching?" Jo went right to Ezra and put her arms around his neck. He stood up, and Helen grabbed on to the hem of his swim trunks. He put his free hand out to Charlie, and the boy finally lifted his ravaged face. Ezra was good. Ezra was safe. She'd done that right at least, that one good thing. She'd chosen a father like Ezra.

THEY WENT INSIDE to watch *Home Alone 2: Lost in New York*. "Isn't that a Christmas movie?" Margaret's father asked.

"It's Jo's favorite," she said.

Neal pushed his chair back from the table, and wordlessly, his wife got up and sat in his lap.

Margaret focused on gathering the dishes. She could hear "Jingle Bell Rock." Jo and Helen loved the movie, had seen it probably twenty times, the little sadists. They always asked to fast-forward through the sad parts and the pigeon lady to when the music kicked in at the booby-trapped town house.

It was so satisfying the way all the boy's defenses worked, the trip wires and zip lines and paint cans on doorframes—so different from her own experience of childhood. But was it wrong to let the girls revel in so much violence? The robbers got pinned against the wall by a plummeting tool cabinet; they fell through the floorboards; they got electrocuted and set on fire; a staple gun shot them in the balls. It was torture porn for children. It was funny when the men screamed.

But she figured kids wouldn't love it so much if they didn't have a need for that precise brand of fantasy, the fantasy being: your family hurts you, but you don't need them; you survive. In the end, they return, chastened and loving you better. She bore the dirty dishes into a house that rang with the demented sound, the pealing shrieks, of children's laughter. Macaulay Culkin was throwing the bricks down onto the bad guy's face.

MARGARET WASHED the plates in the sink, the icing resisting the water. She missed the china they'd had when she was a kid. The plates had been white with a pattern of tendrilous branches that always made her think of English shadows and the cold taste of sliced fruit. She didn't love the pretty new china: It had butterflies on it, and why would anyone want to put food on butterflies? The icing was all over their wings.

"Can I help?" Ezra asked.

"Sure, thanks."

She handed him a plate, and he clanked it into the dishwasher.

"A successful birthday," he said.

"Except for Charlie."

He looked around like someone might overhear. But Neal's family had left. Hugh was in his office with the news on while Elizabeth was watching the rest of the movie with the girls. She handed him another plate. Why was he putting it in crooked like that? Half the plates wouldn't fit. It was never so obvious how rarely he did the dishes as it was when he did the dishes. Wait—that was an outdated complaint. He must do dishes all the time now. She wasn't his wife; she wasn't there to do them for him. Did his girlfriend do the dishes? She hoped not.

"Yeah, poor Charlie."

"And Elizabeth, just sitting there."

"Well, it wasn't her fault."

"Yes it was. Of course it was. He's her son. She could at least have said something. *Stop*, for instance."

"It might have just made things worse."

Ezra was always telling her to let things go. She scrubbed at a butterfly. "Even before that. Did you notice the thing with the camera, how she had to be the one to take the picture? She's always intervening except when you actually need her to intervene."

He turned off the tap and looked at her. "Do you ever wonder," he asked, "if you divorced me just to get back at your mother?"

"Ezra, that's insane."

"Margaret, I know."

She considered outrage. He was wearing a pale blue sweatshirt she'd never seen before, with the sleeves pushed up past his elbows. He'd gotten tan; the hair on his arms looked golden. She watched him put the plates in wrong.

Tomorrow the four of them would go home. They would take a car from Penn Station and the girls might fall asleep on the drive and Ezra would help her carry them up to her white apartment, where no dangers lurked and nothing altered but time, nothing but the angle of the sun through the window.

And when he left she would be glad to be alone again.

She wondered what, if anything, Jo would remember of the weekend. Would she remember cannonballing into the water or her cousin kicking the air? Would she remember the dragon? It was only then that Margaret herself remembered it, that the girls had distracted her at the last minute and she'd never gotten around to doing Elizabeth's chore.

. , .

THE DRAGON WAS LISTING in a corner of the pool and Margaret dragged it out by the tail, its black expanse bumping and bouncing gently on the ground. It was fun that something so big could be so light. Where was the valve? was the next question. It was hard to find in the dark. Margaret felt a little obscene about it, searching the dragon's body for the hole. Finally she found it and popped it open, and out came a blast of the morning's air. The sprinkler started somewhere in the yard; she heard it stutter and release, stutter and release. She was sitting on the dragon, rolling around a bit to expedite the deflation, when Jo came out of the house.

"Bang bang bababang bababang," she was saying, one eye closed and one arm out.

Helen was behind her going, "Pyoom pyoom pyoom"—more of a laser gun vibe. The movie must have ended. They were aiming at each other, at the flower beds, at Margaret, at the dragon. "Pyoom pyoom"; "bababang."

"Hey, shouldn't you guys be getting ready for bed?" she asked them. She knew better parents who had successfully quashed their children's firearm fantasies, but not her. At this point she was only registering a formal objection. She didn't really mind that they ignored her; they were entertained, and she had a dragon to squish.

She was on her hands and knees kneading the air out of a leg when she felt something hard against her back. "FBI, open up," Jo said. The girls were giggling.

She put her arms above her head. "Mr. Dragon, I think we're in trouble."

Whatever Jo was playing with was hard and she wasn't holding it too steady. It kept jabbing into her spine.

"Stop right there," Helen said. The gun in her hand was lustrous. Polished wood and a silver barrel, and the trigger silver too, and Helen's finger on it, squeezing. It looked big. It looked real.

"Helen, that's not a toy," she said.

Helen said, "What?"

"That's a real gun. Don't point it. Don't—Put it down. Just put it down. Carefully."

Helen held the dueling pistol up to her face and for a sickening moment looked at it, turning it side to side. "Helen!" And then she understood. She lowered the weapon to the patio and took three big steps away from it.

Jo was still behind her, poking her. "Is that Grandma's other gun, JoJo? Don't point it at me, it could hurt Mommy. Just put it down." She tried to say it like, There's sunscreen on your hands, don't rub it in your eyes. But her voice shook. She turned around, still on her knees, and there was Jo, barefoot, her hair in the remnants of her birthday braids, holding the other pistol. Margaret held out her hand. "Give that to me, Jo."

"It's mine."

She danced out of reach behind a deck chair, waving the gun over her head like a cowgirl.

"It's not yours, it's Grandma and Grandad's," Margaret said, but that wasn't the right thing to say, it wasn't like they were going to take turns, make it fair. "Jo, it's a real gun, and I don't know if it could go off and hurt someone. You're scaring me, I'm serious," she said.

"It's my birthday, and I'm a robber." She ran to the other side of the pool.

"Give it back, Jo, Mommy said so," Helen said, suddenly the responsible older sibling.

"Helen, go inside right now, fast. Tell Daddy to come out. You stay there, you stay inside."

Helen did it, she ran, shouting for her father. Margaret stood up, her feet tangling in the dragon. She kicked them free and moved slowly, slowly, toward her younger daughter.

"What's going on?" she heard her father say behind her. "What's that she's got?"

"It's your fucking pistol!"

"What pistol?"

"The anniversary dueling pistol, Dad. Tell me it's not loaded."

"Oh god. I'm . . . almost certain it's not loaded," he said.

"Almost?"

"I don't know, the things are two hundred years old. I never thought to check. Even if it's loaded, it would need powder and . . . more likely it would backfire, just—blow up."

"Christ, Dad. Jo, please, please put that down."

She took another two steps forward. "If you put it down right now, you can have a special treat. You can have more cake. But you have to put it down right now."

Jo thought about it. She scratched the side of her leg with the barrel. Margaret took three more steps. "Can we have ice cream too?" Jo was asking when Margaret grabbed her arm, the gun arm, and boxed the child's kicking body behind her. "No," Jo shouted. "I didn't say okay."

"Ezra, help me." He hurried over and pried Jo's fingers off the weapon. Jo was bellowing in outrage. Margaret's arm burned—Jo had bit her. Her father had picked up the other gun. Jo was kicking her, and she barely felt it, she just sat there, breathing.

"What the fuck, Dad. You didn't lock up the dueling pistols?"

"I thought they were, I didn't check. They're antiques."

"They're guns."

"So are they loaded or not?" Ezra asked. "Probably not. I bet they're not."

Her dad looked at the pistol in his hand and fiddled with it, turning it this way and that, just like Helen had done. "I guess I don't actually know how to open this thing up," he said. "I could google it?"

Margaret dragged Jo into the house. Now that the crisis was over, she was aware of only her fury. She was shouting, she had to, for safety, for their own good, to teach them this lesson. "Mommy, my hand," Jo said, but Margaret didn't care.

"Never, never touch something like that again. Those weren't pretend, for fun. Those were real. You could have *hurt* each other!" Helen was already crying with belated fear, and then Jo started too. The guns hadn't scared her, but this, her mother, did. "You have to listen to me, you have to start listening to me!" Margaret shouted. She wanted to cry too, and that made her even madder, though she said as she reached for the children that she wasn't mad, she was sorry, she promised she wasn't mad.

Later they would have a long conversation about real life and pretend and guns and whether they should ever watch *Home Alone* again. For now all she could think about was how thin, how thin to fucking vanishing, was the line between normalcy and horror. Despite the tassels and trim, despite the soldier doll and the gauntlet of wedding photos and the shoes lined up tidily by the door, despite the taboo against tracking a single speck of dirt into the house, danger came from all around—danger from the eaves and the doors, danger like a sudden hole in the wall. No one had been hurt. Everything was fine. But where the fuck was Elizabeth? Where was her mother now?

20

IN THE MORNING ELIZABETH SLEPT IN. IT WASN'T LIKE HER to miss any time with the grandkids. But maybe it had been too much even for her, this endless, impossible weekend.

The girls had asked to swim with Charlie one more time before they had to leave. While they ate breakfast with Ezra, Margaret went out to the patio. The dragon had finished deflating overnight; it lay there, an empty skin by the side of the pool. She rolled it up and put it in the garage before the girls could see it and ask if they could play with it again.

When Margaret got the kids into the pool, she tried to give Charlie some extra attention. Did he want to be the one to choose the game? They could play Marco Polo or dive for quarters. But clearly he just wanted to play with his cousins, for the grown-ups to back off.

A few minutes later the men followed. Ezra wore the Hawaiian-print trunks that she knew so well because she'd bought them herself four or five summers earlier, when he'd forgotten to pack a pair for the beach. He'd lost weight since the divorce; his familiar body was foreign to her

now. Her father behind him wore almost the same trunks, bought, probably, by Elizabeth for the exact same reason. And then there was Neal.
He was wearing tight black trunks and black goggles on his head and a
watch so black and waterproof it looked military-issued. What did he
think he was, a Navy Seal? Just don't look. She wished she could control
it, but she couldn't—the rage that filled her at the sight of his accessories.

Neal was telling their father something about monetary policy. Their
father was asking Ezra something about Silicon Valley. He wanted a copy
of Ezra's magazine. No matter how many times Ezra explained, Hugh
seemed not to get that it was online-only.

"It's just a website," Neal said.

Hugh, sure this was an insult, waited for Ezra to contradict it.

"Well, right—it's a magazine on a website," he said.

"But I can print it off if I want to, right?" Hugh asked.

"You can print off individual articles, but they won't look as good . . .
the interactives . . ."

This bored Hugh, so he changed the subject. "What about those fires?"
he asked Ezra. "They affecting your colleagues out West?"

"Definitely. All the smoke. It's scary."

"What people don't know is it's because of the Endangered Species
Act," Neal said.

"What?" Ezra said.

"That's right. Forty years of protecting habitat at any cost and now
they've got burning houses on their hands," Neal said.

Ezra was fidgeting, sort of patting the surface of the pool. "Oh," he finally said. "I hadn't heard that theory. I thought climate change?"

"Climate change!" said Hugh.

Neal snorted. Two against one.

"But the Endangered Species Act?" Hugh said. "Come on, Neal, that's
real conspiracy thinking." Oh no, Neal hadn't seen it coming. "It's just
ordinary sprawl. People building where they shouldn't build. They're just
putting down kindling."

"Asking for it," Neal said, recovering.

"Though I'd probably do the same, if I could find an insurer dumb enough to cover me," Hugh said.

"Well, sure," said Neal. "Beautiful out there."

Margaret went under, let her ears fill up with water. When she stood again Helen was saying, "Uncle Neal, throw me!"

She wanted to say no. She wanted to say, Helen, I think you're getting too big for that now. But she couldn't, would never. She watched as Neal lifted her up, as the water ran off her child.

THE NIGHT THE RICCI BROTHERS slept over, she was older than Helen, but not by all that much. Elizabeth was excited—Neal rarely had friends of his own by—and she reminded Margaret to be on her best behavior. She had gone to Biddy's after school but couldn't spend the night because Biddy had soccer in the morning. When she got home, she went straight up to her bedroom to prepare.

Fuck fire hazards; she made a bed against the door. She put her pillow by the hinge and folded her quilt in thirds to make a mattress. Then she lay down on top of it, wedging her body against the door.

At night they came. She heard the strike of the latch first, then felt the door knocking against her back. Then whispers:

"It's locked."

"It's not. There isn't any lock. Push it."

"It won't open."

"Let me."

The door pressed hard, and she started to slide forward, the blanket slipping on the floorboards. Silently, she twisted her body to brace her feet. But it wasn't enough. The door pushed against her like it was trying to open not just the room but her body itself. Her knees started to bend.

"It's coming," she heard one of them say.

If she turned completely perpendicular, her feet could just reach the end of the bed frame. When the pushing stopped for a second, she did it, fast—pivoted and jammed her heels against the wood, locked her legs, bore the door against her shoulders like a yoke.

She could have shouted. She could have said, Go away. But that would have meant acknowledging that she knew what was happening, which would have made it real, which would have made her complicit. It could embolden them—if she told them to stop and they didn't—if she shouted and no parent came. Better to be only an inanimate weight, a piece of furniture. Better to be the lock herself.

"She must have blocked it," Neal said.

"For real?"

"Push harder."

"I can't, my parents will hear."

"Come on. You promised."

Neal had made the video, like a commercial. Neal had sold her to them, like tickets. The Riccis had a pool and a goat; Neal had a sister. She braced herself against the door and against the prick of guilt she felt for ruining Neal's deal, for refusing to do this little thing to help her brother make friends.

so much time had passed since then, years and years. Night after night had fallen on the house with Margaret inside it, and then night after night had fallen after she'd gone. On only one of those nights had the Riccis tried to get inside. On only eight or nine or maybe twelve of those nights had Neal touched her. Only ever that summer. Only ever when she was sleeping. She would wake with the blanket at her knees and the afterburn of sensation and the half-seen shape of her brother walking out the door. Just that. She could almost have dreamed it, except that it had happened.

But then again so much had happened—so many worse things. The whole world reeked of aftermath. Elections, convictions, marches, wars, the never-ending news that kept her employed. The death of the goat.

And also: romance, children, joy. Even here, she thought, so much had changed, even within the confines of the swimming pool, the space in the yard that seemed to hold not just her family but time itself open within it.

The lightning bugs had flashed there, and there. Violent green weather had blown in and over, and on cold days the moisture in the ground had frozen so hard the dirt could have shattered like glass. She had been changed too—the sloughed-off dead cells of her past selves long gone, replaced. Inexorably she had been changed, and often for the better. Helen and Jo bobbed past in the water where there had been only stone and soil, life where there had been no life. But through it all one thing, one shameful, barely perceptible thing, remained the same, and it made her furious—furious at herself—that she bore it still, could feel it still: the line on her body that her brother had made.

FOUR

21

EVERYTHING ON THE SURFACE WAS CRISP AND DRY, AND EV-
erything just beneath it was busy with wet decay. In a far corner of the
playground Helen had lost her composition notebook in an enormous leaf
pile, and they were digging for it with their hands through leaves as light
as dollar bills to the composting goo below. Had the girls ever raked up
leaves? It occurred to her with a pang of grief that they had not. They had
never raked, nor shoveled snow, nor watered new flowers with a high-
pressure adjustable-spray nozzle. Because of her they were missing out on
the good labor of childhood, all the splendid chores of the suburbs.

They should visit Elizabeth next weekend, or the weekend after; they
were overdue anyway. But it would have to be soon, the leaves were still
falling but in no time they'd have fallen. She could ask Elizabeth to cancel the leaf-blowing crew. They could go down on a Saturday morning.
They could work together all afternoon, their hair tied back with red
bandannas . . .

"Daddy, look," Helen said, and lumped an armload of leaves into the air.

On the sidewalk side of the chain-link fence there was Ezra, with his hands in his coat pockets. "What are you doing?" he asked.

Margaret, elbow-deep, discarded her leaf-raking fantasy, which no one would ever be interested in executing. "Helen lost her notebook in here," she said.

"How did that happen?"

She stretched out a pain in her back. "Ezra, I really do not know how it happened."

"Are you sure you guys should be reaching in there? There could be bugs. Or needles."

"Needles!" Jo snatched out her hands. "I don't want to get a shot."

Margaret glared. "Look, if there are dirty needles in the playground leaf pile, then I give up. Could you just help?"

Weekends they divided in half, and this was where they handed the children back and forth—in the playground, between the benches and the basketball court. The incoming parent was kissed, distractedly; the outgoing parent was kissed, distractedly; the children played.

Ezra came in through the far gate. Instead of digging with his hands, he kicked the leaves around with his feet, taking big swinging strides, like someone walking through fresh powder. What did he hope to achieve with this method? But Margaret, rationing her criticisms, said nothing.

"I actually need to talk to you," Ezra said.

"What's up?"

It was hard to hear him over the crinkling din. "What?" she said again.

"Just stop with the leaves for a minute. I said I want the girls to meet Anaya."

"Oh."

Duncan, she thought immediately. If the girls met Anaya, they could meet Duncan. They could rake leaves at Duncan's house. His kids did that, and washed his truck, and laid the bricks in his garden path.

But what if they didn't like him? What if he didn't like them? And anyway, this was about Ezra and Anaya. Would Anaya be fun? Would she be too fun? Margaret felt lightheaded from all that bending over, from some vapor wafting up from the leaves.

"Mommy, Daddy, you're not even helping," Helen said accurately.

"We're talking, Hel. Give us a sec."

"What are you talking about?"

"Nothing, go away, please."

"I don't want to go away."

"Isn't that Steffie from class?" She ran off.

Ezra kicked some more leaves around. He was like a little boy, doing that. "I thought—we thought—well, it was Anaya's idea—that you and her should meet first. To make sure you felt comfortable. So there's no atmosphere of anxiety. So there's a process."

Ezra did love a process, and Anaya, she gathered, did too. *Atmosphere of anxiety.* Where did he get these phrases? "Oof," she said. "Do I have to?" Then: "I'm kidding. Okay, sure, yes. It's a good plan."

"Great. This will be good. I really think it's going to be good. Thank you. Thanks. So. What notebook are we looking for, anyway?"

"The black one. The composition one."

"But that's at my place."

"It is?"

"Yeah. I just saw it on the kitchen table."

Helen was leading Steffie and Jo back to the leaf pile, which was apparently more exciting than swings or the monkey bars.

"Helen, you left your notebook at my place."

"Oh, right." She threw more leaves at Jo.

Margaret tried to brush the autumn shrapnel off her sweater. "But why did you think it was in the leaf pile, then?"

She thought about it. "I dunno."

They'd been digging for at least twenty minutes. It didn't seem possible that all that effort was for nothing. "Did you lose something else? Could there be something else in here?"

Helen looked around, wondering. "Maybe . . . but if it was here I think we would have found it by now."

The next Saturday morning she left to meet Anaya at a coffee shop near Prospect Park. She'd dressed down for it—sweatshirt, leggings, braid. It occurred to her, seeing her distorted reflection in the parked cars, that her outfit was so calculatedly nonaggressive it might in fact seem aggressive. Margaret had never seen a picture of Anaya but assumed for some reason that she would be a little less hot than Margaret herself. Bouncy, cute, but slightly dumpy, maybe. This was the word in her head—*dumpy*— when she saw a woman at a table with one of Ezra's tote bags at her feet.

Anaya gave Margaret a hug while Margaret tried not to think about her body—taller, younger, her perky boobs, which were solely a woman's boobs and not a mother's, mushed against Margaret's chest. She had a pixie cut. She was definitely not a little less hot than Margaret herself.

They got their coffees and walked toward the park while Anaya told her—charmingly, relentlessly—everything. She taught kindergarten and volunteered in a community garden and tried to make it to the theater at least once a month because why else live in New York City? The path went up and down through the green and brown undulating park, and Anaya's voice did the same, skimming along the contours of her life. Her mother fundraised for the arts and her father was an econ professor at Columbia and she had been raised by a Peruvian nanny who Monday through Friday was allowed to speak to Anaya only in Spanish, which she'd never become quite fluent in and that, she told Margaret, was why she'd always struggled with intimacy at home.

"Ezra understands me so well," she said, "because he's suffered so much trauma too." By *trauma* she meant Margaret.

And yet Margaret didn't dislike her. Anaya laughed at herself as she said that she truly did believe in the healing power of crystals. She had decided she could never have children of her own because she could not bear to bring a baby into a world doomed by climate change, she said, with good humor. Margaret felt an updraft of relief. Here was hope. Here was vindication. Here was the woman Ezra loved. She was not Margaret. She was not remotely Margaret.

THEY WALKED through the park's open lawn. The ground was patchy with use, except for one jewel-green fenced-off pasture the size of a swimming pool, where new grass was being allowed to grow. Her eyes rested there as if it was a field of flowers or farm animals, like whatever sheltered inside the wire was special, fragile, though it was only grass, grass like all the rest. Soon the parks department would move the fence line, seed a different plot, let the people trample this one. But not yet. The air was so clean and blue, just breathing it in felt like some kind of cure, like it could kill germs and cut through grease. Ezra was in love with someone else. Things could be simpler now.

Anaya had a plan. For the first meeting they should all be together. Anaya felt that if Margaret was there too, it would signal to the girls that they didn't need to feel any guilt or shame about developing a relationship with her. Any question the girls had they would answer in honest but age-appropriate ways. She wouldn't sleep over when they were there. That was something they could discuss down the line. Boundaries were really important, she said, especially for children.

"I'm really grateful you've put so much thought into this," Margaret said.

Anaya hugged her again—oh god, her boobs, they jiggled when she laughed. "Do you ever listen to that relationship podcast—the therapist's?" she asked. "She did a whole episode on it."

But it was hard, by the time they'd looped past the dog beach, to think of much more to talk about. What Margaret really wanted to ask was, What is it like being with Ezra now? Does he still get annoyed when . . . Do you ever feel . . . Is the sex . . .

But Margaret could respect boundaries too. She was thinking of ways to wind it up when both of their phones pinged simultaneously—Ezra. A group text. (The first group text! she could see Anaya thinking.)

Jo had been hurt.

All the minor thoughts made way. She felt the park go flat, flat as a prairie or a parking lot, the rolling scenery bulldozed by urgency. She walked a straight line across it. "Yes, go to urgent care. The pediatric one in Brooklyn Heights," she told Ezra. "I'll be there in twenty."

"Could I come too? Just in case you need an extra pair of hands?"

There was no need for a third adult, but why not let her come? This was what it meant to take care of a child, after all. Things broke; the fever spiked. Pink eye, stomach bugs, strep throat, ear infection, hand-foot-mouth—the basic diseases of childhood, of the fragile, beloved body. If only the car would go faster, she would really rather have run there. She wasn't bothering to speak to Anaya now; she didn't mean to be rude, but she was conserving her strength, she was getting ready to jump out the door and up the steps and there they were, her children in the waiting room, and Ezra, poised between panic and relief at the sight of both women coming through the door.

22

THE URGENT CARE HAD AN APP THAT TOLD YOU HOW MANY people were in line ahead of you, so you never had to bother the person at the front desk. She showed it to Jo. "One more, and then us."

"I'm tired, Mommy."

"I know, I'm sorry."

"It's not fair Helen gets to play with Daddy's girlfriend and I don't."

"You will, I promise. Right after this. And you can choose a treat. Bubble gum, whatever."

She'd suggested that Anaya and Ezra take Helen home, after a brief whispered conversation about what was wrong with Jo. Something had happened to her arm. She couldn't move it, but it couldn't be broken— Ezra said she hadn't fallen down or anything. It was really weird, he told her, so weird it was freaking him out: "What is it when someone's arm suddenly hurts? A stroke?"

"You mean a heart attack?" Margaret said.

"That would be the left arm. Is it her left arm?" Anaya asked.

She promised to call as soon as they'd seen the doctor. Margaret had no clue what was wrong with Jo, but she was fairly certain it wasn't a heart attack.

THE ARM DIDN'T SEEM to hurt if Jo didn't move it, but it didn't not hurt either. She cradled it in her lap like a borrowed doll, looking pale and somehow hollow-cheeked despite all her baby fat. Margaret squeezed her good hand.

"Tell me how it happened again?" she said.

"I was spinning then it hurt," Jo said, staring at the cartoons on the TV.

Margaret watched too. The sound was off. There was a mermaid that was also a cat. And a cat that was also a pillow? There was a water stain on the ceiling above them, with cracks in it. Wouldn't there be mold? Wasn't this itself a health hazard?

They'd been waiting for about half an hour. Margaret was worried, but now that she could see Jo, she wasn't frightened anymore, and all that unspent adrenaline was leaking out of her. Across from her a dad held a glassy-eyed toddler in his lap. A fever, for sure. The flu was going around. As she diagnosed the sick child, she made eye contact with the father. Work boots, stubble, self-consciously nostalgic Queensboro Bridge T-shirt. She shifted against Jo to put an arch in her lower back. She wished she wasn't wearing this sweatshirt. He was looking at her legs. The toddler coughed. She wondered where the mother was.

She got distracted sometimes by these fantasies that were barely even fantasies. She felt no desire to imagine—let alone begin—a conversation, an exchange of text messages, a meeting, an affair. She just wanted him to look at her legs, her eyes, her legs. She needed to make someone focus on her, a man but not always a man.

Near the end of the marriage it had gotten very bad, that need. She would be in the checkout line, at a bus stop, lifting a toddler into a swing, doing any everyday chore—but it would be like she was doing it onstage, her movements extravagant for a distant audience. The action itself meant nothing, had no inherent value; she thought only of how she looked doing it. It was disgusting how desperate she'd been for attention. She had been lonely, was the problem, even with her babies she'd been lonely.

Marriage had isolated her even, somehow, from herself. She wondered if Ezra had changed for Anaya, or if the way Ezra was with Margaret was unique to Margaret—Margaret's fault. For example: She had never masturbated. Not in twelve years. The idea of her having a vibrator had made Ezra uncomfortable. She'd mentioned it once or twice—maybe they could try it . . . But what did she need it for? Sex was something they did *together*. That was the whole point.

It made her angry to think about it now, angry to think about how Anaya probably masturbated guilt-free whenever someone lit a scented candle anywhere in Brooklyn, and how because she wasn't the mother of his children, because he hadn't known her half his life, because he was different now, Ezra probably thought it was so hot.

Eventually she had ordered a vibrator after all. She'd mustered all her courage and marched to Ezra and told him she wanted to experiment and not feel ashamed, and he had said, "Ashamed? Of course I would never want you to feel ashamed of anything."

But then one night, Jo had been fussy and difficult to put to bed, and Ezra had at last taken over to give her a break, and when he came into their room she had her legs spread. It had been summer, and the window was open, the night air getting its fingers in at the edges of things. He had turned his face back into the hallway while she scuttled under the blanket.

She hadn't been sure before what exactly his issue was. Did it hurt his feelings, the idea of her touching herself? Was he worried that if she came too easily, she'd be spoiled? That she wouldn't want or need him anymore? These were simple fears, sort of sweet fears—they could have talked about them. But seeing his face in the doorway she understood. She had frightened and repelled him.

"You couldn't even wait for me?" he said.

They had fought about it later, but that night she had apologized. She had told him he was right, that she was selfish.

She caught the dad looking again. Not that it mattered, not that she needed it. She didn't feel that way anymore, lonely. Really, she didn't. Meeting Anaya brought it back a little, maybe—her fresh body, the minor sense she gave Margaret of fading, diminishing.

She was telling herself the story of the vibrator now, she realized, so she wouldn't be tempted to feel jealousy or regret. She reminded herself: hope, relief, vindication, all that she'd felt in the park's clear air, by the new-seeded grass.

A nurse was calling the next patient. Margaret and the dad exchanged commiserating half smiles.

"Mommy," Jo said. "Mom." She tugged with her good hand on the end of Margaret's braid.

"What?"

"Isn't she calling me?"

Oh. She'd been listening for her own name, for Margaret, but of course it wasn't her name on the list. The nurse walked over, stopped right in front of them. "Is this Josephine?" she asked, annoyed, because it obviously was, there were only two patients in the room and the other was a boy.

"Sorry, so sorry, I wasn't paying attention." Margaret gathered her bag and her injured child. The dad averted his eyes.

INSIDE THE EXAM ROOM, the doctor looked at Jo and put her hands on either side of Jo's elbow. Jo whimpered and turned her face into Margaret's side. Margaret explained that she hadn't been there when it happened, whatever it was—she wanted to imply that it wasn't her fault, though they all knew it was always the mother's fault. She made shushing sounds and stroked Jo's hair.

"Now, what kind of lollipop do you like best?" the doctor asked. "Strawberry? Nursemaid's elbow," she told Margaret.

"What?"

"The elbow popped out."

"But—how?"

"You mostly see it in younger children, but it's not unusual at her age either. Even a tug can do it, if you're swinging a child or hurrying them along."

"How do you fix it?"

"Oh, it's done."

"What?" she said again.

"That's all it takes to pop it back in. A little twist."

"You mean you did it already?"

"That's right. Now, let's see if you can give me a high-five with that hand."

Margaret was dumbfounded. It was like a magic trick—the doctor had barely touched her. Jo couldn't believe it either. She was afraid to move her arm. How could it get better so fast? How could the past just be over?

But then the doctor offered a roll of stickers, held them dangling in the air. Jo reached for them slowly, untrusting, knowing any moment the pain would kick in. But it didn't, and still it didn't, though she lifted her arm up higher and higher. She grasped the stickers. "It doesn't hurt," she said, and Margaret too felt lifted up and up. It didn't hurt! They walked out into the painless world.

23

A FEW MONTHS BEFORE THE END OF THE MARRIAGE, MARGA-
ret and Ezra were having dinner with their oldest college friends, Emma
and Ben, and talking about an essay on consent that had gone viral.
Emma had made chicken and kale salad. Margaret said, "Don't you feel
like—and I would never say this in public, but don't you feel like it's a bit
exaggerated?"

Ezra visibly cringed. "I don't think you can say that."

"I don't mean her story, but the way everyone is talking about it. The
whole Twitter narrative."

"Say more," Emma said.

"I guess I assume people are coming to it with their own experiences,"
Ezra said.

"But to call it rape—"

"Hi, honey."

Jo had wandered in. "Can I have another cookie?"

Ezra and Margaret said "No" and "Just one" simultaneously.

Jo got the cookie. "Can you watch the movie with us, Mommy?"

"Not right now, I'm talking with my friends." Jo climbed into her lap and stuck a finger in her ear. "Argh, Jo-baby, get out of here," she said.

"Can I have one more?"

They waited until Jo had left the room and then Emma asked, "Does she actually call it rape herself? In the essay?"

"No. That's what I mean about the Twitter narrative. What bothers me is the—the flattening effect. If that's rape, if every unwanted"—a spastic shiver went through her—"touch is rape, then what language do we use when rape is violent, or penetrative, or statutory? I don't want to say *actual rape*—"

"No, you're definitely not allowed to say *actual rape*," Ben said. He was the only one who hadn't read the piece, and he was scrolling through it now on his phone.

"I basically think you just have to give people the latitude to use whatever words they want," Ezra said.

"Sure, but it's not *her* word, it's not what *she* said."

"But it's not just about her. The people commenting all have their own traumas, their own triggers. I just think those of us who have never experienced any kind of"—Ezra paused to collect the correct phrase—"of assault on our personhood that a nonconsensual sexual experience would entail, well, we probably shouldn't even weigh in."

The fork went still in her hand. "People like us who have never experienced . . . ?"

Long ago, when they had been nineteen, and in college, and only friends, they had gone on a long walk around campus. It was October, early evening, and the yellow leaves looked even yellower in the lamplight as Ezra's gentle questions drew her life out of her, drew out everything that had hurt and frightened her. She told him—oh, everything.

About Neal—the first night and the ones that came after. About how Elizabeth could not be told—because of the pills, because she wouldn't rewind the camera. And he had pressed her face against his chest and said, "I'm so sorry, I'm so sorry that happened to you. I'm so sorry and I'm so—" She remembered exactly how his voice had stopped there, scrabbling for purchase on the violent upsurge of his feelings. "I'm so angry."

She had cried enough to soak through his T-shirt. When she finally stepped back and saw the wet circle on his chest, she'd laughed, embarrassed, and he'd laughed too. And so she'd loved and married him.

Now she said, "I told you about Neal."

"What about Neal?"

"What Neal did when we were kids. That summer. I told you about that."

Ezra looked at their friends, not at her. Ben had put away his phone. What was she doing?

"You forgot?"

"No, no, of course not." She could see him working backward, dredging that conversation up through the years—a walk they'd taken, something awkward and upsetting. "I mean, I knew something happened. We talked about it, but not since when, like, college? Like, the beginning of college?"

"You forgot."

"No, no, I didn't forget. I just wasn't thinking about it right now. Anyway I don't think you want to talk about it in front of . . ." He gestured at their friends.

This whole time she'd never mentioned it again because she thought she didn't need to—that it was too fundamental to bear repeating, that it would be like reminding him that her name was Margaret, that she was his wife.

"Are you okay?" Emma asked.

"Do you want us to give you some space?" Ben asked.

"Yeah, maybe, this is kind of personal," Ezra said.

"No," she said. "Sit down. Come on. It's just a thing that happened. Ezra's right: we don't have to talk about it."

"What kind of thing, Margo?" Emma asked. "What did Neal do?"

"Who's Neal?" asked Ben.

"It's totally different from the essay, though, right?" Ezra said, sounding hopeful. "It was more, like, a kid thing. Like playing doctor."

"Playing doctor. No . . . it wasn't like that."

"Well, no, of course not exactly—"

"For one, he was thirteen, not five. And he would do it when I was unconscious."

For a long time she had seen that as a mitigating circumstance. If he was going to touch her, at least he did it in this quiet way. How much damage could it do, really, if she couldn't resist, if sometimes she slept right through it? Unconfrontational, that was what it was.

She saw it differently now.

"Right," Ezra said, "yeah, that's bad."

"So if you're interested in questions of consent, I think actually there is some relevancy."

"Right, I hear you." He started stacking the silverware onto a plate. She was getting shrill; their friends might think she was being dramatic. "I guess I just think we all need to be careful not to impose our opinions if we don't have the exact same lived experience," he said.

Maybe that was all it was—her opinion. Who was she to say for sure what happened? Who was she to say it mattered? Ezra had believed it mattered once. What had changed? Only that she was his wife now, and so the events of her life were personal, domestic, shrunk to the scale of everything he knew about her. It was complicated, he was thinking, because he knew Neal, he knew Elizabeth, and therefore what happened did not exactly happen. It was just their life; it wasn't history or news. What he would condemn on Twitter—the story of a stranger, which came with the imprimatur of public outrage—he would shush in their friends' kitchen. She didn't want his allyship anyway. She wanted his sorrow and his anger. She wanted him to bloody every last knuckle and salt the earth, or at least to feel the urge to. She wanted to hear his voice break again in that one moment that even now was slipping away from her.

She had thought, all this time, that he was avoiding the subject out of love and care for her, out of some exquisite sensitivity. Related topics would come up and she would sense that he was watching her and suppressing the desire to punch the wall. She was moved by the idea that talking about it would cause him great suffering. And she had admired how he was able to relate to her family, not as if he had forgiven them, because how could he, but as if he understood that the past was full of shame and regret and all anyone could do now was be careful and kind. She had thought that he knew this line went through her and she was living on the other side of it, and had loved her more because of it.

But no. The whole thing had slipped his mind.

"If you ever want to talk . . ." Emma had said.

But how could she talk to anyone else about it if she couldn't talk to her own husband?

They thanked them for dinner. They gathered their children and went home. She'd thought a husband would keep her safe. But he hadn't agreed to that; he didn't even know that was what she was asking for. If she had been safe all these years, it was only because she'd been lucky or because she herself had made it so.

24

JO BENT TO PICK UP A BIG ONE AND THE OTHERS TUMBLED OUT
of her arms. "I can't carry all these," she said.

"Do you have to be such a baby?" Helen said.

Jo was tugging and tugging, but it wouldn't come. Helen laughed at
her. "That's a root."

"It's not!"

"Okay, keep pulling then."

Jo looked like she intended to, like she would dig up the whole tree if
she had to. It was stuck and straining underground, peeling up sheets of
dead leaves. Jo used to play this game where she would come up to Margaret with a spoon and order, "Eat this," and Margaret would open her
mouth, and then Jo would say, "I tricked you. It's worms!" She always did
it, but Margaret never stopped opening her mouth. Jo really was not going
to give up on that root, was she?

"I think we've got plenty now anyway," Margaret said. "Want to head
back? See what the guys are doing?"

"Okay," Helen said. She was holding a tidy stack of branches like she gathered firewood all the time, like she was a regular colonial girl. Jo hugged a pile of sticks against her chest, and Margaret could tell they were poking her in a thousand different ways.

They walked out from under the trees and through the salt grass. They passed an old rusty boat rotting out on its side. Jo tried to peek in, but "No no let's not"—it was probably bow-to-stern full of rats. In the mud by the bay they were building a bonfire. It was Saturday, and November, and everything was muddy and brown except for the bay, which was a blue-gray that made Margaret think of stones, smooth, cool stones she could lay over each eye. Just looking at it was like applying a face mask, like the vision alone might delay the onset of fine lines and wrinkles. She wanted to go dip her face in the water.

Duncan's sons, Louie and Willis, were crouching down. Despite the chill, they wore basketball shorts, their only accommodation to the weather white athletic socks tugged as high as they could go up their skinny legs. There was a glow right where they were putting their hands. It got brighter and brighter, and they kept almost touching it, which made Margaret nervous, though they were thirteen and fifteen and did this all the time, and she wasn't their mother. She knew they were placing twists of newspaper in the flame, but it looked like they were hand-feeding an out-of-sight animal, sliding treats right past its teeth. Suddenly the fire roared up, fully grown, and even the boys rocked back on their heels.

Duncan was getting out the hot dogs. The kids had met Anaya, so the kids could meet Duncan. It shouldn't have been that simple, but in the end it basically was.

"These are perfect," Duncan said, inspecting the girls' piles of sticks. "But I think we need even more. And some bigger ones too."

Louie stood up. "I'll go."

"I'll help," Helen said.

"Me too," Jo said.

Helen scowled.

"JoJo," Margaret said, "could you stay with me? We can start the hot dogs."

"No."

"I'll give you a marshmallow."

"Okay."

It was important to give Helen some space and independence. But as soon as she started walking away, Margaret regretted it. Louie was the younger brother, but he had already had his first big growth spurt. He looked huge beside Helen. From the back he could have been a man—a skinny man. The brighter the fire got, the darker the sky looked, and it was darkening anyway. In a moment the kids were lost in the gloom.

Duncan, down by the fire, put a hand around her shin and raised his eyebrows at her. The look meant *hey* and *you okay?* and something sexier too. She could see from up here that his hair was ever so slightly thinning, and she loved him more because of it, because he wasn't perfect and therefore not entirely unlike herself. The idea of him losing anything—a strand of hair—made her want to crawl across the ground and look for it.

Willis got a beer out of the cooler. Was fifteen old enough for that? He took a sip, which shocked her less than the way he did it, grabbing the bottle so casually without asking anyone's permission, lifting it up by the neck between two fingers and popping the top off with the edge of a lighter. There was something about using a tool meant for one thing to do something else. It looked cool and competent and ruthlessly masculine. Once she had hoped to have sons instead of daughters. She had thought it would be easier. She wondered now if she would have envied them this, their unapologetic physical authority.

"Excuse me," Duncan said.

Willis grinned. "Just testing it for you," he said, and handed over the bottle.

THE GRIN REMINDED her of Danny as a teenager. Once, only once, had anything remotely romantic happened between them. It was the summer before he left for college, and she'd taken a stack of plates into his parents' kitchen. He'd been sitting at the table. "Come over here," he said, and pulled her onto his lap. She sat, stiff with surprise until she realized what was happening and that it might never happen again, and then she leaned back against him, fit every possible inch of her body snug against his chest and thighs.

"I'm gonna miss you, Margo," he said into the hair at the back of her neck. And then too soon, before she could even say "Same," he stood them up and it was over.

She'd seen him a few Thanksgivings ago. He'd buzzed his hair—he was going bald, he told her, and rubbed a hand over his head, and winked. He was still beautiful. But it was the impersonal beauty of a rediscovered artifact, a bronze vessel that would be only a dented pot except for the sheen of centuries past on it. She had thought of him laughing at the mole, laughing at death, tasting like strawberry daiquiri. She had thought of her own safe lust. He was no one really to her now except for what he symbolized: the good brother, the good man. She had felt a keen wonder at his presence. She could not have hugged him more gently.

When Margaret pulled away from Danny's arms, he said, "You should come visit me sometime."

But Biddy had been watching and gave them both a long, stern look. "Margaret," she said, "don't you fucking dare."

NOW WILLIS LOOKED UP from his phone and asked Duncan: "You mind if I meet up with friends later?"

"Does Louie have plans too?"

"How should I know?" A look went between them. "I don't think so. I think he's happy to just hang with you guys," Willis said.

Willis was a Danny, he had that confidence, but Louie was different. They worried about Louie. He was so sweet and aimless she wondered if his sweetness and aimlessness were a strategy, though to what purpose she couldn't guess.

"Hanging with the girls will be good for him," Duncan had told her when they'd introduced everyone (carefully, casually, hopefully). "It's good for him to be seen as the big kid—the cool kid."

She agreed, she could see it already. Helen and Jo adored him. But it made her uncomfortable, the idea that her daughters were giving Louie something valuable by looking up at him that way, something he needed like milk or vitamins in order to grow into a tall and healthy man. It made her uncomfortable, Helen off alone with him in the dark. Why weren't they back yet? Oh, there they came.

They dumped what they'd collected inside the glowing radius. Louie squatted and placed the biggest branch hatchwise through the flame. She saw Duncan's hand open and close. The boy wasn't doing it right, she could feel him thinking. The hand annoyed her, but the restraint she appreciated.

Louie was gesturing, telling some kind of story, and Helen was listening, herself a kind of kindling.

"What do you think they're talking about?" she asked Duncan quietly.

"I'll read their lips and tell you," he said, smiling up at her again, forgetting about the architecture of the campfire. "He's telling the story of this bay. Eons ago it was all glacial ice. Legend has it—"

She snorted.

"Excuse me," he said, "but legend has it that the six golden eggs of a giant duck"—she sat down, and Jo clambered into her lap—"were stolen by a great evil serpent. The duck searched all the land through the fields and forests for its eggs. Finally it saw the glacier, these great silver orbs of ice—"

"You're making this up," Jo said.

"I would never," he said. "Listen. The giant duck sat down on the ice. Whether out of confusion or heartbreak, the story does not say. But it sat right down and days passed, and nights, and gradually the great heat and weight of the duck melted the ice, melted the glacier away, until all that was left was a pool of deep, clear water."

"Why's this sad?" Jo asked.

"It's not over, don't interrupt. The duck *was* sad, super sad. And it started crying, which for a duck is very pitiful to see, and the salt of its tears mixed with the ice water. And that is why this bay is brackish."

"Seriously?" Margaret said, laughing. "That's the end?"

"Of course not. Now, while the duck was crying, across the surface of that new water suddenly came paddling . . . who do you think?"

"The babies!" Jo said.

"Her six golden ducklings. And that is why today . . ."

"Here we go," Margaret said.

"And that is why today we call this body of water . . ."

"Cold Butt Bay?"

He threw a marshmallow at her. "No, don't be ridiculous. They call it—"

"Can I have one too?" Jo asked.

"Hot dog first. So your point is it's not global warming that's melting the glaciers. It's ducks."

"Doesn't anyone want to hear the punch line?"

Duncan could not be more different from Ezra. She trusted Ezra, felt an exasperated fondness for him. But he had only gotten more impenetrably self-serious in the last couple of years—at least when in her presence. She blamed, in part, Anaya. But it wasn't Anaya's fault. Both Margaret and Ezra had only become more of who they already were.

"What happened to the serpent?" Jo asked.

"What?" Duncan asked.

"The evil serpent that stole the eggs."

But he didn't answer. Louie was distracted, texting, and Duncan seized his chance. He leaned forward and carefully, subtly, rearranged all the branches on the fire.

THEY HAD SPENT the night before together. They didn't do that often. They were too busy in their own separate lives. And the truth was, Margaret wasn't sure she liked it. Ezra had always passed out immediately, like a child, and had to be nagged awake, like a teenager. She had liked his calm, warm inanimacy. She had liked that he had never witnessed her sleep. But Duncan had insomnia. Duncan would be awake when she was not. That meant she mostly lay in bed pretending to sleep until finally sometime after midnight the performance turned real and she passed out. She wasn't sure, yet, if she could get used to that.

But the mornings were a pleasure. That morning, before all the kids had descended, he'd been in her mouth when he took a step backward, and then another. She followed. She was crawling on her knees toward him before she looked up and saw him grin and realized that that was what he had wanted, for her to crawl.

She liked to do what he wanted before realizing she was doing it. She could act without thinking, and so without shame. She liked to feel he had a plan for the small things because for the big things—the two of them, the four children, the house in the Rockaways, the small white apartment, what it did or could mean—no plan was forthcoming.

Being there together with the children didn't quite feel real, despite the water and the fire, despite the heat, which for sure was coming off it. It felt unreal, in part, she realized, because she could not imagine Elizabeth there. She could not imagine her mother walking past the rotting boat to the water's edge. She couldn't picture her meeting Duncan.

But that meant, maybe, only that she was growing up, only that she was freer than she'd been before.

"Look," Jo said.

Ducks overhead—real ducks incoming just ahead of the dark.

"You can really see the speculum when they turn like that," Duncan said.

"The what?"

"The blue feathers on the backs of the wings. It's hard to see when they're on the water, you have to see the wings spread open when they're flying. It's a flock thing—the color helps them recognize one another, know who to stick with in the air."

The kids looked up. The ducks came in flapping to the bay, wing to jostling wing, twenty or even thirty of them, lower and lower, until they settled into a long skid on the surface of the water. She rubbed her cheek against the top of Jo's head, leaned against Duncan's shoulder. The birds slowed, stopped, tucked the blue away, folded up their wings.

25

A FEW DAYS LATER SHE MET HER PARENTS FOR LUNCH. ELIZA-
beth and her father rarely came into the city now that he was retired—
he, who had commuted every weekday in his suit and tie and shoes as
shiny as black sedans. He said he was over it, over the hassle, the crowds,
the crime, and the trash. But he didn't seem over it. He returned to the
topic of the changing city as much as some of her friends talked about the
exes who had betrayed them—obsessively, tediously. But he'd made an
exception that day. He didn't say why, just that they felt like coming in,
and could Margaret squeeze in a meal?

She couldn't remember the last time they'd done something just the
three of them. She got there first and waited. It was one of her dad's old
restaurants in Midtown, full of businessmen in red booths peeking around
silver ice buckets. A booth always made her feel like a little girl, her legs
dangling, her feet kicking, the backs of her thighs sticking to the red
leather. Everywhere, red leather shined at her.

In the year of The Affair, her father had driven a sports car just that color. For some time after, Elizabeth had been obsessed with red cars—anything red and shiny, anything that moved and clipped the eye. One day in winter when Margaret was eleven or twelve, a red car had passed them on the highway. The inside of the minivan went dead flat, as if someone had air-locked them in. She knew what Elizabeth was thinking—though had it ever been explained to her? What would anyone have said? For years now your mother will be fixated on red cars because she imagines every red car she sees has your father in it, with his mistress beside him, even if he is at that very moment driving another car, the one carrying you and your brother and herself beside him. She will see the red car pull away and she will think she's the one being left behind, though the mistress has been dumped, though the red car has been sold, though the husband is right there.

"Don't look at it," her dad said.

Margaret pressed her cheek against the window, combed her hair with her fingers so it hung across her face and made a private room. Her hip pressed the door handle. The seat belt strap was a blade against the jaw.

"Did she touch you while you drove? Did she put her mouth on you?"

"Enough." Sometimes her father tried to stop Elizabeth, shame her. But it never worked. "You can't punish me forever," he often said, incorrectly.

Sometimes he tried the children—"Do you want them to hear these things from their mother?"—but she didn't care, that was something she truly didn't care about. "You're the one who did *those things*; why shouldn't I talk about them?" Or: "Punish you? You think you're the one being punished?"

The Affair, or rather Elizabeth's furious grief over it, was the family's monumental event. No pain could rival it, no pain would dare. The first weeks were the worst, of course, when Elizabeth lived on rage under the robin's-egg bedspread and the immaculate room began to stink like bad breath, a smell that Margaret associated not with the mouth itself but with the words that came out of it, with her mother saying, that whore, that cunt, that woman. But years after the appearance of normal life recommenced, something would happen, anything—a word, a look, a car—and *bam* there was the past again, trailing its bloody hem across the floor.

Margaret willed the red car gone, but it wouldn't go. They slowed down; it slowed down too. They sped up to pass; the red car blocked the lane. Then suddenly the highway exploded into the car's dead air. She thought the word *hole*. She thought *fuselage*, thought *under fire*, thought, insufficiently: *wind*.

But what was happening?

In the front seat, Elizabeth had opened the door, was bracing it with her leg, pushing hard against the juddering highway velocity. Her body was half out of the car. Neal yelled and lunged, throwing his arms around the seat in front of him and his mother on the other side of it. The door swung in; Elizabeth kicked it open again. The wind was in Margaret's hair, forcing her eyes shut. The highway was right there, a black grind abrading the interior.

Hugh braked and swerved, and then they were on the shoulder, parked. The red car was long gone. The doors were shut.

What happened after? She couldn't remember. Maybe her father had yelled, but she doubted it. Maybe Elizabeth had wept or looked satisfied. Would she really have done it—jumped? Plunged out into the highway as if into a pool? It seemed plausible then that she might do anything.

The next morning they had to go to school, which meant they had to get back into the minivan. It sat there in the driveway, as shiny as a commercial on top, scummed with road salt and snow grime below. The air inside was so much colder than the air outside. "Hurry up," Elizabeth said to her and Neal, as she tossed her pocketbook on the seat and slotted her thermos of tea into the cup holder. Margaret didn't understand how she could act like nothing had happened. But as Elizabeth turned the key, Margaret saw for a moment the flash of her eyes in the rearview mirror—bright, wet, frightened-looking eyes. "Seat belts, everyone," she said.

. . .

MARGARET TEXTED HER PARENTS: "eta?" After all this time, did Elizabeth see red and still think: sex; rage; death? Would the booths look like sports cars to her? Or had Elizabeth, without Margaret even noticing, one day moved on, moved past it all? Maybe it was only Margaret who still lived with these associations, with the metaphors that her parents had made.

At last her dad walked in, white hair and a white polo glowing under the blue blazer. He was talking on the phone, looking off into the middle distance, so he didn't see her until he was right at the table.

"Hi, Dad," she said, and he spoke into the phone, "Yes, yes, I'm fine, Margaret's already here, see you in a few." She stood up to hug him.

"Where's Mom?"

"Oh, late as always . . ."

"Shopping."

"Sure—yes, probably." He gestured for the wine list.

He'd always been a big people watcher, especially interested in the minor grotesqueries—the obese or the boob-jobbed, the over- or under-dressed, the improbably coupled, the conspicuously lonely. A tall woman alone in a severe black suit—check out the battle-ax, he'd say. An old man with a young woman—escort. And in fact there was a man his age at the table next to them, wearing basically the same blazer, and a woman her age across from him in a wrap dress just like her own. Father-daughter, she tried to think, but—being her father's daughter—thought otherwise.

Today he didn't point out the battle-ax, didn't spare a glance even for the young woman's dress.

"Is everything okay?" she asked. "*Dad?*" Loudly, in case the other table suspected what she suspected.

"Actually, something alarming just happened. To me. I was assaulted in the subway."

"Assaulted! Christ, Dad, what happened?" He was a big man, tall, broad-chested. He was her *father*. She looked him over, but he seemed unharmed, his polo shirt lay as clean and unwrinkled as a laundered napkin across the swell of his belly. She'd been busy thinking about the violence her parents did to each other. But here was a wholly new danger, from a wholly unexpected direction.

"Well, I don't know if that's the right word for it. Accosted, I guess. I was in a crowd walking through the tunnel and this man got right in my path and he . . . he chest-bumped me. On purpose. He saw me coming, and he got right in my way so I couldn't get around him. He rammed right into me like a linebacker. And—here's the thing—he wasn't homeless or on drugs. Not that I could tell. He was Black but"—she cringed at that *but*—"professional-looking, you know? He was quite, I guess, quite handsome, really. I don't know why it should matter so much, him being handsome. But it does. He had a sweater on—cashmere. I felt it."

"What did you do?"

"I guess I sort of shouted something, but no one else really noticed. I almost fell, and I reached out and kind of grabbed hold of him, of his sweater. That's why I remember about the cashmere. Actually, I have one just like it, it's a Brunello, a sort of butterscotch color. It slipped out of my fingers and he kept walking. And I just carried on, came here."

He was shaken. Nothing like this had ever happened to him, at least not since he was a boy, a child. This was exactly what he'd been afraid of. This was why he didn't come to the city. She wanted to say, Don't blow this out of proportion. Don't make it a whole worldview. She wanted to say, You're safe now.

"Your mother's in a panic, of course. She never wants me riding a train again."

"She does know I ride the train every day, right?" But this wasn't about her. The bread basket came with an ice-cold dish of butter. Elizabeth entered the room.

She was dressed in a coat of silvery-yellow that matched the shade of her hair lately, and its hem dipped and swung about her. She gave the impression of giving little gracious nods to the diners she wove between, as if thanking them personally for coming. Margaret unfolded her menu flat on the table like a map, a map that would get her through the next hour and then out the door.

"Have you talked to your mother much recently?" he asked before she reached the table.

"The normal amount. Why?"

Elizabeth went to Margaret's father first. She grabbed him by his big white head and smashed it against the buttons of her coat. Then she pulled away, looked him up and down, and, taking a fainting sort of seat, began to berate him.

"What were you thinking? What subway station were you in? For god's sake, Hugh, you should have known better. And parading around with a blazer on in the city these days, you may as well be wearing one of those— what are they called, that the gas station people wear?"

"Sandwich boards," Margaret said.

"Sandwich *what*? No, not that. One of those signs with advertisements on it, that people wear on their chests. You may as well have had the words *Wealthy Retiree* on your chest. *Rob Me!* it might have said. I told you to take a taxi from the station. I *told you*. Who cares about the traffic, what's the big hurry? You're *retired*, remember? And did you even call the police to report what happened? That madman could have followed you. He could be here right now." Her head swiveled around the dining room. "Margaret, look, my hands are trembling. Butter a roll for me."

Her father relaxed under the onslaught of Elizabeth. Here was why you weathered the disappointments and betrayals of a long marriage. Here was safety. Elizabeth put the event in proper perspective: it was not scary and inexplicable; it was a bad thing that had happened because Hugh had not listened to his wife.

When they went home, would they tell the story at the white dinner parties of the suburbs, with people like the Riccis? They wouldn't like the other couples seeing her father that way, frightened and fragile, knocked free of his money and authority. But they would be dying to talk about it, to make meaning of it. How it proved what they already knew about the lawless city and the changing times. It was practically news, and it had happened to them.

Margaret handed Elizabeth the roll, and she took a bite. "Only red wine? You know I'm not drinking red right now."

"I figured you'd want a cocktail."

"I do want a cocktail. But where is the waiter?"

Certainly every one of them deserved to be knocked over in train stations. But they were her family. She didn't actually want them to get hurt.

The waiter recited the specials. Elizabeth wasn't hungry; she would just have three appetizers.

They talked about the girls. They talked about Charlie, who Elizabeth thought was developing some behavioral issues. They talked again about the man in the subway station. Margaret looked at her phone. She felt like she'd been in that restaurant for a year, ten years, all her life. Would it ever be possible to see her parents without digging up quite so much of the past, without slotting each new crisis into the catalog of ancient disasters? No, probably not, never. And all that red was giving her a headache.

Finally, when the plates were taken away, she remembered to ask: "Wasn't there something you'd wanted to talk about?"

And Elizabeth said, "Yes, it seems I've got something."

"Did you find that table you wanted?" Elizabeth had mentioned she was thinking of redoing the dining room. She'd been looking at antiques.

"Well, yes, I did actually find the most—but no. That's not what I'm talking about."

"So—what?"

"It's just high blood pressure, really. But I may have had a bit of a stroke."

"Your mother's sick," her father said. And the wheeling booths all came to a halt and did not move again.

FIVE

26

IT WAS SPRING AND THE STREET WAS FULL OF PEOPLE, BEAU-tiful people with their arms full of white-blossomed branches. They carried the bundles like delicate trees. What were they? Where had they come from? Cherry blossoms, maybe. Someone must be selling them at the farmers market by the park. The trees themselves were in their last outrageous flower; any second now they would shrug and settle down to green. The people knew it, that was why they wanted the branches, wanted to buy them, to take them home and keep them there, so it wouldn't matter so much tomorrow, when they walked outside and the petals had all fallen underfoot.

Margaret bought them too, of course, when she found the stand and the branches in buckets going for $12 a bundle or two for $20, though she felt ridiculous carrying them home, almost dropping them onto the sidewalk when she tried to check her phone—not at all a beautiful person with a tree in her arms.

But it was worth it for how nice they looked now in the vase in her window, like an April Christmas tree. The girls were with Ezra for the afternoon, the windows were open, she loved the smell of her apartment when the windows were open, the familiar diluted with freshness. The afternoon light was thin and pale, an old light, it made her think of charwomen and factory workers trudging home from their labors down the city streets. Not her. Not laboring, not trudging. Biddy was coming over later. She had to be in the city for a meeting in the morning. Until then she was going to lie in bed and read and look out the window at the tree outside, the tree heavy of course with white flowers, each one like a drop at the lip of a faucet, fat and glistening and almost ready to fall.

Her phone buzzed—a text from Duncan. Elizabeth was sick, she reminded herself—she had another doctor's appointment on Monday to adjust her medication. She must not forget that her mother was suffering. But Margaret was not suffering, not now. She felt full, ripe, quivering out on the far edge of a stem. Instead of reading, she jerked off.

Was it weird? Did she do it too much? She masturbated maybe every other day now, whenever she had the time and felt a little pleasant and decadent, or a little tense—which maybe was all the time, actually, the anxiety thrumming under even the most languid moods. Because any moment the fruit would fall, the blossom would wither, spring would pass . . .

She had told Duncan about this anxiety, and he'd said, "I wish you didn't always have so many worries." And the next time they were together, he took off his belt, bound her hands behind her back with it, bent her over the dresser, and said, "You don't have to make any decisions. You just have to do what I tell you." Pleasure. Impossible pleasure.

You don't have to make any decisions, she thought now. You just have to— She came. Too fast. She always felt disappointed when that happened. Like: I allotted more time for this. Now she would have to get out of bed. She would need to tidy up. She would need to get dressed. But not yet.

. . .

ONCE, OUTSIDE her apartment window late at night, she'd heard two people arguing. The woman kept saying, over and over again: "I'm not doing this right now, I'm not doing this right now, I'm not doing this right now." When she paused, the man said: "I'm not a pervert, you're the pervert." She assumed they were drunk. She assumed they were married. Once a monogamist, always a monogamist.

Was there a difference between the way her sexuality had existed for Ezra, as only the necessary precondition for sex with him, and her feelings for Duncan? She stepped into the shower. She thought of Duncan saying, You belong to me. She thought of him saying, Open your mouth. Where did this desire to submit to him come from exactly? She had resented feeling controlled by Ezra, feeling manipulated by Ezra. But maybe that was only because he'd always denied that he was doing it?

"I feel bad leaving you all night with the baby," she used to say, if invited out to dinner with a friend.

"If it makes you feel bad, you don't have to go," he'd tell her.

And she'd agree with him: "You're right, I'll say I can't make it."

He never told her no. He made her tell herself no.

He would have objected to this, of course. He would say he never wanted anything but for her to feel fulfilled. He'd say she had only herself to blame. Exactly. She ran the razor around her kneecap. Ezra had made her dominate herself and submit to herself, both at the same time.

At first, with Duncan, she'd asked him what he liked, what he wanted, until finally he said: "Don't ask. If I want something, I'll tell you." It was a relief. The other day, they had finished lunch at a restaurant, and when she'd walked out of the restroom he was waiting right outside. He pushed her back and locked the door and fucked her against the wall. Middle of the workday. She had said, after, as they walked casually away down the street, "We can do anything we want, can't we?" She was curious about that feeling, the feeling that he was leading her somewhere and she didn't

know where. She wanted to know more about it. She wanted him to tell
her to do things that she'd have to trust wouldn't hurt.

Right after she'd left Ezra, she had looked at porn for the first time.
That was normal, right? She was a full-grown woman. How had she never
watched porn? She had looked, briefly, at all the regular shocking things.
She wanted to search for something, to figure out what it was she liked.
That was one reason to leave a relationship, the fact that she'd arrived at
middle age without quite knowing what she liked, that Ezra had made
her feel ashamed of even asking the question. But what were you supposed to search for? How could you possibly reduce all your shifting desires into the confines of a search term? The categories that popped up
seemed absurd if not insane. Big, tight, ass, load, stepmom. She started
typing something into the search bar. She wrote: "touched while lying
there."

A warning had come up. This content may include images of the abuse
of children.

Horror.

She had pushed the phone away from her like it was leaking something
filthy, like it was getting on her hands, an acid or an oil. She curled up in
the other direction, pressed her face into the pillow. Horror and nausea
and shame.

She'd never looked at the site again. In fact, she'd never looked at any
porn again.

She had confessed this to Duncan only recently. She had made herself
do it—tell him. Telling him things was another kind of submission. She
needed to be different with Duncan than she'd been with Ezra. What
was the point of starting the whole thing all over again if she was going to
make the same mistakes, if she was going to end up just as lonely?

They'd been out at lunch, she'd been holding bread in her hands,
good, crusty bread, and she was not eating but dismantling it, destroying
the bread to crumbs. She told him about the phrase—"touched while lying there"—and about the warning. There was a capaciousness to Duncan, a sense that he could take it all in, which made it easy to talk to him.

Still, she had dropped the bread and covered her face with her hands before she got to the end of the story.

He'd been confused—gentle, and kind, but confused. For the first time, he'd seemed not quite to understand her. He'd asked about the phrase. "Did you look for it because you wanted to see it? Do you feel like that's something you might like?"

Because, if it was, he could try to give it to her.

"No!" She didn't like it. And yet she'd written it.

Her phone was ringing now: Biddy was early, already outside. She wrapped a towel around herself and buzzed her in, gave her a damp hug.

"Geez, girl, you shouldn't have gone to so much effort," Biddy said.

"I know, I know, sorry. I was jerking off."

"Seriously?"

"Just give me a minute."

She pulled on a dress and toweled her hair as they talked about what they wanted for dinner. Biddy never had a night free from Steve and the kids. It was glorious to have her all to herself. They would do whatever she felt like doing.

"So how many puzzles did you bring?"

"Shut up. I'm dying to go out."

"How was the week?"

Biddy stood crammed between the laundry basket and the shower door talking at Margaret's reflection. "Fine, but I'm tired. I feel like I can barely see around the bags under my eyes. Alice keeps climbing on top of me in the middle of the night. Can I try that lipstick?" She hip-checked her way in front of the mirror.

"Did I tell you I planted all these tulip bulbs last fall? White tulips, all through the backyard. I planted them and they just popped up everywhere. I keep going out to look at them, early in the morning, late at night. The other night Steve made us dinner after Alice went to sleep and he was waiting for me to come eat it and I was just out there, looking at the tulips. I feel bad. He's been sharking around trying to have sex with me for days, and I'm just out there, looking at flowers."

Margaret was glad she hadn't gotten ready earlier. It was lovely, like being in high school again, talking with Biddy in the mirror. "So did you go inside? Did you eat Steve's dinner?"

"Oh my god wait never mind about the dinner, I can't believe I'm telling you about these fucking tulips when I have the most amazing gossip. The most amazing gossip. Kendra Cleary has an OnlyFans page."

"Kendra? No way."

"She does. She does! And guess what it's called. You'll never guess. Ass Playground."

"*Ass Playground?*"

"It's not what you think. It's better than you think. She makes these little, like, dioramas and photographs them on her butt, on one of her butt cheeks. Out of clay, I think? I ran into Chloe and she showed me on her phone, but our kids were with us so it was hard to get a good look. It's like—miniature monkey bars, a swing set, and then her black thong like some country lane through the hills."

"Is there a market for that?"

"I guess there's a market for everything."

Silent for a moment, they marveled at Kendra Cleary. How did she get the playground on there? Did her parents know? Who took the pictures? Well, probably you could set a timer on your laptop camera or something. But who arranged the swings? It sounded difficult—just, logistically—twisting around to art direct your own ass. She felt a burst of admiration for Kendra—for the effort that must go into it, for how hard she must be working.

"Speaking of sex work . . ." While she did her mascara, she started telling Biddy the story about telling Duncan about the story about the porn. "This is gross, I'm ashamed, I'm sorry, I don't know why I keep wanting to talk about it," she said. "You told me about your beautiful tulips, about Ass Playground, and in return I'm telling you this."

It's hard to put mascara on when you're trying not to cry. Biddy, perfect Biddy, took the wand away from her. "Oh, Margaret, you idiot. What woman doesn't want to just lie there and get fingered sometimes? Sometimes you're just tired. There's nothing wrong with you. Look up." She took Margaret's chin in her hand and drew the mascara through her lashes. "And FYI, there actually is a search term for that, a totally normal search term: next time try *erotic massage*."

27

IT WAS THE FIRST WEEKEND IN JUNE, THE BEGINNING OF AN-
other summer. Behind the playground was a tiny, ice-cold public swimming pool. It was both so dirty and so chlorinated you could feel the two
forces battling for supremacy, churning the Windex-blue water between
them. Jo and her friend Fiona were doing jumps off the side. They had
names for the different jumps and announced each one ahead of time:
"barrel roll"; "ninja"; jackknife"; "mermaid." Each one looked basically the
same to Margaret. Helen had her calves up over the edge and was floating on her back, her arms spread out and her eyes shut, the sunlight gathered in her face.

The pool was plan B. She'd been planning to take the kids to the
Rockaways with Duncan, but he'd called the night before to cancel.
Something had come up, something that his wife (ex now, but wife always) wanted to do with the family. Priorities. Margaret didn't give him a
hard time about it. By leaving her marriage she'd relinquished the option

of giving anyone a hard time, the license that was granted to you by monogamy's stable admixture of love and resentment.

At least she hadn't told the girls about their plan yet, so no one besides her had to feel disappointed. But his canceling had upset her, given her a bad lower-belly feeling—embarrassment or impending doom. She knew she was blowing it out of proportion, but she was grateful for the check in her comfort, for the reminder of how tenuous any relationship would be now that she was out somewhere beyond marriage. There was love but no safety here.

"You can be rougher with me," she'd told Duncan the other day, while he worked his fingers into the base of her ponytail. She'd been the one to say that.

BIDDY WAS SKEPTICAL about Duncan. She'd thought Margaret was crazy to leave Ezra at first. She'd come around, but she still felt this Duncan thing was too much, too soon. She didn't think it was healthy for Margaret at this stage in her life to be obsessing over some man and the weird sex she wanted to have with him.

It didn't much bother Margaret that her best friend was sometimes wrong about her. It was Margaret's own fault. Biddy knew how Elizabeth was, but not about the pills; she knew how Neal was, but not about his coming into the room at night. Year after year, like a habit, Margaret had kept her secrets. Why? It wasn't too late. It wasn't like Biddy was some innocent baby. Biddy could handle it. She could have told her that night in front of the mirror. After Biddy said "Margaret, you idiot," she could have said—

But she didn't.

When they were little, it was because she didn't want to go anywhere Biddy hadn't gone. She didn't want to be different, damaged, the one who grew up first.

Then it was because she didn't want to hurt her. Biddy would feel terribly

guilty that she hadn't known, that Margaret hadn't given her a chance
to help.

But more than that, it was because Margaret didn't want her to know
that something in their shared childhood had been mutilated, perverted.
It would creep toward Biddy, the wrongness—creep over from Margaret's
side of the bed. It had happened to Margaret, but telling Biddy would be
like making it happen to her too. Like after the meat loaf—when Biddy
had said her stomach hurt and Margaret had run to the bathroom and
barfed. Because as children they had wanted to be one girl, one body.

Why do that to her? Why drag her down there, through the black sew-
ers of sleep? It would have been like letting Neal touch Biddy too, and she
would rather have killed or died than let that happen.

Though in fact it had almost happened, once.

She rolled over early one morning to find Biddy already sitting up in
bed. She'd had a strange dream, she said, or maybe not a dream. In the
night, she'd seen Neal.

"Huh," Margaret said.

"I thought it was your mom at first. But then I said something and he
moved and I saw." Under the blanket, Biddy's knees were pulled up against
her chest.

"Weird." Margaret turned her face back into the pillow, as if she was
still drowsy, though in fact she was wide-awake, dread making her heart
beat fast. "Did he say anything?" she asked.

"No. I don't think so. What was he doing here? What'd he want?"

"I dunno. You said it was a dream."

"Right, yeah."

Finally Margaret said, "I'm hungry. Let's go downstairs."

She never mentioned it again. It was terrible—how close she'd come
to letting that happen. And after, it was even more impossible to tell her
the truth. What sort of person must she have been to let Biddy come
over, to let her sleep in the same bed? To fail to even warn her of the risk?
Biddy might think it was almost—she cringed—like she had offered her
up. And then when Biddy said what she had seen, to act like Biddy had

dreamed or imagined it, to pretend she didn't know that it was real. She was no different from Elizabeth. She would have done anything not to have to talk about it.

Biddy would have been angry. That was the real reason. She would have known that Margaret was a liar.

After that night, for a very long time, she made sure they had sleepovers only at the Murphys' house. Biddy's mother never went around the house shouting about fire hazards, and Danny was there, being funny at dinner and offering to fight any kid who teased them at school. She thought she'd have to make up excuses, but Biddy never asked why, never asked to stay over at Margaret's instead. It had made her wonder—though she tried very hard not to—if Biddy had known more than she said. What if it wasn't a sound that had woken her, but something else? Maybe she'd felt the blanket lift. Maybe she'd felt the hand. Maybe Biddy had lied too.

A SPLASH AND A SHRIEK. Jo had gotten bored of jumping off the edge and jumped on her sister instead, plunging Helen under the water. Margaret was off and moving, knowing exactly what would happen but too slow to intervene. Helen came up spitting. "Helen just wait don't—"

Helen lunged back at her sister, knocking her off her feet.

Margaret pulled Jo up, streaming and wailing about the water up her nose. "Please don't drown each other," she said.

"She jumped on me for no reason."

"I know, I saw. Don't do that, Jo."

Jo was making big hacking noises, and snot and pool water dripped from her nose.

"But, Helen, remember you're still bigger."

The injustice. When her sister had attacked her for no reason. Helen dove under and away. Margaret watched to see where she would surface. The pool was full of dark wet heads and—though a mother must never admit this—they all looked the same, she couldn't tell which child was hers.

Margaret held Jo against her chest and thumped her on the back like a baby. In the water she was as light as a baby. When Margaret was pregnant, she was always bumping into the edges of things. It didn't hurt the baby, the internet assured her—the baby was safe in all that water. She felt proud of childbirth, of having gone through it, as if it were a quest her native village had sent her on. But there was nothing special about it— every woman in the pool had done it. Elizabeth had done it. She made herself think of it that way, intimately. Margaret had been born of Elizabeth. Elizabeth's insides had had to be sponged off her skin. Traces of Elizabeth were probably on her still.

When Jo got hurt, she would cry, "I want Mommy!" She did it at Ezra's, but she did it at Margaret's too. Weeping against Margaret's chest, she would say, over and over again, "I want Mommy."

"But I'm here, Mommy's here," Margaret would say, as if she didn't know precisely what she meant.

There was something Margaret wanted to express now, if only to herself, an idea that was gathering around her in the swimming pool. She needed only to draw it up to the surface. It had to do with an individual life, about the portion that was obligation, the portion that was freedom. If she could grasp hold of it, she could say: Here I end; there you begin. But it was too big, too fluid—less an idea she had than an idea that had her. She would have had to draw up the whole pool, and the playground and sidewalks around it, and the parents and the children and herself inside it.

She felt suddenly the snug application of a sun-warm cheek and Helen's cold arms back around her neck. "Hey, Mom," she said, "we need you. We want you to throw us in the air."

While the child fell up through the air, Margaret looked down. There was grass in the pool, verdant splinters floating all around her. That was odd—the closest park was blocks away. How had they gotten there, these blades of grass from some mowed green lawn, this new green grass in the water?

28

ELIZABETH'S DOCTORS WERE ALL IN MANHATTAN, WHICH MEANT that Margaret had spent more time with her mother in the past few months than she had in decades. Elizabeth didn't want her to go to the doctor with her. She wasn't senile, she said, she didn't need a babysitter. What she wanted was to go out to lunch after every appointment. It didn't matter if she got out at 10:15 or 3:00. She wanted lunch, somewhere nice, one of those glossy uptown bistros. She said she saw Neal all the time, she never saw Margaret. She could have chosen a doctor in New Jersey. Had she chosen Manhattan solely so Margaret would have to go to lunch with her? She felt a flush of happy annoyance at the thought.

A few months earlier, after the second stroke, they'd begun a routine. Every few weeks Margaret would find herself waiting at a table in the middle of the workday for Elizabeth to blow in. She was always full of energy at first. But by the time the food came she was flagging. She never seemed hungry. Margaret would ask about her blood pressure, about how she was feeling, looking for any decline in speech or memory. But Elizabeth revealed nothing. Margaret knew how handsome and attentive the doctor was, how much he'd laughed over the story of Charlie's piano recital. She knew that Elizabeth had been running late but then had to wait ages to get in and there had been an appalling woman ahead of her, all skin and bones, smoking right in the office out of one of those computer cigarettes. What were they called?

"A vape."

"A what? No, that's not it. You know, it's a small cylinder—it looks like people are putting the lighters themselves in their mouths."

"It's called a vape, Mom."

"An electric cigarette! That's what it's called."

But of her condition, Margaret knew vanishingly little. This woman who had sat her down and told her more than any child would ever want to know about her father's sex life and the pills she'd taken and demonstrated precisely how many crunches you had to do as you aged to keep your abs tight was now silent about the private world of her failing body. After each lunch, Margaret had taken to calling her father so he could fill her in on what was actually happening.

It was funny that Margaret hadn't quite noticed this before: that Elizabeth never answered questions. She imposed plenty of intimacies but said only what she wanted to say, like a politician representing the world's most cryptic party. There were so many things Margaret wanted to know about: boarding school, Barnard, Elizabeth's parents, her marriage, her past and what she thought of it. She could not understand her mother if she could not make her answer, and the only thing she understood about her mother was that she could not make her answer.

"What did the doctor say?" Margaret asked. Elizabeth looked skinny and her posture was off, folded forward, like she was protecting some fragile bone inside her chest.

"Oh, this and that. How is Helen's reading going? I was talking to Jeannie Ricci. You know her granddaughter is the same age? Well, she's on the spectrum. She can barely read at all."

"Which one has the daughter?"

"Jeremy, the older brother." Unfathomable: Jeremy Ricci married; Jeremy Ricci, a father. There were ways to transfer videotapes to DVDs to files to the internet, but she didn't like to think about that.

"But at least," Elizabeth added, "the Ricci boys still live in town; they didn't insist on moving to a whole other city."

"New York is hardly a whole other city. It's *the* city."

"Well, that's a bit provincial, don't you think?"

"Sorry, what were we talking about?"

"Helen's reading."

"Oh, Helen's doing great. She started reading my old copy of *The Secret Garden*. Do you remember giving that to me? You wrote an inscription for my birthday. I'd forgotten all about it."

"Did I?" She picked at a roll.

"Yes. You wrote, 'To Margaret on her tenth birthday. May you always love flowers and secrets.'"

Elizabeth looked directly into Margaret's eyes for a moment, a shock. "What a lovely inscription," she said.

"It is, isn't it? Beautiful and a bit strange."

"Well, I don't know if there's anything strange about it."

"Flowers *and secrets*."

Elizabeth sipped her ice water, daring her to impart any meaning to this.

—

The truth was that for all her asking, she didn't really want to know about Elizabeth's illness, about the frailty of the body that had orchestrated her introduction to the world, the mother's body that had created and then controlled her. She feared her mother's body in the same way she feared her mother's knowledge of her own body—her height and weight, shots and fillings, the texture of her shit, the date of her first period—the original intimacy that now seemed an intolerable trespass. She had resented Elizabeth's lapses in understanding and attention, and yet she had spent years trying to evade Elizabeth's oversight, to maintain some privacy in the face of all that information, to become a person instead of a child, which is to say, a kind of patient. Now Margaret wasn't ready to see their positions reversed.

The first time she saw a doctor without her mother in the room, she was eleven. She'd gotten her period young, and right away, Elizabeth had made her an appointment at the gynecologist. Later she'd wondered why. She was years away from having sex. But at the time she'd just assumed that was part of becoming a woman: someone had to look.

They went to an office park where every building was the same red-faced brick. She put on her first paper gown and put her heels up in the footrests they called stirrups though they weren't anything like stirrups because stirrups were down below while these held her legs up high. "Scooch down," the doctor kept saying. "Scooch down to the edge here." It was almost impossible to spread her knees—like holding her mouth wide open at the dentist but so much worse—but she did as she was told. She could feel how hot the lamp was, how bright the light must be down there.

Then the doctor showed her the tool she was going to use—a silver tool with a handle and what looked like a blunt blade. She compressed something, and the blade separated into two pieces, like a duck's bill. This was what she was going to insert into Margaret to open her up. She had them in different sizes. "I'm going to use the smallest one here," she said. "You'll just feel some pressure, maybe a little discomfort."

The pain was incredible and the thing was barely inside her. She felt like she was burning or tearing or both, and her body bucked halfway up the exam table, the paper gown billowing away from her skin. "Let's try that again," the doctor said. "Just relax. Scooch down."

Again the pain, and then a click, and the pain got worse, and another click, and the pain got worse again. It was cranking her open. Women did this every day, she knew in theory, but the courage it took to lie there holding her body still through the ratcheting pain was stupendous. If she had had any choice in the matter, she would have fled the room. But she didn't have any choice. And anyway, it couldn't possibly get worse, she told herself, and then she felt another click, and it did.

"I'll just take a swab now," the doctor said, and there was a tickle somewhere deep inside her and then suddenly it was over. Release, withdrawal, the pain swapped out so completely for something minor—she smarted, she ached—that it seemed a kind of trick. How could something so violently invasive leave no mark?

Margaret was permitted to sit up and clamp her thighs back together. But the doctor wasn't done. The exam was normal, the doctor explained, but the way she'd responded to it wasn't. It didn't hurt other girls this much, she explained. Other girls were not this afraid.

When she got into the car Elizabeth wanted to know why she was crying.

"She asked me if something happened to me."

"What does that mean, *something*?"

"Something bad."

"What did you say?"

"I said no." Because nothing *had* happened to her. Nothing like what the doctor suspected.

Elizabeth turned off the car and opened the door. "No, Mom, don't," Margaret tried to say, but it was too late. Elizabeth stormed into the office. What had the doctor been thinking, to ask a child a terrible thing like that? There was nothing wrong with her daughter's body. She went off to protect Margaret in the one way she knew how: by asking to speak to the manager, by berating someone for the quality of the service.

Where was the waiter? Margaret hoped he would hurry. She always felt disoriented by the submersion of a restaurant lunch, the underwater feel of a dark room in the daytime. Between those hours with Elizabeth and meals with colleagues and dates with Duncan, she felt like she lived half her life in restaurants, worrying about all the other places she needed to be. Lunch was late that day, and she would barely have any time to work before picking up the kids.

She needed to work. She had taken on more freelance editing—a writer had asked for her help on a book. She'd never edited a book before, but it wasn't so different, just longer, ever so much longer, but that was okay because she charged by the hour. Her apartment was more expensive every year. There were so many things she wanted to do—rent a car, rent a cottage, buy a linen slip dress, take the girls on vacation—and for that she needed money, more money than she had, money that Elizabeth might give her if she asked, but she didn't want to ask, didn't want to know what Elizabeth would demand in return for that show of weakness.

"What can I get you ladies?"

Margaret asked for the omelet. Elizabeth ordered the pea purée.

"Just the purée, ma'am? Just to confirm—the side dish?"

"Oh no, it isn't a soup?"

"No. I'm sorry, no."

Elizabeth glared at the waiter, for the outrage of the purée not being soup. Could they not simply mix in some water and make it so? "Well, fine, I'll have the caviar, then."

"Very good."

The waiter began to sweep back into the current of the room but then stopped, snagged for a moment on doubt. "I'm so sorry, I'm just making sure. You don't want the pea purée. You want . . . the caviar."

"Yes, that's what I said." She looked at Margaret like, *really.*

Margaret, full of sudden pure fondness, wanted to laugh. Elizabeth was still Elizabeth.

"Ezra called me the other day."

"He did?"

"Yes, to see how I was feeling."

"That was nice of him."

"He calls me every couple weeks, actually."

"That's weird."

"Why should it be? He's always been lovely to me. He says the girls have been spending more time with his girlfriend. I don't know if I approve of that."

"Yeah, they have. She's fine, she might be kind of perfect for him."

"Hm."

"It's true."

"Well. I hope he'll have an easier time of it now." Easier than with you, she meant but did not say, and that was something; Margaret appreciated that. She thought about how, that day at the gynecologist, even though they were already late to pick Neal up from school, her mother had marched back into the building. That she had tried, in her own way, to help.

At last their lunches came. "Lovely," Elizabeth said, and the waiter smiled, gratified. She lifted the tiny spoon, offering to share a bite of the glistening black eggs. Margaret hesitated, and then opened her mouth. They tasted good, so good, of all the concentrated salt of the amniotic sea. She was still Elizabeth, she was still her mother. Her hand shook.

29

AT THE BACK END OF THE GARDEN WAS A TREE HOUSE, STUR-
dily built a decade earlier by Duncan's best friend, Dante, for his daughter. It was pleasingly cartoonish, with a rope ladder and boards nailed at
janky angles that she hoped were just for show. Wild green jungle vine
grew up one side and over the roof. "The girls are going to lose their shit,"
she said when she saw it.

"Can we . . . go in there?" Helen asked. They'd never seen a tree house
outside a storybook. (Never raked, nor shoveled snow, nor seen that hall-
mark of childhood—her fault.)

They were nervous about the rope ladder. A boy pushed past them,
holding a stuffed pig in his teeth. Small faces peeked over the edge. To
Helen, Margaret said, "You can do it." To Jo she said, "Let me help you."

The party grew, filling the backyard. These were Duncan's people. She
drank her wine and introduced herself. So how did you meet Duncan?
How long have you and Duncan been dating? So I hear you're an editor?

So how did you meet Duncan? She hadn't met any of them before, was invited this time only because Duncan's ex, June, was out of town. Otherwise June would have been there instead.

What was she like? Meeting the women of Duncan's circle, that was mostly what she was thinking about—that June would be like one of them. They all seemed to have unimpeachable jobs—doctors or environmental engineers or deputy commissioners in the mayor's office for things she didn't catch. They wore what Brooklyn mothers wore, linen dresses the colors of the earth or rompers like sexy toddlers. They were fit with good hair getting quickly ruined by the heat. One after another they flipped their heads forward, tied it up.

Above the adult conversations floated the tree house. An occasional shout—they're coming, hide—and the sound of bodies hitting the floor. Now and then a grubby foot emerged, reached blindly for the ladder. Occasionally she caught a glimpse of her own children through the tree house window or darting across the planks. She wished she could be up there too, free to kick her feet above the sea of snacking grown-ups.

A soccer-jerseyed boy came down, scuttled to the picnic table, took a whole plate of cheese, and then faced the impossible obstacle of climbing back up again with the plate in his hands. She watched him for a while, wondering if she should help. When he started putting the cheese in his pockets, she averted her eyes. She needed to make a good impression on the parents, not the children.

She found Duncan with Louie and Dante, the host, whom she complimented on the party and the tree house.

"I remember playing in there so much," Louie said.

"Get up there, you can make sure no one falls off the edge," Duncan said, seeing that he was yearning to. But he was so tall, comically tall. They knew it would be an ordeal, watching him try to fold his limbs inside.

"Go on," Dante said. "It's sturdy as hell."

"Nah, I'm cool. Where's Willis and Mira?"

The dads exchanged a grimace. In a bedroom, she gathered. Their older kids had a casual thing going on, Duncan had told her. Poor Louie. She felt a pang of envy on his behalf and then some pangs of her own.

She wanted to be the one to sneak off. She wanted Duncan to pull her inside, upstairs, into a dark bedroom, where the party's hum would remind them that anyone could walk in at any second, as he tugged her underwear down to her thighs and pushed her face into the coat pile. But it was summer, there was no coat pile—the fantasy already diverging from the possible. Duncan could have pulled it off; he was good at that type of thing, unlike Ezra, who would never. But he wouldn't want to do it there, in front of June's friends. And anyway, who would watch her children?

"Can you watch the girls for a moment?" she asked Duncan. "I'm just going to use the bathroom."

"They're fine, don't worry."

"Just—can you keep an eye out?"

He thought she was hovering, overprotective. But he forgot how little they were. If Jo came down alone, she might fall. She would not have had to explain this to Ezra because he would simply have known it, done it. But they were his own children, of course. Someday she should tell Duncan more about her childhood—all that she feared and why. But for the moment it seemed too exhausting—an endless, tedious, impossible undertaking—this attempt to bring a new person up to speed on the annals of her life. This is my language, these my holidays, my congresses, my restaurants, my rivers and the dams in them that make my lightbulbs go, and here on crumbling scrolls are the accounts of every famine, purge, and civil war, every revolution of government and industry, all that I made and lost and more. She was thirty-six years old. It was too much to ask.

THE HOUSE WAS QUIET after the blaze of the backyard. The bathroom's white doorknob glowed in the gloom and was cool under her hand. She was tired, and her head hung low as she peed. She let herself just sit there for a while, thinking of nothing.

Outside again, she stood under the tree house. "Hey, guys, all good up there?"

No answer.

"Helen and Jo, poke your heads out, please, it's your mother."

An older girl in a tank top leaned out, her ponytail brushing the railing. "Those kids aren't up here anymore," she said.

"What?"

"They got down."

"When?"

"I dunno."

They were hungry, or they needed the bathroom. But she should have passed them coming out or in. She looked around the yard, dodging conversations. "Lost my kids," she repeated pleasantly. She went back in to check the bathroom, but it was empty. "I can't find the girls," she told Duncan.

"I wouldn't worry."

"You didn't see them get out of the tree house?"

"I must have missed it. But come on, they're fine, they're just playing somewhere."

"I'm sure they're fine too, but I still need to find them." He really didn't understand, did he? Jo was only six—she might still follow dogs into streets. "I'm going to look inside."

Again the cool dark. She called their names. Nothing. No one in the kitchen but the blank-faced cabinets, a cutting board smeared green, the scouring smell of vinegar and mint.

She went upstairs. Some Constructivist art on the landing, a child's drawing of an ambiguous four-legged animal, many family photos— Dante, his wife, the unseen daughter. In the upstairs hallway everything was lines within lines—the hall itself, the molding down the baseboard and up against the ceiling, the red runner underfoot, the panels on the three shut doors. The house was old, beautifully updated at what must have been monumental expense, allowed ever since to go pleasingly shabby in a way that Elizabeth would have despised. It was just the kind of house Margaret would have wanted, if she'd had much more money and a husband.

Downstairs everything had been impeccably tidy, the party-prep deep clean involving what must have been a thorough process of depersonalization. But up here things had slipped by. A single white ankle sock lay on the floor like a dropped envelope. If someone caught her, they'd think she was snooping. She tiptoed, which made it worse.

From behind one of the doors came the sound of beating drums. They got faster and louder, a melody beginning to skirl, voices chanting in words she didn't understand, except that she understood what they meant—that something heroic was about to happen, here, maybe, to her, in the hallway.

She opened the door, and the song was all around her. She saw a TV, and a couch, and four kids on it watching a movie. The screen was blue; the perspective changed, and she understood it was an ocean. A boat darted over the water, the wind animating its sails.

"Hi, Mom," Helen said.

"You okay?"

"Mm-hmm."

"Where's your sister?"

"I dunno."

Margaret wanted to say, Your sister is your responsibility, you're supposed to watch her. But Jo was Margaret's responsibility. She was the one who was supposed to watch her.

Behind the next door was a bathroom. Then the parents' empty bedroom, the blanket taut across the king-size bed, a stationary bike crouched in the corner, sharp angled and insectile. Margaret went up another flight of stairs. How big *was* this house? It was doing something confusing to her—boggling her urban depth perception. No one Margaret knew in the city lived like this. The black banister slipped through her hand like so much doled-out ribbon. More doors, another hall, the same repetitive linearity, the same molding in the other direction.

Strange actually to think that this was a home, that many times each day a person walked around this corner, put her hand right here where the banister ended. She would know the meaning of every creak and shadow. All that was flat surface to Margaret would for her be utterly familiar, utterly specific—like this, the divot in the wood her thumb had found. She heard a sound, a voice but no word. "Jo?" she said softly.

She opened a door and there was Willis, leaning back against a headboard, his eyes shut tight, and a girl straddling his lap, her ponytail swinging to a cheerful rhythm. Margaret gasped, slammed the door, heard the girl giggle. Please let them not have seen her face. She would never mention this, never, ever.

She would have run downstairs, but there was one door left, and she was beginning to be frightened. The light through the third-floor window reminded her of Elizabeth's house, of the excess upstairs daylight when no one was there to see it, of the unreal light of movies or dreams. She felt like the child approaching the hole in the wall through which she might see anything—the enchanted forest, the camera lens, the whistling void.

She opened the door, and there was Jo in a bed, her hand under her cheek, breathing the slow breaths of a deep, deep nap. It looked like a guest room, a bit dusty and anonymous, a rocking chair filling up a spare corner. She saw Jo's purple sandals on the ground next to a big pair of sneakers. Then Louie sat up.

He'd been lying on the other side of Jo and sat up in a jangle of teenage limbs.

"Oh, hey," he said. "Jo fell asleep."

"What are you doing?"

"She fell asleep."

"But what are you doing?"

He was scooching down to the end of the bed, trying to get out without waking Jo. "She fell asleep watching TV and I carried her in here." Now that he was standing up, his tone had turned a bit defensive. He said it like, I already told you.

Margaret said nothing.

"I was bored of the party, I don't have any friends here." Did he look guilty because he had reason to be guilty, or was he reacting only to something in Margaret's face, some cumulative expression like a chord hit by every feeling she'd had walking through the house—her social anxiety and real estate envy, her missing children, Willis getting laid, Louie in the bed, the many disparate notes of her own personal history? Did her face reflect all that? Did she look suspicious? If it had not crossed his mind before, it did so now—the possibility.

He was looking for his shoes. "I didn't do anything," he said.

She was across the room, she was in his face, her hands went up, and he stumbled back against the wall. He had touched her child. Her sleeping child with her warm, abandoned limbs. She would shove him, hurt him, make him say what he had done—tried something, taken something—comfort, pleasure—from a child—he had no right. Fury, like a convulsion, locked her jaw.

"I was just trying to help." He said it with his face turned in to his shoulder. He said it like he was afraid.

She took a step back. He lifted a hand, rubbed his head where it had knocked against the wall. Something dinged, and he looked at her, as if to make sure it was safe to take his phone out of his pocket, as if he wasn't sure what she might do. "Dad's wondering where I am," he said.

Her arms felt weird, hanging by her sides. The violence was draining down and away, pooling in her extremities like blood. She found it hard to speak.

He was smashing his feet back into his sneakers. He leaned down to pull up one of the jammed heels, touched the wall to steady himself.

He was a kid. He was Duncan's baby—Louie, who felt forgotten, who did not always know where he fit in. It was Margaret who poisoned things. It was Margaret who had wanted to hurt someone.

He would tell his mother. He would tell June, and June would tell her friends, and Margaret would be revealed, exposed. He would tell Duncan, and Duncan would not love her anymore.

Or maybe, she thought, he wouldn't tell. Maybe he'd feel that he must have done *something* wrong, for a grown-up to react that way. And besides, what had really happened? She had not actually touched him. If he'd hurt his head, it was only his own fault, his own clumsiness. How terrible, she thought, as he backed out of the room, that this was now what she hoped for: that he'd be too ashamed to speak.

She slumped down against the door. Jo was still sleeping. She didn't know that her mother was scary, was dangerous, had tried to protect her in all the wrong ways. The door, the bed, the boy—the world heaved up the buried past.

30

SHE WAS HOME ALONE IN THE PAST. FIFTEEN—NOT A BABY. For once she had known exactly what it was, the sound in the night. The sound of breaking, and then the sound of what had broken falling, the pieces spinning and colliding. She recognized it not from real life but from scary movies, and its crystal clarity was like a movie too, how precisely, even a floor away, she heard the window shattering.

She knew what came next: the creak of footsteps. She thought the word *intruder*. She thought: deadly home invasion. The pumping of her blood berated her ears. All she could hear was the wind.

Neal was away at college, and her parents were out at dinner. But they had a phone in their room, so she crept there, shoved Elizabeth's dresser in front of the door, put her hand on the phone's beige plastic, and waited. She didn't want to call 911 until she was sure it was a real emergency, until someone tried to open the door.

"Margaret!"

She'd fallen asleep. The door was straining, juddering the dresser forward. She got up to pull it free. "This is such a *fire hazard*," Elizabeth was saying.

But then she looked at her. "What's wrong?"

Margaret explained. "Hugh!" Elizabeth shouted down the stairs. "Margaret heard a window breaking."

"Well, she heard right," he called back.

It was in the dining room. They went to look, and there behind the head of the table was a black hole in the wall, a jagged-edged square that let in the sweet night air. Blades of glass shone from the carpet, an upside-down chandelier. She stepped closer. There was something in the hole. Not the glinting shards, but something with its own brightness: the blossom-covered end of a branch.

"Didn't I say that cherry tree was too close to the house?" Elizabeth said. "I'm getting the vacuum. Didn't I tell you? Margaret, don't. You'll cut yourself."

She was holding a big piece in her hand. She held it up to her eye like a camera and looked through it, then through the window decked with white petals. It was only a tree. It was only some passing weather. For once she'd been wrong to be afraid.

SHE THOUGHT of this now as the ice cream truck man handed down a cherry dip. Pigeons pecked at their feet, going at the fallen sprinkles like so much rainbow chicken feed. Jo kicked; the birds shuffled just out of reach.

"I want a tree house," Jo said.

"Me too," said Margaret.

"Could we build one in the park?"

"I wish we could. But there are probably rules."

"Can we go play at that house again?"

"Maybe sometime. You guys had fun?"

"I didn't get to finish the movie."

"You fell asleep," Helen pointed out. "And I didn't get to either. Mom made us leave, remember?"

"Jo, do you remember falling asleep?" Carefully, casually: "Louie carried you to bed. Do you remember that?"

Helen, jealous, reached over and flicked her sister's ear.

"Ow!"

"Helen, don't."

"I wanted to go back up the tree house," Jo said.

"But do you remember?"

"I never fell asleep."

Margaret gave up.

IT HAD PROVEN impossible to leave the girls and go back to the party, impossible to sidle under Duncan's arm and make more polite conversation about how they'd met. She'd looked but hadn't seen Louie, or his brother, downstairs.

"But we had a whole plan," Duncan had said. He was confused, then annoyed. "The guys were going to babysit and we were going out to dinner. I've already promised them forty dollars each."

"I know, I'm sorry, I just . . . Jo seems overtired. I think she needs a quiet night at home with me."

"Sure, but Willis and Louie can put them to bed. Look, is something wrong? Oh no—you hated my friends."

"No," she said, and laughed like she was supposed to.

"You did. I agree, they're terrible, they suck. I hate them all too. Did someone say something that upset you? Don't go."

She thought she should be honest. For once, she should be honest. At least to head off the story Louie himself might tell. She said, "Something a little weird happened. When I found Jo, Louie was there too."

"So?"

"In the bed."

"Wow, okay. What exactly are you saying?"

"I'm not."

"Implying?"

"Look, I—"

"Louie would never."

"Of course. I don't think so either. It's just boys do, sometimes . . ."

"Margaret, please don't even think it. She's six. He would have to be some kind of monster, and he's not. He's a smart teenager and a sweet kid, he would never—"

Louie was his son. It was his job to protect him. Jo was her daughter, the same. Maybe this was it, proof that their experiment had failed. She would need to tell him about Neal and the Riccis, or he would think that she was crazy. Even if she told him, he might think that she was crazy. Anyway, she couldn't do it then—not by the cheese plate, in the heat of the meat vapor billowing off the grill.

"Louie is a great kid. You *know* I think he's a great kid," she said.

"Yes."

"It just made me nervous. And we weren't there."

"Jo would tell you if anything had happened."

"She couldn't, she was asleep."

She noticed her hand was holding her own throat. Nobody gets over that, the woman in the book club had said, and maybe she was right after all.

And maybe that doctor was right too, the doctor who'd looked between her legs and known, from the depths of her clinical experience, that something was wrong with her—the doctor who'd told her that it wouldn't have hurt so much if she hadn't been so frightened.

Oh—she had to go. She wasn't ready to be angry at Duncan, she didn't want to be. She should go before she committed real violence, kicked over the grill, burned down the tree house, said what she thought about people being more afraid of the possibility of an accusation than the possibility of a violation.

"Let's talk about it later, okay? I'm sorry. Thank Dante for me."

He let her go. He did not kiss her goodbye.

. . .

OUTSIDE THE SIDEWALKS were dead silent—the stoops abandoned, the windows blank slabs of glass. Even the ice cream truck was too subdued to play its song. She needed the gates of matter to swing closed again, for the world to be pure phenomenon. The soft serve was cold and sweet as a fact, the girls were quiet, and their bodies made blue shadows on the ground. When they finished eating, they put their sticky hands in hers, and she let go only when her phone rang.

She thought it might be Duncan saying Louie had told him everything, saying she'd behaved like a freak, unforgivably. Or it might be Duncan saying it was okay, that he wanted to talk about what had happened, that they could figure it out.

But it was her father, asking her to come home.

SIX

31

NO RENOVATION—NOT THE HALL BATHROOM OR THE KNOCKED-out back stair, not the new kitchen, or the new kitchen after that, or the new kitchen after that—could have prepared her for the change at Elizabeth's house.

The dining room table and chairs had been moved into storage. In their place stood a cot, tidily made up with yellow and white sheets, and glinting below, the metal wheels that gave it all away, that rolled in the hospital with it. The tea set and topiaries had been replaced by a cloudy glass, a paperback, a small family of prescription bottles. An armchair had been maneuvered in; Elizabeth was sitting in it, a big book in her lap, glossy photos of the farmhouses of New England.

"I didn't feel safe going into the city anymore. And the hospital in Millburn is just as good as NewYork-Presbyterian, if not better. So much less crowded."

"How are you feeling?" Margaret asked. "Are you tired?"

Elizabeth had had yet another stroke, a worse one this time. She wanted to know how frightened Elizabeth was, so she would know how frightened she should be.

"What do I have to feel tired for? I don't do anything. Neal comes, but I never see you or the girls."

It was an in-between time. Summer camp was over, but school wouldn't start for a few more weeks. Until then, Margaret had told her father, they might as well be in New Jersey. Margaret called it helping out. Hugh called it lifting her mother's spirits. Ezra was finishing a big project— relaunching, once again, the magazine. There would need to be a new name and a new logo to go with it, and a very long inclusive process leading up to it, beginning with a four-day brainstorming retreat. Go, she told him. She could work remotely, do the bare minimum for a while, save on babysitting. The girls could swim and see their cousin. She would put off talking with Duncan.

There were good moments and bad moments, Hugh had said. Elizabeth often seemed her normal old self—reorganizing the spice drawer, nagging the pool company about the pH balance. Then suddenly she'd be too weak to manage the stairs.

But she didn't look sick to Margaret. Thinner, but Elizabeth would consider that a plus. Sometime during the stroke or after, at the hospital, she'd bitten her bottom lip, hard. The lip was swollen, and it made her pout. Elizabeth gave the impression that her sore lip was the worst part. Forget the fact that behind her skull the slow blood crept and clotted through the contracting vessels; this was the real problem, this ordinary discomfort. She kept asking Margaret to find her more ChapStick.

It made her wonder if Elizabeth was playing it up, just a bit—her role as the invalid at the heart of the house. Hugh's call had scared Margaret. She'd thrown clothes in a bag and rushed the girls on the train first thing in the morning. And now here she was, jumping to attention while Elizabeth shouted out orders from the dining room, less a sickroom than a command center. She gave no sense of retreating or withdrawing, of accustoming herself to her illness; it was the house that accommodated, the rooms that changed.

If the sight of anything worried Margaret, it wasn't Elizabeth. It was the house.

"Has it been hard for Dad? Keeping up with the place lately?" she asked now.

"No, why should it be? Lorinda still comes every week to clean; your father doesn't need to lift a finger."

That wasn't what he'd told her. The house was too big, he'd said. Things kept breaking. A door handle—the screws got loose, and its tongue fell off. And the doors themselves, half of them warped by humidity. If you wanted any privacy, you had to jam each door into the threshold and then jam it out again with your shoulder. Even the bats were back, roosting in the attic.

All around she felt the creeping disarray, like the house was declining in tandem with Elizabeth's body. A plastic CVS bag holding tubes of something—toothpaste or ointment—had come to rest amid the white wedding pictures. Half the chessmen lay on their backs. As Elizabeth talked, Margaret noticed the wastepaper basket in the corner. It was a decorative one, embroidered with medieval-looking roses, and there were used tissues inside. She realized she had never before seen trash in this trash can before. Garbage was to be disposed of only in the kitchen; the wastepaper basket was there for show or for guests who didn't know better.

Nearby on the carpet was a small plastic wrapper. She stepped closer. Someone must have tossed it toward the bin and missed. It was square with a ghost of a circle inside. A condom wrapper? A condom wrapper in Elizabeth's dining room.

She bent over and picked it up. The plastic crinkled between her thumb and finger. The label was cherry red. She had to get rid of it before Elizabeth saw, because if she saw she was sure to assume it was Margaret's— that Margaret's pockets were spilling over with sex trash and drug paraphernalia.

She kept her back to Elizabeth and looked closer. Never mind, no, it wasn't a condom. It was only the cellophane from a lollipop. All summer the girls' camp counselors had been doling them out for good behavior. She laughed at her mistake and put it deep in the kitchen garbage can where it belonged.

—

At one of their last lunches in the city, Elizabeth had been talking about Margaret's apartment, how disorganized it was, how Helen and Jo's closet was crowded with outgrown clothes. "You're like my own mother. You just don't care if something is out of place," she said.

"I care. It's just that I'm busy."

"Look at you, right now. Your elbow is in the bread crumbs and you don't even know it."

She was right. But Margaret would not get distracted by self-defense. "Your mom was a bad housekeeper?" she asked.

"Well, they always had a maid, lived half out of hotels."

"But was she messy?"

"Oh, she was a slob. Not that she didn't look impeccable. But at home she was a slob. She had such beautiful things, but she didn't take care of them. Didn't know how to or couldn't be fussed. She had this beautiful black coat with a fur collar and cuffs. I remember at Christmastime I was always picking it up from the floor."

"What was their house like?"

"This menu has far too many appetizers—I always think that makes a restaurant look insecure, don't you?"

"But wait, tell me about the house. I want to know what it was like."

"Stylish. But there was no warmth or color in it. The only color was mess, trash. What I mean is—your eye would seize at last on something pretty, something gold or green, seize on it from across the room, but when you got close, it would just be a bill or a plate of limes from the night before. Flowers in a vase, maybe, but even then: white. It was less a home, really, than a place for their dinners, parties, what's the word— a *venue*. It was either crammed with people or completely vacant. Like somewhere you'd expect to have to sweep the litter from the floor each morning. It wasn't something that even bothered them."

"It must have bothered you."

"Well, but I was barely there."

"The home you made for us was very different," Margaret said.

Elizabeth was pleased; she lowered her face to the menu. "Oh good," she said, "they have a bisque."

"I'll have the same."

A happy weight had settled over Margaret then, the feeling that she and her mother had something in common—they cared about things being beautiful. Nothing about Elizabeth's vision was stingy or cold, you had to give her that. It was all abundance. She just cared about things matching, that they fit together and aimed toward an absolute coherence. So they had a different style; so the things that didn't fit had to be left out; so what?

Margaret would be different now; she would be generous. If she couldn't give up her grievances entirely, she could at least give her mother a chance. She could be honest with her.

Maybe, if it came to it, if she really had to.

For now she said: "You've got some chores for me to do? Let's do some chores."

"I want you to clear out my wardrobe."

"What do you mean clear it out?"

"I want it taken care of now so no one has to worry about it after."

"After what? Come on, Mom. Don't talk like that. You're not dying."

Elizabeth shut her book of photographs, smacking the cottage on the left page with the full force of the big red barn on the right. "Dying? Don't be absurd. I mean after we sell the house."

⌒

They'd been planning to tell her.

"I think it's very wise," Neal said.

Margaret was setting the table for dinner in the kitchen, now that the dining room had been repurposed.

"You knew?" she asked Neal.

"We've been discussing it for a while. You'd be aware if you visited more often."

"I get that the house is too big. And with Mom not feeling well it makes sense. It just seems sudden."

"It's the right time to sell," said Neal. "Interest rates are low; the market has never been hotter."

"Where will you go?" Margaret asked. Don't say the city, she thought. "Don't say Florida," she said.

"God, no," said Elizabeth.

She was sitting at the table. Hugh set down a drink in front of her. "We'll find somewhere smaller around here," he said. "It might take a while to sell anyway."

"This house? Don't be ridiculous. Someone will want it immediately," Elizabeth said.

"And like I told you, *we* want the house," said Neal.

"What?" said Margaret.

"I need to figure out the financing. But if possible we should keep it in the family."

"You want to live here?" she asked her sister-in-law, who had taken one of the counter stools and was looking silently at her phone.

"Why wouldn't she want to?" Elizabeth said.

"It's our dream," Neal said.

"It's a very nice house," his wife said, and both Elizabeth and Neal looked at her like—*Nice?*

Well, why not? Why shouldn't it all be Neal's? She didn't want the house, with the bats and the soldier doll; she didn't want to live in the suburbs. Anyway, she couldn't afford it.

And yet. That the house would belong to Neal. That he could go anywhere within it. Do anything to it. She imagined his fist against the walls, knocking.

"Well," Hugh said, "we'll have to see. The house is worth a lot now."

"I can manage it."

"Let's just get it on the market and see."

"I can *manage* it, Dad."

Just then the children came in, saying they were hungry, asking when dinner was. Hugh didn't think Neal had enough money. Neal must hate that. But if he expected their father to give up anything for less than it was worth, he must not have been paying attention.

32

ALL THE NEXT DAY IT RAINED. IT WAS HOT AND POURING, soaked and steaming, dark at 2:00 p.m. The summer storm degraded the day, and that was how it should be; the day should be ruined. Elizabeth had taken charge of time. Her to-do lists would govern the hours and her illness would govern the days, the rain-dark days of her decline.

The sweaters had to go. No need anymore for all those sweaters. No, not *every* one, obviously. Save a few cardigans, the summer-weight sweaters, a few things she could throw over her shoulders. The rest she should take to Goodwill. The dresses Elizabeth wanted to go through one by one. She had ideas about who might like them—Margaret herself, of course, but also more distant relatives, Lorinda the cleaning lady, Biddy and Mrs. Murphy, Helen and Jo someday.

She began in the guest room closet where Elizabeth stored her off-season clothes—the wool skirts and coats and corduroys, the itchy sweaters with silver buttons. Then she moved into the main walk-in. She brought the clothes down the stairs in great armloads, the swan necks of the hangers snagging on every rung.

But when she got it all down there, ready for inspection, Elizabeth was too tired to look. She was in bed, her face to the wall. The arm that lay on top of the blanket was as narrow as Helen's.

"Mom?"

"Mm."

"Are you okay?"

"Resting."

"Can I get you anything?"

No answer.

She started to leave but then came back and sat in the armchair. She watched her mother sleep.

She was thinking of a question, the perfect question. It should be something about the past. When she asked it, her mother would know that she cared. She tried to imagine Elizabeth at Helen's age, at Jo's. It was hard, but it shouldn't be impossible. Margaret would ask the question right when she woke up. Elizabeth would be more open then; she wouldn't have a chance to get distracted by the things of the world, how they needed to be rearranged or replaced. Margaret would take advantage, she would ask her question in that murmurous moment between sleep and wake.

But she waited and waited, and Elizabeth didn't wake up. She coughed, and opened and shut the door, and still Elizabeth slept.

Eventually the girls came down, saying they were bored. All they wanted to do was swim but not in the rain—it was no fun getting wet if you were already wet. They wanted her to find them umbrellas so they could go outside and see if the rain was slowing down, so she did that. Then they wanted her to go outside with them and twirl their umbrellas like in the musical, so she did that too. By the time Margaret got back, Hugh was in the kitchen, rinsing a pan in the sink.

He lifted it out of the water, examined it, and squirted another round of soap. She went to help unload the dishwasher.

"I hate that they changed the dish soap," he said.

"They what?"

"They changed the soap. It used to cut right through the grease. Now look—it's still full of oil."

"Right." She stacked some cups. "Wait. Are you really saying they don't make dish soap like they used to?"

"Don't laugh. It's a fact. Ask anyone my age. They must have changed the chemical composition or something. Some new environmental standard. It's like the dishwasher. They say 'high efficiency,' and maybe it uses half the water, but it takes twice the time."

"That sounds frustrating but . . ."

"Don't say it's for the good of the planet."

"I would never. I mean—not to you. I just think the woke progressives have better things to do than to go after your Palmolive."

"Tell it to the pan," he said, and they both laughed a little. She looked at him, bent scrubbing over the sink, his glasses fogged, spatters of water or grease on his polo shirt. Then he lifted his head—he'd heard it before she did—her mother calling from the other room.

She was awake. Margaret had missed her moment.

There in the sound behind the familiar querulous impatience was a new note, something more delicate—actual need, actual distress. Her father's face looked different too, like something had been taken from it or added to it. A renovation around the eyes, a ground-down look.

"I'll go," she said. "Let me."

The dining room had gotten dark, and Elizabeth needed Margaret to flick the switch, and then she wanted a cup of tea. When Margaret got back with the mug, both girls were in the cot, snuggled up to Elizabeth.

"Don't smoosh Grandma," Margaret said.

"They're not smooshing me; they're perfect."

"Can we have a bed like this at home?" Helen asked.

"Look, it moves," Jo said. She had a remote control in her hand. She pushed a button, and the bed made a sound like an engine and all their heads started tilting upward, and then she pushed another button, and up cranked their feet.

"Higher!" said Elizabeth.

"JoJo, that's high enough, that doesn't look comfortable for Grandma." The bed was now in the shape of a hammock, and both ends were still rising. There must be a limit, right? A point at which the machine would stop before the head and the foot turned in on themselves and made a perfect circle.

"You're pushing the wrong button," Helen said. "It's my turn anyway."

The bed stopped moving.

"You had it for longer."

It started again. Elizabeth was sitting up practically at a right angle now. "Did not."

Helen reached over Elizabeth to snatch at the remote and Jo dodged, burrowing under the blankets with it, her sister close behind her. The bed began to reverse.

"Guys, don't roughhouse. You'll hurt Grandma."

They were kicking each other down at the foot of the bed. It was incredible—they had no idea how terrifying Elizabeth had once been. Above the sheet line, she smiled serenely at the children's antics; below: shrieking and shouting, one shrouded, many-limbed body seemed to be attacking itself.

"Stop that right now," Margaret said. "I'm not kidding. Give me the remote. Stop fighting!" She tried but failed to find a handhold on a child. A foot shot out and kicked her in the belly. "Fuck," she said.

At last she pulled the whole blanket off the bed and the girls sat up, looking cheerful, their hair sizzling with static electricity. The remote control lay at her feet.

"Mom," Helen said, "we're bored."

SHE'D PACKED an activity for them, something she'd been saving for a rainy day. It was a jewelry-making kit, with trays of beads with letters on them. Margaret brought it downstairs. "How about you each make some-thing for Grandma? But do it quietly, please."

Once the girls were set up with the beads on the floor, and Elizabeth settled back comfortably in the armchair with her drink and the farm-house book, Margaret sat down on the bed.

She'd missed her moment, but she had her question. She asked it now:

"Hey, Mom, I've been meaning to ask you something. I was thinking. Tell me about Rome."

"Why—are you going to Rome?" Elizabeth glanced at the girls and then whispered loudly: "With *that man?*"

"With Duncan? It's fine, Mom, they know Duncan."

"When?" Jo said. "To France?"

"No, Rome is Italy."

"We want to go with Duncan too."

"Okay, but I'm not going anywhere, with or without Duncan. Do the beads. I just meant I wanted Grandma to tell us about Rome when she was little."

"What about it?" Elizabeth asked.

"About traveling with your parents. How you went to the Colosseum. I thought you could tell me about seeing all that art. I don't know if the girls have ever heard about all the trips you used to take."

Elizabeth's hands were moving in her lap, as if she was stringing her own necklace, but no one had given her any beads.

"Mom?"

"I never went to Rome."

"Yes, you did."

"I was at school. It was my parents who went. I always wanted to, but they left me behind."

"But you told me about it, about seeing the ruins. You got a new dress. Remember?"

"Never Rome," she said again. "They went without me. That was the point."

But Elizabeth had talked all about it, Margaret was sure: how she went to the Colosseum, how she saw the frescoes on the walls, how she'd never forgotten the portrait gallery and that was the reason she'd wanted to study art in college. The ruins—she'd talked about the ruins. The roofs of the homes had fallen in, and the walls had crumbled, and all that remained as proof that a family had lived there were four columns demarcating a room, columns freed of all burdens, pointing straight up at the sky.

"If you muss that bed," Elizabeth said, "please fix it up again. This is still the dining room."

I didn't muss the bed, it was you and the kids, she thought but did not say. She wondered if Neal would remember about Rome, but she knew she'd never ask him. She would never understand Elizabeth. Never, never! She stood and smoothed the sheets, smoothed them mercilessly flat.

Elizabeth had always commanded so much sympathy, and Margaret, not knowing why, had always withheld it. Was this why? Because her mother was a left-behind child? It was good they were selling this house, this house her grandparents' money had paid for. But why had Elizabeth told so many stories? Why had she lied?

"Here, Grandma," Helen said. She had made a bracelet with all their initials on it. But when Helen went to put it over Elizabeth's wrist, the knot slipped loose, and the beads bounced on the floor. Helen looked like she might cry.

"Don't worry," Margaret said. "We'll just fix it, I'll help you." She knelt and ran her hands over the carpet. "We'll make it even better this time. I like these pretty green ones. Green is Grandma's favorite color, isn't it?"

She stopped and looked up at Elizabeth. "Isn't it?"

She thought she'd picked up all the beads, but she kept finding ones she'd missed. All that day and the next she stepped on them, the fallen beads rolling gold and green.

33

MARGARET RAN A LOAD OF LAUNDRY. IT WAS FUNNY HOW utterly domestic her life remained after marriage. She took little field trips outside, little glamorous field trips to dinner and the office, but her real life was this—closets, clothes, the drumbeat of the washing machine, the cavalry charge of those last three minutes when it hit the spin cycle.

But no, that couldn't be the spin cycle—she'd only turned the machine on five minutes ago. And the noise was even louder than that. It was an actual stampede, feet pounding, the girls running down the stairs.

"Charlie's here," Jo shouted.

Neal was back again. She didn't watch them run out into the rain toward his car. She retreated to the kitchen instead. She was draining the pasta when they came inside. Pouring boiling water from inside a cloud of steam, she was exempted from the mandatory hugging. Elizabeth called from the dining room. She needed a glass of water. She needed a different book. She wanted someone to look for a specific blouse that she wanted to give Neal's wife. She wanted to see her grandchildren.

"You hear McCarthy on the debt ceiling?" Neal asked Hugh. He was leaning over, looking at something inside the oven. "Do you like this range better than the Viking?"

"Are you thinking about renovating?" she asked.

"I'd like to have multiple ovens."

He didn't even bake.

"So much better for hosting."

"How many ovens?"

"Two, maybe three."

"Will that be enough?"

He considered it.

"Uncle Neal, come play hide-and-seek," Jo yelled from the other room.

"Jo, don't yell from the other room," Margaret yelled from the other room.

Jo came to the threshold and said, quieter, "Uncle Neal—" but Margaret interrupted her. "Let Uncle Neal and Granddad talk. I'll play with you."

"We want Uncle Neal to play."

"We can both play," Neal said. "I'll be It."

"But it's dinnertime anyway."

"Go on," Hugh said. "I'll shout when it's all on the table."

SO SHE WAS THIRTY-SIX under her parents' bed, hidden behind the dust ruffle. She rested her cheek against an arm and waited. Distantly she heard Neal discovering the children one by one. "Where could they be now—are they in the *closet*?" and she knew by the delighted yelp that he had torn a door open and found a child inside.

It was fun, it was good fun. But she wished she'd hidden somewhere less hidden. Somewhere where she would have been found sooner. And at the same time, she did not want to be found. She wanted to stay there in the good dark under the safe weight of the mattress, the day reduced to a gray stripe laid against the floor.

But ready or not they were coming, she could hear them in the hall, she could hear the latch's iron jingle. Someone thumped to their knees and lifted the ruffle and said, "I found you." She blinked in the light, and Helen grinned.

"Dinner," her father shouted.

ELIZABETH ENTERED the kitchen last. Hugh held her arm and led her slowly, carefully. Now she looked weak. Each step was charged with a new unsteadiness, a sense of danger, which made the whole thing feel processional, formal. She was not simply joining her family for dinner. She was the symbol of a nation giving succor to the crowds, the great leader emerging from clouds of rumor. She tottered, there was no other word for it. Neal pulled out the chair.

It was strange to see her move like that, stranger even than eating in the kitchen, not that Elizabeth ate anything—not the spaghetti, not the salad, not even the chocolate cake that Margaret had bought specially to tempt her. But when Margaret put the cake on the table Elizabeth exclaimed over it. "Now this is too beautiful to be a regular cake. It must be a special cake, a birthday cake. Whose birthday should we pretend it is?"

"Mine!" all the children shouted.

Once Margaret would have glowered. Why did she have to make a whole thing out of the cake; why did she always have to make herself the center of attention? Now she saw the magic in it, in making a center at all. Her mother couldn't hold the knife, but she held the moment, made it an occasion. Elizabeth looked happy, Margaret thought, and she realized that she felt jealous. She had always wanted to be the one to make her happy.

WHEN DESSERT WAS FINISHED, she set up the children in front of the TV and went back to the kitchen to help clear the table. They were talking about the house again.

"I'm sorry, Neal, I just can't see it working," Hugh was saying.

"What working?" Margaret asked.

"Subdivision," said Neal. "I buy the house and subdivide the property into two lots. We'll move in here and sell the other half."

"But it's not big enough to subdivide—you can't get another plot out of the backyard."

"You can, I've paced it off."

"How? How can you?"

"You can if you cut the pool in half."

Hugh was banging, lightly but persistently, the cork from the wine bottle against the face of the table. "You take that pool out, you lose substantial value. People who'll pay what this house is worth want a pool. They want a decent yard. They don't want another house right out their window. It'd look terrible, and anyway, no zoning board would approve it."

Subdivision? That was worse than renovation. So gross somehow, that Neal had gone out to the yard and paced it off, his lips moving, perhaps, as he silently counted his steps, as he drew that line down the unresisting grass.

"Trust me on this," Neal said.

Elizabeth said, "We should at least consider—"

"No, enough, come on. We're putting it on the market."

"Honestly, it's irresponsible *not* to do this. Money on the table. You help me buy the house, I'll make it back, plus forty, fifty percent."

"Stop," Margaret said. "He's telling you he's not going to do that."

"Stay out of it. You have no idea," Neal said.

"I'm just hearing what Dad's saying. It's their house. They're not going to cut you some shady deal."

"Margaret, there's no need to be a bitch to your brother," Elizabeth said. "Someday I'll be gone and you'll have to be more loving toward him. You and your father are always ganging up on him."

"Ganging up on him? How have we ever ganged up on him?"

"Hugh, tell her she can't talk to me that way."

"Talk to you what way?" Margaret said. "I literally just repeated what you literally just said to me."

"Don't shout at me."

She wasn't shouting. Was she?

"Hugh, are you going to back me up or not?" The weakness was gone; Elizabeth was her old ferocious self again.

"I'm sorry," Hugh said. "Back you up on what? I think we've got off topic."

"Never mind," Margaret said. "Do whatever you want."

"Dad doesn't gang up on me," Neal said.

"I'm on everyone's side," Hugh said.

"Please," Elizabeth said. "All you care about is peace and quiet."

"What's wrong with peace and quiet?"

"What's wrong is you're a coward," Elizabeth said.

"Mom, stop," Margaret said.

"What am I supposed to do, say nothing? Look at her, giving real estate advice. She tore up her own family. What kind of mother would do a thing like that? She doesn't even look ashamed."

Margaret was still holding the silverware, halfway to the sink, the dirty knives and forks turning hot in her hand.

"Elizabeth," Hugh said.

"I can say what I want, I'm sick."

"When did you ever not say what you wanted?"

"Why are you guys shouting?"

Helen was standing in the doorway, Jo and Charlie behind her.

"I'm shouting because my daughter's a whore."

The kitchen was silent while they all marveled at it, the word *whore*, like something out of one of Elizabeth's novels, or the Bible, or history.

"What else do you call someone who trashes their own marriage? A tramp who spits on everything everyone else thinks matters? Look what she did. She's cold. She can't even love her own brother."

Suddenly Margaret wanted to laugh. She was saying it all, and Margaret felt only an awful relief. She flung the silverware into the sink and it made a clashing sound, the sound of a sword being thrown to the floor in a gesture of violent surrender. She could feel and say and do anything she wanted now because who could possibly blame her?

"You know why I don't love him," she began.

And then she saw Helen's and Jo's faces. She saw the way Helen had taken her sister's hand. She saw the door and what came through it: care and consequence. She went to the children. She stood between them and the past.

"It's okay, guys," she said. "Grandma is just being silly. Let's go somewhere else. Let's go outside."

"What are we doing?"

"Just lie here and look up."

"Why?"

"So we can see something happen."

She lay on her back in the grass, a kid on each side.

"Do you see my bedroom?"

"You mean our bedroom?"

"Yours now, yeah. Look just above it, where the roof is, and then to the right? We're going to watch that spot."

"Why?"

"To see if we can catch the bats come out."

"Ew," said Helen.

"Cool," said Jo.

"What if they come down here?" Helen asked.

"They won't. You're not a mosquito. They're going to fly up and away."

The sun had just gone down, and the sky was a gold-rimmed, expensive-looking blue.

"Why do you like the bats so much?" Jo asked.

"Do I like them? Maybe. *Like* isn't the right word, exactly. I used to be afraid of them. I wouldn't want to be stuck inside with one. But I like that they're wild. I like that they live here and we can't control them."

"Are there bats at home too?"

"Sure. In the park mostly, but probably in old buildings too. Church spires and stuff. Wild things can live anywhere."

"How long do we have to wait?"

"I don't know."

"I'm bored."

"Me too."

"Don't whine."

"Is it true you don't love Uncle Neal?" Helen asked.

"Yes."

"But that's not nice."

"I know it's not. But I love you. I love you both more than anything."

"I don't think the bats are coming."

"Maybe you're right. Maybe we missed them."

"The grass is wet."

She felt it too—the earth's cold sweat seeping up through her shirt.

"Just stay with me a little longer, okay?"

And then it was dark. It happened quickly, more quickly than she remembered. When she was young, the gloaming had seemed to last hours. She had played whole games of tag in it, eaten whole bowls of ice cream while the day diminished imperceptibly into evening. Now, it lasted minutes, moments, seconds. She lay and watched it happen, time. The grass turned black, the bushes turned black, only the sky held the blue of deep water.

And that was when they came, slipping out of the house like a ribbon. Immediately the ribbon began to fray, to separate, and then one after another each small darting self wheeled up and out so fast that Margaret barely had time to raise her arm and say "Look!" before they were gone.

By 9:00 the next morning, Margaret and the girls were gone too.

SEVEN

34

THEY WERE GOING TO BE LATE FOR SCHOOL. JO WAS HOLDING two leaves. They were magic; they made her fly. Margaret was holding her upper arm so she couldn't dart off the sidewalk. Helen was a few paces in front, stopping to tell them again that they were going to be late to school.

It was the first week of classes and Helen had a spelling quiz. She'd been struggling the night before. New or knew, there or their, whole or hole. It was difficult. "See if this helps," Margaret had said, as she looked over the practice sheet: "A hole is a small thing, like in a wall, for a mouse. But the whole has everything in it, so it gets that silent W."

She'd said they would practice again in the morning, that in the morning it would be easier to remember: "At night the brain consolidates information. Neurons, they make, like, wires or roads in your brain—they grow while you're sleeping." (Was this quite accurate? She hoped so.) "Anyway, let's quit for tonight, let's read a story."

But as soon as Jo handed her the book she said, "Oh no. Anything but that one."

It was *Heckedy Peg*, about a witch who turns a family of children into roast rib and porridge and other English foods. A gift from Elizabeth, who'd read it to Margaret as a child.

"We love this one," Jo said.

The witch is about to take her first bite—knuckle-deep in the pie that is a child—when the mother bangs on the door of her hut. The witch says you can't come in your shoes are dirty so she takes them off. The witch says you can't come in your socks are dirty so she takes them off. The witch says you can't come in your feet are dirty so she cuts them off.

Margaret had read it so many times she didn't need to look at the page to say the words. The girls were snug against her side. Behind Helen's back she snuck a look at her phone, answered one-handed a work email about when an article would be ready for the copy desk. The witch saw the mother had no feet so she let her in, Margaret recited while writing back, "Soon, tonight."

The mother crawls inside, breaks the spell, and the children spring out of their dishes into human form and do a jig on the witch's fine table-cloth. It turns out the mother hadn't really cut off her own feet; she was only pretending, hiding them under her skirt. Suddenly she leaps up and says to the witch, Now you'll be sorry. They chase her out of the hut, through the fields, and over the bridge, where she throws herself into the water and is never seen again.

"Now it's bedtime. I need to do some work. We can read it again to-morrow. I said no. Fine, just one more time."

Margaret had always hated *Heckedy Peg*. The witch's creepy hunger. Those consumable children. Come now, sweet chickens, she says, and shows them a sack of gold. How like Elizabeth.

But lately the book had grown on her a little. She liked the good mother who breaks the spell by knowing the children for who they are, guessing which child is fish and which is cheese, etc. Plus she's pretty, with an apron around a tiny waist. You'd never believe she'd borne so many children (seven: each named for a day of the week).

So this is it, the feminine ideal, Margaret thought: a mother willing to take a knife to her own limbs to protect her children. And even better, nobody has to feel any guilt or sorrow about it, because when the time comes, she just jumps up, whole and unscathed, magically regenerated like some kind of zombie or gecko. Overidentifying with the characters in children's picture books was a symptom of loneliness and of a lack of intellectual stimulation. She needed to read a real book, a grown-up book. She'd brought home from Elizabeth's her old high school copy of *To the Lighthouse*. But she kept opening it up and cringing at her teenage handwriting in the margins: *lily feels dissapointed*. (She had not learned yet how to spell that word.) Nobody cared if she reread *To the Lighthouse*. Nobody cared about her feminist dissertation on *Heckedy Peg*. Just be present, here, now, with your children, she told herself. Now you'll be sorry, she said again.

But then a genuine surprise, on reading number 29 or 40 or 76. The titular peg was literal. Despite all that kidnapping, and the strenuous-looking flight over field and bridge, you can see that under Heckedy Peg's rags, in place of the limb, is a twisted piece of wood.

It made her ask for the first time: Who had the witch cut off her own leg for?

She had spent a furiously productive few days at the office making up for lost time. Give her the essays on health policy and infrastructure, give her a border crisis and the decline of democracy. Give her even the president. Give her a problem and a prescription—anyone's voice that was not her own. That was why she'd chosen this work. Not to tell people what was right or wrong; not to explain or persuade, but for her own selfish, private purposes.

After the kids went to bed, she stayed up late editing. She was trying to fix a piece about free speech in higher education, working toward that moment when the argument's logic fell into place, when the progression of thought began to seem inevitable instead of arbitrary. But she just couldn't do it. She kept moving lines, paragraphs, up and down. On the right-hand side of the page, in the red tracked changes, her own name repeated over and over, the record of each one of her demands.

She kept on editing right until she fell asleep and then after. She dreamed about a Word document, the copy-paste motion of her fingers. But the essay made no sense. A sleigh slid over the snow. An elderly servant with a fever polished everyone's boots. A man fought a duel at dawn for honor, a word that had lost its meaning, that was only a tassel on the handle of an ornamental saber, only the sparkle of the revolving clock-face of a spur that jingled as it turned.

She'd been reading a novel lately about the end of the Austro-Hungarian Empire, and her subconscious had turned it into an op-ed. It was laying out some kind of argument about Cossacks galloping through the borderlands with their bellies flat against horses because God had abandoned the kaiser. The cost of silence, we can no longer, now is the time. Something was in the room; something had come to wake her. The empress was dead, but the peasants would never believe it.

⁓

She caught herself as they walked to school half remembering the dream, thinking nonsensically: It needs a clicky headline, something that plays well on social. Jo had dropped her magic leaves and needed new ones. Margaret lifted her up into the branches.

"Next weekend we should go back to New Jersey," she said.

"No," said Helen.

"Grandma was mean," said Jo.

"I guess. But I didn't need to get so angry. Sometimes it doesn't really matter what people say." That seemed wrong. "I mean you should always be kind, but you don't have to get too upset if other people aren't."

"Anyway we don't want to, we're sick of it there," Helen said. "Can we go to the beach and see Louie and Willis instead?"

"Maybe. I could ask . . ."

She would love to take the girls to the beach. The morning was milky with the day's abeyant heat. But soon the sea would be warmer than the air, and then the heat would retreat even from the water, and then summer would be over; it would be too late.

But she hadn't seen Duncan yet. They'd been busy—they hadn't talked about their children, the party, the past. Duncan was capacious but not infinitely so. She understood now that it would never work.

And still she thought: But maybe?

"It's hard to explain," she'd told him when he'd called to ask what had happened in New Jersey. *Hard* didn't capture it, the great bearing-down pressure required to open and shut her mouth around each word.

But she kept thinking about him. How when he was on top of her, she felt all body. She had her children, she had her work. She was fine. But she didn't want to lose him. As long as they delayed the conversation, the possibility remained. He'd said he wouldn't hurt her, and he didn't. She kept thinking about that. Her face was down in the sheets. She felt the palm of his hand. She felt the palm of his hand again.

Why did that mean so much to her? Picturing it as she walked, she could feel him kneeling above her, looking at her—regarding her. She could feel his look even more than she could feel his touch. What moved and excited her was the fact of lying there under him, naked and not in danger and very, very wide-awake.

JO WAS PETTING someone's tiny dog, shrieking at its leaping kisses. "Jo, come *on*, we're going to be late," Helen said again. "Mom, can I just go? Can I go ahead?"

Margaret considered it. Maybe Helen was old enough this year to walk a few blocks alone. But then Helen stopped and said, "Dead rat!"

"Where?" said Jo.

"Over there."

"Just keep walking."

Jo refused to move. "I want to see."

Margaret tugged on her hand. "Absolutely not. It's disgusting, and we're going to be late."

Margaret had seen the rat already, between two cars in the gutter. It had rained so much lately that the body was more stew than corpse. There was a tail, and paws, and some material slushed between that she didn't want to look at.

"I want to see," Jo said again, and tried to twist away, but Margaret held on to her hand, and for a moment they both pulled in opposite directions until Jo cried out and clutched her arm.

Oh god, she'd dislocated her fucking elbow again. No— How could she let this— What kind of mother—

Never mind. It was fine. It was totally fine. Jo's arm was moving normally by her side. In Margaret's relief she no longer minded about the rat. So much of parenting was this: the instantaneous lowering of expectations. Her children were safe. Nothing else mattered. They went back and looked at what was left of the rat. The girls seemed pleased that they lived in a place where you could find something that interesting just lying in the street. But did they understand that this was death? This final, catastrophic puddle?

"Just don't go any nearer," she said.

Then a kid from Helen's class caught up with them and the girls pointed. The other child stepped closer.

"Morning," Margaret said to the girl's dad.

"You're Helen's mom? I'm Ralph, I think I've met your husband."

"Ezra, yeah. Not husband, though."

"Oh, sorry, your partner."

"No, sorry, not partner."

"Oh, sorry—"

The poor guy, why was she making this so hard? "No, it's my fault! Ezra's my ex. I'm Margaret."

"Nice to meet you. What are they looking at?"

"A rat. I mean—a dead one."

"What? Amelia, come back here."

He reached for his daughter just as Helen gave the girl a little shove in the direction of the curb.

The dad gasped, the child wailed. Jo said witheringly, and very distinctly, "Don't be a whore."

"Jo," Margaret breathed. "No! Apologize! Helen too. I'm so sorry," she said to the dad. "I have no idea where she could have learned that word."

"Yeah you do," Helen said helpfully. "Grandma called you a whore last week. Remember?"

Margaret put a hand to her forehead in a gesture that she hoped looked rueful. Maybe the man would laugh, but he didn't. He just held tight to one of the shoulder straps of his daughter's backpack and said they'd better go.

They waited a moment so it wouldn't be so awkward and then followed the girl and her father.

"Guys," Margaret said.

"Sorry," Helen said.

"Just—can you—"

"We will," Helen said.

Jo held her hand and for three straight blocks was good.

And then the girls were gone, into the school, and straightaway the feeling came. Everything went very far away from her. There was a distance between her skin and clothes, a sort of exterior crawl space. Everything that made Margaret Margaret withdrew, diminished, because no one wanted or needed anything from her. She walked by the homes behind stoops behind gates. Shadows were laid over her and then stripped away again by the exposure of every intersection at the end of every block. Around her, alterations of space and density. Other people, sometimes. Down the entrance to the subway they descended. The dad from before rushed past with no sign of recognition. No one could recognize her now. Not her face nor the nameless not-wife, not-daughter, not-even-mother nub of her that was her deepest stubborn self.

35

IT HAD BEEN RUINOUS, THIS LAST STROKE. WHEN MARGARET got to the hospital, the doctor explained the extent of the damage. Elizabeth was barely conscious. She was not speaking. Her features were out of focus or out of place—there was some paralysis, the doctor said, but Margaret was confused. Which part was paralyzed? Was it the mouth, where it drooped, or the eye, with its new rigidity? She kept thinking—stroke of what? Stroke of luck, stroke of fortune, stroke of genius. Stroke: an artist's line. As she listened she held a straw, futilely, to Elizabeth's mouth. Nobody ever said a stroke of disaster, stroke of death. You'd just say stricken.

Margaret had thought there'd be more time, but she was wrong. Sometimes you have to do something extreme so people understand how much pain you're in. Elizabeth had said that once, a long time ago. There was so much they had not spoken of, and now there was no longer any point in speaking of it. What would she have said? That she was angry at this person who deserved only mercy, whose suffering was at last beyond any possible comparison? Come back here! she wanted to say. Come back here this instant.

Soon there was nothing to do but watch HGTV. *Love It or List It* was on. While a couple was fighting over which of their desires—garage or closet space—could be fulfilled and which would have to be discarded forever, Neal came in. Someday, Elizabeth had always said, she would have to be more loving toward her brother. He hugged Margaret, and she patted his back. They looked at the patient, two people in early middle age, clearly siblings. All those side-by-side years watching the same things happen, all that unavoidable proximity, it must add up to something—a set of references, a language. But when he said, "Terrible to see Mom like this," she couldn't think of anything to say.

Was she sleeping, or was she unconscious? It mattered, though Margaret wasn't sure why. Either way, Elizabeth was lying there defenseless, exposed. The fact that it would have been so easy to hurt her made her feel that someone, maybe Margaret, maybe Neal, would have to hurt her. Neal straightened Elizabeth's blanket and leaned in close to kiss her. His torso hovered. She saw his belt with the holster for his cell phone, and the wallet shape fat in his back pocket, and the splayed hand that bore his weight on the mattress.

Was Elizabeth still Elizabeth now? She seemed to know nothing of Neal, of the passing nurses, the coursing tubes. Did it matter what happened to her body in the bed?

Yes—she would wake up.

If she did not remember?

Still yes.

It was hers, yet, if nothing else was—the dignity of the body, of an animal moving in response to the world's stimuli, toward or away from pleasure or pain.

But someday she would not wake, and then? The record of her body would be real only to other people, who would know only what they chose to; Elizabeth herself would be insensate, forever.

Well, obviously. That was death. That was the whole point. That was all anyone really knew about it.

But there were approximations. That was why people hurt children—because they wouldn't remember, because they wouldn't tell, because people didn't think they were quite alive. That was why Neal had done things to her when she was a child, sleeping. That was a little taste of death.

She watched Neal touching their mother's forehead, her unmoving arm. She thought it again: Someday she won't wake up.

And now Margaret flinched, and now Margaret fled the room.

‗

Her phone read 5:19. She was sure something had woken her, but all was quiet. Quiet too in the hallway. She had brought the girls to New Jersey for the weekend while they waited to see what would happen, and now she went to check on them. Jo was fast asleep in the far corner of the bed, but Helen was missing.

She flicked on the hall's overhead light and, squinting, went into the bathroom. Empty. Her eyes dropped, as they always did, to the wall below the shelves. The hole had been there for only a few days before she came home from school to find the bathroom smelled of fresh paint and the wall was perfect again. She'd felt relieved, but not entirely. The flat white surface was a different kind of madness. At times she had wanted to kick the hole back into existence, just to prove that it was real. "Helen?" she said softly, beginning to feel afraid.

Maybe she'd gone down to Elizabeth's room. But Elizabeth wasn't here. Elizabeth was at the hospital. Elizabeth might never come home.

At last, going down the stairs, she heard something. Pling. Pa-pling. Pa-pling? A robotic note, but musical. And under that, as she descended, a metal sound, like an engine going hard around corners. Rrrrr pa-pling.

They were in the living room playing *Mario Kart*, Helen and Ezra. Ezra was in a hoodie and basketball shorts, Helen in her nightgown, both of them flickering in the colors of the nineties, leaning from side to side as they barreled through stacks of coins.

"You're here!"

"I'm here."

She had texted Ezra after dinner, told him what was happening, that she'd keep him in the loop. She didn't realize until now that she'd known he would come. He was Ezra, he was family, he would be here.

"But how did you get here?"

"I called Chris, he said I could borrow their car. I got in around midnight and crashed on the floor of the girls' room. This one woke me up."

"Where did you find that?" she asked about the video game.

"Hang on." He did something with a ramp and rocket boosters. It looked like Helen's Mario had fallen off the track into a pool, but it didn't matter, the dirt bike was zooming along just fine through the deep water. Ezra was picking off a princess. He was in first place. He had won. "I love her too, you know," he said. He set the controller aside so they could cheer on Helen. She made it out of the water. She bumped off the sides and spun around and righted herself.

"Mom, look."

"I'm looking."

"Sixth place. Is that good?"

"I think it's very good for your first time playing."

"I got it as a back-to-school gift for the girls," Ezra said. "I figured we could use it now to take our minds off things. Helen's not bad."

"It's hard to keep it straight, but I'm getting better. Mom, I'm hungry. Can we have pancakes?"

"Helen, it's not even six a.m."

"But can we?"

She got out the skillet and the oil, the bowl for the Bisquick, asked, "Do you want to stir?"

"You do it. Is Grandma coming home today?"

"No, sweetheart."

"I don't want Grandma to die."

"Neither do I."

"But she's not immortal." You could tell by the way she said the word that she'd never said it before—*i-mor-tal*—the syllables as stiff as new shoes.

"No, she's not immortal." Margaret stopped whisking, tried to think of what to say. "Grandma's body is really tired. Sometimes that means it's time for a person to die."

She could say it only because she was saying it for Helen. For herself alone she would not have been able to admit it, allow it, the fact of Elizabeth not being immortal.

It didn't matter, of course, if she could say it or not. Because it had already happened—it was over. Before she searched the dark house for her missing child, before she woke without knowing why, it was over, though Hugh waited until 7:00, a more reasonable hour, to call and tell her the news. Elizabeth was dead.

SHE HAD IMAGINED a better ending. She had imagined Elizabeth's last days in the dining room, sunlight thrown like a yellow blanket across the bed. Margaret would have leaned over, laid her head in the light, her cheek in her mother's cupped palm. She would have asked the perfect question, the one that would have finally let her be known.

One morning, she had been trying to talk to Elizabeth, trying to draw her mother back into herself and her attention back into her daughter. But Elizabeth turned her face away, looked toward the window like she was snubbing her, like something far more interesting than Margaret was out there. It gave her a funny stab of jealousy toward the numinous light, the numinous light that didn't even need her. Like sibling rivalry with death.

"That glass needs washing," Elizabeth said, though it looked clean to Margaret, though the morning sun was streaming through in bright, relentless torrents. She raised a hand as if lifting a Windexed rag, then let it fall back to the bed.

That had been her chance.

Now there were shoes in the hallway. Chaos had come to the house, chaos without Elizabeth. Margaret had failed everyone, she thought as she put away the shoes. She had left and not come back in time. And then she felt: Elizabeth did it on purpose, to punish Margaret for her selfishness, for losing her temper, for leaving her husband. She died without looking at the camera.

But Elizabeth hadn't wanted to die—not ever and certainly not then.

In the room that was now only her father's she put fresh sheets on the bed. She smoothed the blue bedspread, blue as the morning. There was a sound behind her, a beating sound. People were running, from what, to what, unclear, then clearer.

It was the children coming through the door.

Helen stood off to the side. She had entertained Jo and Charlie, kept them safe. "Thank you for being such a helper," Margaret said.

But that was the wrong thing to say—it was something you said to a little kid, and Helen wasn't little anymore.

"How are you doing, Helen, really?" she asked. "I know this has been a lot to cope with."

But that wasn't right either. That was something Margaret's grown-up friends said to Margaret herself.

Helen just looked at her. All her secret girlhood shone within her, shone like dark berries on the innermost branches. If something was wrong, she would say, right? If someone hurt or damaged them, these girls would know better than she had how to talk about it. Talk to me, she thought but did not say.

"Mommy, throw me," Jo said. She did. She picked Jo up and sailed her through the air toward the new-made bed. Up there she could see more than Margaret could see, up over the trees, up through the uppermost panes of glass.

She thought for a moment of Elizabeth, long-ago Elizabeth on that icy day, turning around in the minivan, suppressing all her grief and rage, and saying brightly to her children with what could only have been courage: "Seat belts, everyone."

36

THE KIDS WENT HOME WITH EZRA, AND THEN IT WAS ONLY Margaret and Hugh left behind to get the house in order. He didn't want to wait: the listing was already online. He had changed his mind about getting another place in town. He was thinking he might rent an apartment in the city after all, start going to museums or something.

She missed not just Helen and Jo but also the noise they made, how they ran up and down the stairs as if trying to fool the house into thinking that the bluster and bustle of everyday life was ongoing. They dropped things—toys and pillows and water bottles—on the floor and then kicked them, here and there, as they moved around the space, as if they wouldn't be satisfied until the mess was uniformly distributed.

"Why do you do that, instead of just picking it up?" she asked Helen, out of curiosity as much as frustration, as she kicked a stuffed bear across the threshold of a room.

"Do what?" Helen asked, kicking.

It was easier to feel the familiar yearning for her kids than it was to admit that she missed her mother. Now they were all gone, and stillness had taken the house in its arms. A knocked-over picture frame stayed that way, face down. The soldier doll hung paralyzed. Each tassel on each curtain looked pinned to the wall. Even the armchairs looked two-dimensional, since no one ever sat in them.

All that changed in the house was the light—its reaching in each day to knead then stretch then knead then stretch the shadows across the dusty floors. The house was not, after all, an extension of Elizabeth. It was simply big, and indifferent, and difficult to clean.

Biddy came over one night to look through the giveaways. A Diane Keaton–ish movie played in the background, about the widowed or divorced having one last adventure. Biddy was lying on the couch in one of Elizabeth's skirts. "I cannot imagine washing Alice's mouth out with soap," she said.

"Neither can I."

"Remember that time your mom got mad at you for saying . . . what was it? Like barely a swear. Hell?"

"Sucks."

"No."

"Yes. I think I said, This sucks."

"Incredible."

"And she didn't just use a bar of soap. She used dish detergent. You had to swish it around like mouthwash until she let you spit."

"Legendary. My mom did that too, but only once to Danny when he was really bad. She keeps asking me what she can do to help—I keep telling her you don't need lasagna or whatever. Also Danny texted, wanting to know if I thought he should call you."

"What did you tell him?"

"I said absolutely not, don't call that whore with her filthy cunt of a mouth."

She laughed, tried not to cry. Biddy knew her, knew her entirely.

"I'm sorry, Margo, I wish I knew what to say."

"I know. Just—are you going to take that skirt? There's a blouse that goes with it." She rifled through the shirt pile.

"Honestly, *Elizabeth's* clothes. How can I?"

Before the last stroke, Elizabeth had chosen for Margaret three A-line ball gowns; five wool suits (one with actual epaulets); six knee-length belted shirt-dresses; and innumerable sundresses. They were up in her childhood bedroom for now. She'd need to rent a storage unit—they'd never fit in her closet back home.

"You don't have to wear it," she told Biddy. "You just have to take it. If you don't choose I'm going to make you take a ball gown, and those things are fucking voluminous."

The rest she took in clear trash bags to Goodwill.

The girls had been asking about death and after. You're still part of the universe—she'd tried that out as an answer. People still love and remember you. And your body (this bit was harder), well, it becomes part of other things—flowers that feed the birds and so forth. Biddy said she told her kids that death was not an end, it was only a change. But Biddy was Catholic. Obviously, it was the end of something.

She dumped the trash bags at the drop-off location and walked back through the cluttered store. She looked at the price on an Instant Pot, touched the belt on a man's beige raincoat. Here was a kind of afterlife—in the radiant aisles, among the arcing silver racks. Maybe someone would choose her dresses, bring them forward, lay them down by the altar of the cash register. They would go back into the world, then, skirts flounced by living legs, flashing buttons proclaiming to everyone who passed: *Elizabeth!*

When she got home her dad was sitting on the porch steps. It didn't seem like something he would do, sit on something that wasn't a chair, alone, outside, in the evening.

"What are you doing?" she asked.

"Just resting," he said.

A bat got down the chimney through the open flue and flapped horribly in the curtains. Margaret ducked and shrieked while her father got out his racket. He took a few practice swings, as if he might swat it down, but he didn't even try. Instead they just left the windows open, and in the morning the bat was gone.

She roasted a chicken. She scrubbed the pan. Was it possible he was right about the soap?

She gasped awake from a nap in the armchair.

"Just checking on you," Neal said.

She swam in the pool in the rain.

She went outside. The house was clean, the for-sale sign staked in the yard. She could go home soon. But she would miss this yard. It had given her something, a sense of possibility—there was danger out there but freedom too, past the property line, in the wilder dark, where her family would never go.

She wandered across the driveway down to the blackberry bushes. There might be some berries left, if she could see to pick one. But she heard something, the hiss of steps through the grass. Someone was coming.

Neal. She hadn't seen his car, hadn't realized he was there. Since Hugh had refused to keep talking about subdivision he hadn't been around as much. He'd only come to get some things. But it was good he'd run into her, he said. He'd been meaning to take her aside, find a time to talk.

He wanted to make sure they were aligned on what was best for Hugh. She didn't understand about the house. His idea was too good to pass up; it would give everyone the greatest financial security possible; it would mean he could make sure that Hugh was properly cared for no matter how long he lived. There wasn't as much cash on hand as she thought. But it wasn't just about the house. He had also asked Hugh to give him power of attorney, in case of incapacity. So—that would be handled. Well, Hugh hadn't agreed yet, but he would. *Formality*, he used that word. He was being polite by including her—he found a way of making this clear.

"But there's nothing wrong with Dad."

"Well, he's getting older too. You know how fast things can happen now. It wouldn't kick in until it was necessary, obviously. But he's already so emotional about these decisions."

Could she make him go away? She would like to. "I think maybe I should have the power of attorney."

"That's ridiculous."

"Why?"

"You have no experience managing finances, no experience with the law. You can barely pay rent on your crappy apartment. No offense. I'm the one who lives here, I'm the one who was here for Mom. You barely even visited, and then you stormed off at the last minute in a temper tantrum. Not that anyone's blaming you, of course."

"At least my main concern isn't my parents' money."

"Don't you dare speak to me that way."

I'll speak to you any way I want, she thought but did not say. He was angrier than she was, and that made her feel powerful. *Power of attorney.* Neal was right—she had only the vaguest sense of what that entailed.

She could hardly see his face now. The lightning bugs had turned on and were flashing, flashing.

"Why did you do that to me?"

She had not planned to ask him this; had in fact never imagined asking him. She asked it now clinically, casually, as if it was only of academic interest, and maybe it was—the interest of a historian trying to make sense of the ancient past, of some barbaric, long-forsaken pattern of behavior.

"Do what?" he said.

"Why did you do that to me? When we were children."

"I don't know what you're talking about."

"Yes, you do."

"Come on, Margaret, seriously. Do what?" It was the tone you used with a madman, with a child, with someone incapable of listening to reason.

"Touch me. Film me. Bring the Riccis to my room. I was your sister."

"What film? What are you even talking about?"

He took a step toward the house, but she moved in front of him, blocked his way. "Why did you do it?" she asked.

"I barely even— It was like three, four times. Those guys didn't even get in."

"What happened to the tape?"

"Have you been obsessing over that all these years? It was nothing. It was barely anything. The tape—it didn't even work. I mean the angle was all wrong. It was, like, the edge of the bath mat, and your feet going by. Hardly anything else."

"Hardly anything?"

"It was a waste, a joke—they were actually mad at me. This isn't healthy, to be fixating on that. You really need to be in therapy, you need to be talking to someone about this."

"But why did you think you could do it?"

"I'm not having this conversation, this is crazy. I'm going inside."

She did not want to be this near him. She couldn't see his hands in the dark. But she would make him answer. "You've never thought about it, all this time? You've never wondered what it was like for me?"

"*It, it, it*—it was nothing. We were kids, we did dumb things all the time. The Riccis were bullies. They made me, they wouldn't give it up. Kids do that kind of thing all the time."

"I don't think so. I don't think they do."

"It didn't hurt you."

"I was sleeping."

"Exactly."

He pushed past her—she felt his shoulder, his arm—and all her loathing and terror returned, slicked out of her pores.

"Look," he said, walking away, "I can see that this has been bothering you a lot. I apologize. But this isn't about you now. This is about Dad. This is about us coming together in the memory of Mom."

He sounded so sane, so right and rational. She followed him into the porch light, followed him up the steps. He was wearing black loafers, and the leather was covered in the lawn's dead grass.

They had come from the same place, been made by the same people, learned the same words from all the same stories. With the loathing at last came pity, and sorrow for whatever it was in their upbringing that had failed him too. And yet she did not know him, could not love him.

She tried again. She asked him one last time before he opened the door to the house. "Why did you do it?"

And he answered the question. He answered without turning around. He said:

"I was curious, and you were there."

37

ELIZABETH HAD BEEN RIGHT: THE HOUSE SOLD FAST. AND A few days after the service Margaret was back, back for the last time.

Two small children, a boy and a girl, were in the yard. "Look," they were saying, running over to things she couldn't see. The girl put a hand inside the blackberry bush, tugged at what must have been a berry there. Margaret was surprised they had found one this late in the year; it was probably shriveled or rotten. Don't eat it, she wanted to tell them. And also: Go ahead and eat it. It can't hurt you.

They bent their heads together over the girl's hand, their foreheads almost touching, and she watched them, the lancet-window shape of their brother-sister bodies.

She was waiting in the driveway for We Take It All Away, a junk-removal company that charged $500 for taking as much as would fit in the bed of its truck. She had on one of Elizabeth's dresses—a lime-green number with a pattern of pink umbrellas. It looked hideous on her, and it was sleeveless, and she was cold in the new fall air. Behind her on the lawn stood a mountain of the unwanted: books, box fans, toys, beach things, snow things, some things so disconnected from their original context that their purpose was entirely obscure—mysterious metal hoops and rods, spools within wheels. The pile kept snagging her vision, jagged bits like fins or blades glinting dangerously on the lawn, though it was only the sun that did that, only the sun shining off plastic or glass. The chaos suggested violence, as if the house had been bombed and this was all that was left, though the house was fine. The house was clean. The house wasn't theirs anymore.

That day the new family had brought over an architect to begin drawing up plans for a renovation. She was trying to stay out of the way, but there was so much to get done. Neal had helped her clear out the basement that morning. She had waited for him to come up the stairs before she went down; she gave him a wide berth in the hallway; she navigated around him the same way she'd been navigating around him for twenty-five years, and would for twenty-five more, her arms full of the heaviest boxes she could find.

The We Take It All Away guys pulled in and got to work. She was worried they would ask her, You sure you don't want this? about all the things she was paying them to trash. She was afraid they'd ask her what on earth had happened here, how had it gone so wrong. But your life, they might say, as she threw it all away.

Of course they didn't. Probably all their customers were women like her, looking sweaty and sad beside their stuff.

"Stand back, kid," one of the men said, and obediently, she stepped back. She was thinking how long it had been since the moving van had come to her and Ezra's apartment, and the men they were paying by the hour had had to stand there listening while they discussed in polite despair who should take which piece of furniture. Now she watched everything go into the truck and it wasn't so bad. She could feel an echo of the work in her own body—the heave and release, the rhythm suggesting some more honest and archaic labor, the hauling up of bales of hay or buckets of water.

"Hey, lady," the man said. "Hello? Can you get your kids to stand back?"

Oh, right. When he said *kid* he didn't mean her. The brother and sister were standing by the truck's big wheels, too close to the line of tossed junk.

They're not my kids, she thought but did not say.

"Sorry," she said. Then: "Come on, you two, let me show you something."

They followed without asking who she was.

"This is where I grew up," she told them. "I was a little younger than you when we moved in." She remembered—the house, the yard, the statue of the naked man, the strangeness that dissipated, the strangeness that never would. She thought they might have questions, but they didn't. That was something she liked, how children were never curious out of manners alone.

"Do you like to climb trees?"

"Sometimes," the girl said.

"Okay, well, this is the best climbing tree, and that one is the second best. This one is harder to get up into, but you can go really high once you're in it, and you can see into all the windows of the house. And in the spring it's covered with blossoms. You want to try it?"

"Okay," the girl said, and raised her arms and waited to be lifted. Margaret laughed. That was just like Jo. She felt a shiv of anger toward these children. Because they were taking her house, her tree, her blackberries. And because they were not her own children, whom she missed suddenly with a feeling more like panic or grief, though it was no big deal, really it wasn't—she'd be home again tomorrow.

She lifted the girl, then her brother, then followed herself. They accepted this as normal, though she was a grown-up, though grown-ups didn't climb trees. She sat on the lowest branch, her back against the trunk, kicking her sneakers into the air. "You'll be able to climb up yourselves in no time," she told them. "My friend Biddy could do it when she was seven."

"Who's that?" the boy asked.

"Biddy, my best friend."

"No, who's that man there?"

"Where?"

He pointed toward the road. Walking up the driveway was a hard-bellied man in jeans and white sneakers, his hair in need of trimming, walking as tentatively as a stranger toward the big house, as if he wasn't sure what he might find there, what kind of people lived inside.

"Dad," she called, but he didn't look up. She called his name. "Hugh!"

What would he do now? He didn't know who he was without Elizabeth—he'd told her that. She had always been so . . . *Elizabeth*, the center of all action and interpretation, and he a benign presence slinking around the edges.

She knew her father loved her, in the sense that he sincerely wished her well. She had never been angry with him because she'd never, she realized, expected very much of him. She'd treated him always the way she'd treated Elizabeth only at the very end of her life—like someone you demanded little of because you knew they could do no more. Was it because he was a man? Gross. She wanted, out of long practice, to blame that on Elizabeth, but surely it had something to do with him himself, her father, Hugh.

But that couldn't possibly be the big twist—could it? That she should have been more pissed off at her father?

She felt in place of anger only tenderness, an exasperated generosity for them both. There in the driveway he reminded her of that other man—what was his name?—Mrs. Ricci's dad from Baltimore, who had been kind to her. She felt the ghost urge to run and get her mother, to tell her it was an emergency, an adventure, an occasion—to see her rise up from the flower beds.

Someone's mother was shouting from the porch, but it wasn't hers. "Jessa, Theo." She swung out of the tree and turned to help the children.

They clambered down her impersonally and ran off without saying goodbye.

The men finished packing up the truck. The We Take It All Away truck took it all away. Gradually the silver patches of crushed grass unfurled, turned green again, left no trace.

SHE WOKE IN THE NIGHT. It was not that something disturbed her, but that nothing had. She was woken by the sudden startle of new silence, like when you realize the AC has switched off, or the cycle of the dishwasher ended, something that you hadn't realized was going until it stopped, the quiet its own alarm. She didn't bother trying to go back to sleep.

She stripped the sheets from the bed and walked down through the house. The rooms were emptier than she'd ever seen them. The chessmen and the soldier doll were gone. The glass box with the dueling pistols was gone, packed away like an impostor's reliquary. Moonlight shone off clear counters. Tassels and trim hung around an empty center.

She had some chores to do. She opened the fridge and dumped out the condiments—her mother's mint jelly, her mother's cocktail sauce—all of it slurrying around the drain. Then she got the china, the white plates covered in butterflies, and started wrapping each one in yesterday's newspaper.

Soon, she told herself, I will take the train home: I will get the kids; we will eat, and play, and read, and in the morning I will be there, in my own life—tomorrow when I wake. And when the sun rose, she was there to see it happen—there as it dawned for the last time on Elizabeth's house. The light ratcheted up through the windows, and when it hit the cabinets, a revelation: they were covered in dust, milky fingerprints all over the glass, a long scummy smear of jam like the first stroke of a message written in blood.

Ichor! She reached for her mother's cloth.

38

"DON'T, YOU'LL TIP US OVER," SAID BIDDY.

The cuffs of Margaret's jeans were sodden, and a ribbon of algae was stuck between her toes. She was lying against the back of the canoe, a knee hooked over the edge, trying to swish the mud off her foot.

On the shore things moved through the weeds—rats, probably, or small birds easily mistaken for rats. Take-out cartons flashed. The place smelled of mud and salt and things rotting past all recognition, all that rankness whirled up in the fresh air. It was a sense experience too profuse to be redolent. Nothing reminded her of anything else.

"This place is really part of the city?" Biddy asked. An edge of the skyline was visible, but very far off and insignificant compared to the gray water lapping around them.

"Yeah. It feels so far away, doesn't it? Like the edge of everything."

"But you're not going to move out here, are you?"

"With Duncan? No. It's his place, not mine. We're not together that way. And anyway, it's too far from Ezra, for the girls." She pointed across the bay. "Last time we tried to make it to that island out there, but it got too stormy. You want to go?"

It was only a small island, with nothing on it—rocks, sand, some grass at the pinnacle. But it was set apart, a destination, while still being close enough that they could see the kids on shore, come back quick if they were called.

"Sure, let's do it."

"But first you have to tell me what you really think."

"He's so different from Ezra."

"Biddy! Come on. Aside from Ezra, what do you think?"

It was Duncan's forty-fifth birthday, and he'd invited his friends and neighbors out for a bonfire. He'd said Margaret should bring anyone she wanted, and she'd asked Biddy so they could finally meet. Margaret recognized some of the guests from Dante's party, and the boys were there, and even June, their mother. She was wearing coveralls and old sneakers in a way that looked insanely chic and had said hello in the friendliest way possible, and yet Margaret, a coward, was hiding from her now. The kids were playing with a dog; Helen and Jo were taking turns with the tennis ball. A pack of neighbors had brought out a garage-full of rusted beach chairs and arranged them in a gossipy circle, their butts inches from the damp sand. Duncan was squatting at the center, building the fire that she couldn't yet see.

"I like him," Biddy said begrudgingly, so Margaret would know she meant it.

Margaret had told Duncan what there was to know. He had taken it in, and then stormed around the room as if the past was something you could punch in the face, and then put his arms around her. She loved him for making just the right amount of big deal about it. She would start over with Louie. She would be watchful and hopeful at the same time. That was basically parenting, right? Joy and vigilance.

They paddled deeper, inexpertly, sweating in the cool air. Soon they got better at matching each other's rhythm. Biddy was in front, and Margaret was glad; she could watch her total devotion to the task. Her curls were sticking to her neck; she'd started getting highlights and her hair was suddenly once again the exact color it had been when they were children. Biddy! There was nothing Margaret didn't love about her—her sarcasm and steadfastness, her conventionality shot through with sudden rebellion, her puzzles, her tulips, her saying "You idiot."

The other day Margaret had had to explain to a writer that his essay wouldn't work. You're trying to do too much, she'd said. It can't be about everything at once. But couldn't it? It was a question only of distance, of putting some things at the right remove and bringing others very close—the suburbs, the city, the sky, the bay, the mud, the children, the fire.

The fire! Careful, she wanted to shout, but didn't, because she was too far away now to make a difference. She had smelled it before she turned to see it. Red and gold the flames rose up, red and gold the light in the air.

Suddenly she was frightened. They were halfway to the island and she couldn't make out Helen and Jo by the fire, the fire that was both a warning and a summons. The island was for another trip or another person. She was a mother. She didn't want to miss the party.

She waited for a moment, hoping Biddy might say it at the exact same time, trying to place the thought in her mind. "Hey," she said. "What would you think about—"

"Heading back? Sure."

Biddy stuck her paddle down and the boat pivoted slowly around it. Margaret leaned over the edge. Nothing was coming from below to drag her down. Nothing was coming from above to pin her there. She put one finger onto the surface, drew a line. But the breeze and the currents were harrying the bay, and the canoe slapped down a wave, and a moment later she couldn't distinguish the mark she'd made from the sign-filled surface of the ever-moving water.

We're coming, Margaret thought. She pulled her paddle hard toward her chest. She pulled the world toward herself an armful at a time.